NGAIO MARSH

Singing in the Shrouds

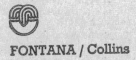

FONTANA / Collins

First published in 1958 by William Collins Sons & Co Ltd
First issued in Fontana Books 1962
Sixth Impression April 1976

© Ngaio Marsh Ltd 1958

Made and printed in Great Britain by
William Collins Sons & Co Ltd Glasgow

FOR

CONTENTS

CAST OF CHARACTERS

P.C. MOIR

A TAXI-DRIVER

A SAILOR

MRS. DILLINGTON-BLICK

HER FRIEND

MR. CUDDY—*A draper*

MRS. CUDDY—*His wife*

MISS KATHERINE ABBOTT—*An authority on church music*

MR. PHILIP MERRYMAN—*A retired schoolmaster*

FATHER JOURDAIN—*An Anglo-Catholic priest*

HIS FELLOW-CLERIC

JEMIMA CARMICHAEL

DR. TIMOTHY MAKEPIECE—*Medical Officer, Cape Farewell*

MR. AUBYN DALE—*A celebrity of commercial television*

HIS DEAREST FRIEND

THEIR DEAREST MALE FRIEND

THEIR DEAREST FEMALE FRIEND

MR. DONALD MCANGUS—*A philatelist*

DENNIS—*A steward*

A WIRELESS OFFICER

CAPTAIN BANNERMAN—*Master, Cape Farewell*

SUPERINTENDENT RODERICK ALLEYN
—C.I.D., New Scotland Yard

CHAPTER ONE

Prologue with Corpse

IN THE Pool of London and farther east all through the dockyards the fog lay heavy. Lights swam like moons in their own halos. Insignificant buildings, being simplified, became dramatic. Along the Cape Line Company's stretch of wharfage the ships at anchor loomed up portentously : *Cape St. Vincent*, Glasgow. *Cape Horn*, London. *Cape Farewell*, Glasgow. The cranes that served these ships lost their heads in the fog. Their gestures as they bowed and turned became pontifical.

Beyond their illuminated places the dockyards vanished. The gang loading the *Cape Farewell* moved from light into nothingness. Noises were subdued and isolated and a man's cough close at hand was more startling than the rattle of winches.

Police Constable Moir, on duty until midnight, walked in and out of shadows. He breathed the soft cold smell of wet wood and heard the slap of the night tide against the wharves. Acres and acres of shipping and forests of cranes lay around him. Ships, he thought romantically, were, in a sort of way, like little worlds. Tied up to bollards and lying quiet enough but soon to sail over the watery globe as lonely as the planets wandering in the skies. He would have liked to travel. He solaced himself with thoughts of matrimony, promotion and, when the beat was getting him down a bit, of the Police Medal and sudden glory. At a passageway between buildings near the *Cape Farewell* he walked slower because it was livelier there. Cars drove up : in particular an impressive new sports car with a smashing redhead at the wheel and three passengers, one of whom he recognised with interest as the great TV personality, Aubyn Dale. It was evident that the others, a man and woman, also belonged to that mysterious world of glaring lights, trucking cameras and fan mails. You could tell by the way they shouted " darling " at each other as they walked through the passageway.

P.C. Moir conscientiously moved himself on. Darkness engulfed him, lights revealed him. He had reached the boundary of his beat and was walking along it. A bus had drawn up at the entry to the waterfront and he watched the passengers get out and plod, heads down and suitcases in hand, towards the *Cape Farewell*—two clergymen, a married couple, a lush bosomy lady and her friend, a benevolent-looking gentleman, a lovely young lady with a miserable expression and a young gentleman who lagged behind and looked as if he'd like to ask her to let him carry her luggage. They walked into the fog, became phantoms and disappeared down the passageway in the direction of the wharf.

For the next two and a half hours P.C. Moir patrolled the area. He kept an eye on occasional drunks, took a look at parked vehicles, observed ships and pubs and had an instinctive ear open for any untoward sounds. At half past eleven he took a turn down the waterfront and into a region of small ambiguous ships, ill-lit and silent, scarcely discernible in the fog that had stealthily accumulated about them.

" Quiet," he thought. " Very quiet, this stretch."

By a strange coincidence (as he was afterwards and repeatedly to point out) he was startled at this very moment by a harsh mewing cry.

" Funny," he thought. " You don't often seem to hear seagulls at night. I suppose they go to sleep like Christians."

The cry sounded again but shortly as if somebody had lifted the needle from a record. Moir couldn't really tell from what direction the sound had come but he fancied it was from somewhere along the Cape Company's wharf. He had arrived at the farthest point of his beat and he now returned. The sounds of activity about the *Cape Farewell* grew clear again. She was still loading.

When he got back to the passageway he found a stationary taxi wreathed in fog and looking desolate. It quite surprised him on drawing nearer to see the driver, motionless over the wheel. He was so still that Moir wondered if he was asleep. However he turned his head and peered out.

" Evening, mate," Moir said. " Nice night to get lost in."

" And that's no error," the driver agreed hoarsely. " 'Ere ! " he continued, leaning out and looking fixedly at the policeman. " You seen anybody ? "

" How d'you mean, seen ? "

" A skirt. Wiv a boxerflahs."

" No," Moir said. " Your fare, would it be ? "

" Ah ! My fare ! 'Alf a minute at the outside she says, and nips off lively. 'Alf a minute ! 'Alf a bloody ar, more likely."

" Where'd she go ? Ship ? " asked Moir, jerking his head in the direction of the *Cape Farewell*.

" 'Course. Works at a flah shop. Cartin' rahnd bokays to some silly bitch wot'll frow 'em to the fishes, like as not. Look at the time : arpas eleven. Flahs ! "

" P'raps she couldn't find the recipient," P.C. Moir ventured, using police-court language out of habit.

" P'raps she couldn't find the flippin' ship nor yet the ruddy ocean ! P'raps she's drahned," said the taxi driver in a passion.

" Hope it's not all that serious, I'm sure."

" Where's my fare comin' from ? Twelve and a tanner gone up and when do I get it ? Swelp me Bob if I don't cut me losses and sling me 'ook."

" I wouldn't do that," P.C. Moir said. " Stick it a bit longer, I would. She'll be back. Tell you what, Aubyn Dale's on board that ship."

" The TV bloke that does the Jolyon Swimsuits commercial and the ' Pack Up Your Troubles ' show ? "

" That's right. Dare say she's spotted him and can't tear herself away. They go nuts over Aubyn Dale."

" Silly cows," the taxi driver muttered. " *Telly !* "

" Why don't you stroll along to the ship and get a message up to her ? "

" Why the hell should I ! "

" Come on. I'll go with you. I'm heading that way."

The driver muttered indistinguishably but he clambered out of his taxi and together they walked down the passageway. It was a longish passage and very dark, but the lighted wharf showed up mistily at the far end. When they came out they were almost alongside the ship. Her stern loomed up through the fog with her name across it.

CAPE FAREWELL
GLASGOW

Her after and amidships hatches had been shut down and, forward, her last load was being taken. Above her lighted gangway stood a sailor, leaning over the rails. P.C. Moir looked up at him.

" Seen anything of a young lady who brought some flowers on board, mate ? " he asked.

" Would that be about two hours back ? "

" More like half an hour."

" There's been nobody like that since I first come on and that's eight bells.

" 'Ere ! " said the driver. " There must of."

" Well, there wasn't. I been on duty here constant. No flowers come aboard after eight bells."

P.C. Moir said : " Well, thanks, anyway. P'raps she met someone on the wharf and handed them over."

" No flowers never come aboard with nobody. Not since when I told you. Eight bells."

" Awright, awright, we 'eard," said the driver ungratefully. " *Bells !* "

" Are your passengers all aboard ? " Moir asked.

" Last one come aboard five minutes back. All present and correct including Mr. Aubyn Dale. You'd never pick him, though, now he's slaughtered them whiskers. What a change ! Oh, dear ! " The sailor made a gesture that might have indicated his chin ; or his neck. " I reckon he'd do better to grow again," he said.

" Anyone else been about ? Anyone you couldn't place, at all ? "

" Hallo-allo ! What's wrong, anyway ? "

" Nothing so far as I know. Nothing at all."

The sailor said : " It's been quiet. The fog makes it quiet." He spat carefully overboard. " I heard some poor sod singing," he said. " Just the voice : funny sort of voice, too. Might of been a female and yet I don't reckon it was. I didn't rekkernize the chune."

Moir waited a moment and then said : " Well, thanks again, sailor, we'll be moving along."

When he had withdrawn the driver to a suitable distance he said, coughing a little because a drift of fog had caught him in the throat : " What was she like, daddy ? To look at ? "

The taxi driver gave him a jaundiced and confused description of his fare in which the only clear glimpse to emerge was of a flash piece with a lot of yellow hair done very fancy. Pressed further the driver remembered pinheels. When she left the taxi the girl had caught her foot in a gap between two planks and had paused to adjust her shoe.

Moir listened attentively.

"Right you are," he said. "Now, I think I'll just take a wee look round, daddy. You go back to your cab and wait. *Wait*, see?"

This suggestion evoked a fresh spate of expostulation but Moir became authoritative and the driver finally returned to his cab. Moir looked after him for a moment and then walked along to the forward winch where he was received by the shore gang with a degree of guarded curiosity that in some circles is reserved for the police. He asked them if they had seen the girl and repeated the driver's description. None of them had done so.

As he was turning away one of the men said: "What seems to be the trouble, anyway, Copper?"

"Not to say trouble," Moir called back easily. A second voice asked derisively: "Why don't you get the Flower Killer, Superintendent?"

Moir said good-naturedly: "We're still hoping, mate." And walked away: a man alone on his job.

He began to look for the girl from the flower shop. There were many dark places along the wharf. He moved slowly, flashing his lamp into the areas under platforms, behind packing-cases, between buildings and dumps of cargo and along the dark surface of the water where it made unsavoury but irrelevant discoveries.

It was much quieter now aboard the *Farewell*. He heard the covers go down on the forward hatch and glancing up could just see the Blue Peter hanging limp in the fog. The gang that had been loading the ship went off through one of the sheds and their voices faded into silence.

He arrived back at the passageway. Beyond its far end the taxi still waited. On their way through here to the wharf he and the driver had walked quickly; now he went at a snail's pace, using his flashlight. He knew that surfaces which in the dark and fog looked like unbroken walls, were in fact the rear ends of sheds with a gap between them. There was an alley opening off the main passage and this was dark indeed.

It was now one minute to midnight and the *Cape Farewell*, being about to sail, gave a raucous unexpected hoot like a gargantuan belch. It jolted P.C. Moir in the pit of his stomach.

With a sudden scrabble a rat shot out and ran across his boots. He swore, stumbled and lurched sideways. The light from his flashlamp darted eccentrically up the side alley, momentarily exhibiting a high-heeled shoe with a foot in it. The light fluttered, steadied and returned. It crept from the foot along a leg, showing a red graze through the gap in its nylon stocking. It moved on and came to rest at last on a litter of artificial pearls and fresh flowers scattered over the breast of a dead girl.

CHAPTER TWO

Embarkation

I

At seven o'clock on that same evening an omnibus had left Euston Station for the Royal Albert Docks.

It had carried ten passengers, seven of whom were to embark in the *Cape Farewell*, sailing at midnight for South Africa. Of the remainder, two were seeing-off friends while the last was the ship's doctor, a young man who sat alone and did not lift his gaze from the pages of a formidable book.

After the manner of travellers, the ship's passengers had taken furtive stock of each other. Those who were escorted by friends speculated in undertones about those who were not.

" *My dear !* " Mrs. Dillington-Blick ejaculated. " *Honestly !* Not *one !* "

Her friend made a slight grimace in the direction of the doctor and raised her eyebrows. " Not bad ? " she mouthed. " Noticed ? "

Mrs. Dillington-Blick shifted her shoulders under their mantling of silver fox and turned her head until she was able to include the doctor in an absent-minded glance.

" I *hadn't* noticed," she confessed and added, " Rather nice ? But the others ! My dear ! Best forgotten ! Still——"

" There *are* the officers," the friend hinted slyly.

" My dear ! "

They caught each other's eyes and laughed again, cosily. Mr. and Mrs. Cuddy in the seat in front of them heard their laughter. The Cuddys could smell Mrs. Dillington-Blick's expensive scent. By turning their heads slightly they could see her reflection in the window-pane, like a photomontage richly floating across street lamps and the façades of darkened buildings. They could see the ghosts of her teeth, the feather in her hat, her ear-rings, the orchids on her great bust and her furs.

Mrs. Cuddy stiffened in her navy overcoat and her husband smiled thinly. They, too, exchanged glances and thought of derisive things to say to each other when they were private in their cabin.

In front of the Cuddys sat Miss Katherine Abbott ; alone, neat and composed. She was a practised traveller and knew that the first impression made by fellow-passengers is usually contradicted by experience. She rather liked the rich sound of Mrs. Dillington-Blick's laughter and deplored what she had heard of the Cuddy accent. But her chief concern at the moment was for her own comfort : she disliked being ruffled and had chosen her seat in the middle of the bus because people would be unlikely to brush past her and she was out of the draught when the door opened. In her mind she checked over the contents of her two immaculately packed suitcases. She travelled extremely light because she loathed what she called the " fussation " of heavy luggage. With a single exception she carried nothing that was not positively essential. She thought now of the exception, a photograph in a leather case. To her fury her eyes began to sting. " I'll throw it overboard," she thought. " That'll larn her."

The man in front of her turned a page of his newspaper and through her unshed tears Miss Abbott read a banner headline : " Killer Who Says It With Flowers. Still no arrest." She had longish sight and by casually leaning forward she was able to read the paragraph underneath.

"The identity of the sex-murderer who sings as he kills and leaves flowers by the bodies of his victims is still unknown. Investigations leading to hundreds of interviews have proved clueless. Here (left) is a new snapshot of piquant Beryl Cohen, found strangled on the 15th January, and (right) a studio portrait of Marguerite Slatters, the second victim of a killer who may well turn out to be the worst of his kind since Jack the Ripper Superintendent Alleyn (inset) refuses to make a statement, but says the police will welcome information about Beryl's movements during her last hours (see page 6, 2nd column)."

Miss Abbott waited for the owner of the newspaper to turn to page 6 but he neglected to do so. She stared greedily at the enlarged snapshot of piquante Beryl Cohen and derisively at the inset. Superintendent Alleyn, grossly disfigured by the exigencies of reproduction in newsprint, stared dimly back at her.

The owner of the paper began to fidget. Suddenly he turned his head, obliging Miss Abbott to throw back her own and stare vaguely at the luggage rack where she immediately spotted his suitcase with a dangling label : " P. Merryman, Passenger, S.S. *Cape Farewell*." She had an uncomfortable notion that Mr. Merryman knew she had been reading over his shoulder and in this she was perfectly right.

Mr. Philip Merryman was fifty years old and a bachelor. He was a man of learning and taught English in one of the less distinguished of the smaller public schools. His general appearance, which was highly deceptive, corresponded closely with the popular idea of a schoolmaster, while a habit of looking over the tops of his spectacles and ruffling his hair filled in the outlines of this over-familiar picture. To the casual observer Mr. Merryman was perfect Chips. To his intimates he could be hell.

He was fond of reading about crime, whether fictitious or actual, and had dwelt at some length on the *Evening Herald*'s piece about The Flower Killer as, in its slipshod way, it called this undetected murderer. Mr. Merryman deplored journalese and had the poorest possible opinion of the methods of the police but the story itself quite fascinated him. He read slowly and methodically, wincing at stylistic solecisms and bitterly resentful of Miss Abbott's trespassing glances. "Detested kite!" Mr. Merryman silently apostrophised her. "Blasts and fogs upon you! Why in the names of all the gods at once, can you not buy your own disnatured newspaper!"

He turned to page six, moved the *Evening Herald* out of Miss Abbott's line of sight, read column two as quickly as possible, folded the newspaper, rose and offered it to her with a bow.

"Madam," Mr. Merryman said, "allow me. No doubt you prefer, as I confess I do, the undisputed possession of your chosen form of literature."

Miss Abbott's face darkened into a rich plum colour. In a startlingly deep voice she said: "Thank you: I don't care for the evening paper."

"Perhaps you have already seen it?"

"No," said Miss Abbott loudly. "I haven't and what's more I don't want to. Thank you."

Father Charles Jourdain muttered whimsically to his brother-cleric: "Seeds of discord! Seeds of discord!" They were in the seat opposite and could scarcely escape noticing the incident.

"I do *hope*," the brother-cleric murmured, "that you find someone moderately congenial."

"In my experience there is always someone."

"And you *are* an experienced traveller," the other sighed, rather wistfully.

"Would you have liked the job so much, Father? I'm sorry."

"No, no, no, please don't think it for a moment, really. I would carry no weight in Durban. Father Superior, as always, has made the wisest possible choice. And you are glad to be going—I hope?"

Father Jourdain waited for a moment and then said: "Oh, yes. Yes. I'm glad to go."

"It will be so interesting. The Community in Africa——"

They settled down to talk Anglo-Catholic shop.

Mrs. Cuddy overhearing them, smelt Popery.

The remaining ship's passenger in the bus took no notice at all of her companions. She sat in the front seat with her hands thrust deep into the pockets of her camel-hair coat. She had a black zouave hat on the back of her head and a black scarf wound skilfully about her neck and a great studded black belt round her waist. She was so good-looking that all the tears she had shed still left her attractive. She was not crying now. She tucked her chin into her scarf and scowled at the bus driver's back. Her name was Jemima Carmichael. She was twenty-three and had been crossed in love.

The bus lurched up Ludgate Hill. Dr. Timothy Make-piece put down his book and leant forward, stooping, to see the last of St. Paul's. There it was, fabulous against the night sky. He experienced a sensation which he himself would have attributed, no doubt correctly, to a disturbance of the nervous ganglions but which laymen occasionally describe as a turning over of the heart. This must be, he supposed, because he was leaving London. He had come to that conclusion when he found he was no longer staring at the dome of St. Paul's but into the eyes of the girl in the front seat. She had turned, evidently with the same intention as his own, to look out and upwards.

Father Jourdain was saying: " Have you ever read that rather exciting thing of G.K.C's: *The Ball and the Cross* ? "

Jemima carefully made her eyes blank and faced front. Dr. Makepiece returned uneasily to his book. He was filled with a kind of astonishment.

II

At about the same time as the bus passed by St. Paul's a very smart sports car had left a very smart mews flat in Mayfair. In it were Aubyn Dale, his dearest friend (who owned the car and sat at the wheel in a mink coat) and their two dearest friends who were entwined in the back seat. They had all enjoyed an expensive farewell dinner and were bound for the docks. " The form," the dearest friend said, " is unlimited wassail, darling, in your stateroom. Drunk, I shall be less disconsolate."

" But, *darling* ! " Mr. Dale rejoined tenderly, " you shall be *plastered* ! I promised ! It's all laid on."

She thanked him fondly and presently turned into the Embankment where she drove across the bows of an on-coming taxi whose driver cursed her very heartily. His fare, a Mr. Donald McAngus, peered anxiously out of the window. He also was a passenger for the *Cape Farewell*.

About two and a half hours later a taxi would leave The Green Thumb flower shop in Knightsbridge for the East End. In it would be a fair-haired girl and a box of flowers which was covered with Cellophane, garnished with a huge bow of yellow ribbon and addressed to Mrs. Dillington-Blick. The taxi would head eastward. It, too, was destined for the Royal Albert Docks.

III

From the moment she came aboard the *Cape Farewell*, Mrs. Dillington-Blick had automatically begun to practise what her friends among themselves, called her technique. She had turned her attention first upon the steward. The *Farewell* carried only nine passengers and one steward attended them all. He was a pale, extremely plump young man with blond hair that looked crimped, liquid eyes, a mole at the corner of his mouth and a voice that was both strongly Cockney, strangely affected and indescribably familiar. Mrs. Dillington-Blick took no end of trouble with him. She asked him his name (it was Dennis) and discovered that he also served in the bar. She gave him three pounds and hinted that this was merely an initial gesture. In less than no time she had discovered that he was twenty-five, played the mouth-organ and had taken a dislike to Mr. and Mrs. Cuddy. He showed a tendency to linger but somehow or another, and in the pleasantest manner, she contrived to get rid of him.

" You are wonderful ! " her friend exclaimed.

" My dear ! " Mrs. Dillington-Blick returned, " he'll put my make-up in the fridge when we get to the tropics."

Her cabin was full of flowers. Dennis came back with vases for them and suggested that the orchids also should be kept in the refrigerator. The ladies exchanged glances. Mrs. Dillington-Blick unpinned the cards on her flowers and read out the names with soft little cries of appreciation. The cabin, with its demure appointments and sombre décor seemed to be full of her—of her scent, her furs, her flowers and herself.

" Steward ! " a querulous voice at this juncture, had called in the passage. Dennis raised his eyebrows and went out.

" He's your slave," the friend said. " *Honestly !* "

" I like to be comfortable," said Mrs. Dillington-Blick.

It was Mr. Merryman who had shouted for Dennis. When it comes to separating the easygoing from the exacting passenger, stewards are not easily deceived. But Dennis had been taken in by Mr. Merryman. The spectacles, the rumpled hair and cherubic countenance had led him to diagnose absence-of-mind, benevolence and timidity. He was bitterly disappointed when Mr. Merryman now gave unmistakable signs of being a Holy Terror. Nothing, it seemed, was right with the cabin. Mr. Merryman had stipulated the port side and found himself on the starboard. His luggage had not been satisfactorily stowed and he wished his bed to be made up in the manner practised on land and not, he said, like an unstuck circular.

Dennis had listened to these complaints with an air of resignation ; just not casting up his eyes.

" Quite a chapter of accidents," he said when Mr. Merryman paused. " Yerse. Well, we'll see what we can do for you." He added : " Sir," but not in the manner required by Mr. Merryman at his minor public school.

Mr. Merryman said : " You will carry out my instructions immediately. I am going to take a short walk. When I return I shall expect to find it done." Dennis opened his mouth. Mr. Merryman said : " That will do." Rather pointedly he then locked a case on his dressing-table and walked out of the cabin.

" And I'll take me oaf," Dennis muttered pettishly, " he's T.T. into the bargain. What an old bee."

Father Jourdain's brother-priest had helped him to bestow his modest possessions about his room. This done they had looked at each other with the hesitant and slightly self-conscious manner of men who are about to take leave of each other.

"Well——" they both said together and Father Jourdain added: "It was good of you to come all this way. I've been glad of your company."

"Have you?" his colleague rejoined. "And I, needless to say, of yours." He hid his hands under his cloak and stood modestly before Father Jourdain. "The bus leaves at eleven," he said. "You'd like to settle down, I expect."

Father Jourdain asked, smiling: "Is there something you want to say to me?"

"Nothing of the smallest consequence. It's just—well, I've suddenly realised how very much it's meant to me having the great benefit of your example."

"My dear man!"

"No, really! You strike me, Father, as being quite tremendously sufficient (under God and our Rule, of course) to yourself. All the brothers are a little in awe of you, did you know? I think we all feel that we know much less about you than we do about each other. Father Bernard said the other day that although ours is not a Silent Order you kept your own rule of spiritual silence."

"I don't know that I am altogether delighted by Father Bernard's aphorism."

"Aren't you? He meant it awfully nicely. But I really do chatter much too much. I should take myself in hand and do something about it, I expect. Good-bye, Father. God bless you."

"And you, my dear fellow. But I'll walk with you to the bus."

"No—please——"

"I should like to."

They had found their way down to the lower deck. Father Jourdain said a word to the sailor at the head of the gangway and both priests went ashore. The sailor watched them pace along the wharf towards the passageway at the far end of which the bus waited. In their black cloaks and hats they looked fantastic. The fog swirled about them as they walked. Half an hour had gone by before Father Jourdain returned alone. It was then a quarter past eleven.

Miss Abbott's cabin was opposite Mrs. Dillington-Blick's. Dennis carried the suitcases to it. Their owner unpacked them with meticulous efficiency, laying folded garments away as if for some ceremonial robing. They were of a severe character. At the bottom of the second suitcase there was a stack of music in manuscript. In a pocket of the suitcase was the photograph. It was of a woman of about Miss Abbott's own age, moderately handsome but with a heavy dissatisfied look. Miss Abbott stared at it and fighting back a painful sense of desolation and resentment, sat on the bed and pressed clumsy hands between large knees. Time went by. The ship moved a little at her moorings. Miss Abbott heard Mrs. Dillington-Blick's rich laughter and was remotely and very slightly eased. There was the noise of fresh arrivals, of footsteps overhead and of dockside activities. From a more distant part of the passengers' quarters came sounds of revelry and of a resonant male voice that was somehow familiar. Soon Miss Abbott was to know why. The cabin door had been hooked ajar so that when Mrs. Dillington-Blick's friend came into the passage she was very clearly audible. Mrs. Dillington-Blick stood in her own open doorway and said through giggles : " Go on, then, I dare you," and the friend went creaking down the passage. She returned evidently in high excitement saying : " My dear, it is ! He's shaved it off ! The steward told me. It's Aubyn Dale ! My dear, how perfectly gorgeous for you."

There was another burst of giggling through which

Mrs. Dillington-Blick said something about not being able to wait for the tropics to wear her Jolyon swimsuit. Their further ejaculations were cut off by the shutting of their door.

" Silly fools," Miss Abbott thought dully, having not the smallest interest in television personalities. Presently she began to wonder if she really would throw the photograph overboard when the ship was out at sea. Suppose she were to tear it up now and drop the pieces in the wastepaper basket ? Or into the harbour ? How lonely she would be then ! The heavily-knuckled fingers drummed on the bony knees and their owner began to think about things going overboard into the harbour. The water would be cold and dirty : polluted by the excreta of ships : revolting !

" Oh, *God !* " Miss Abbott said, " how hellishly unhappy I am."

Dennis knocked at her door.

" Telegram, Miss Abbott," he fluted.

" Telegram ? For me ? Yes ? "

He unhooked the door and came in.

Miss Abbott took the telegram and shakily opened it. It fluttered between her fingers.

" Darling Abbey so miserable do please write or if not too late telephone, F."

Dennis had lingered. Miss Abbott said shakily : " Can I send an answer ? "

" Well—ye-ees. I mean to say——"

" Or telephone ? Can I telephone ? "

" There's a phone on board but I seen a queue lined up when I passed."

" How long before we sail ? "

" An hour, near enough, but the phone goes off earlier "

Miss Abbott said distractedly : " It's very important. Very urgent, indeed."

" 'Tch, 'tch."

" Wait. Didn't I see a call box on the dock ? Near the place where the bus stopped ? "

" That's correct," he said appreciatively. " Fancy you noticing ! "

" I've time to go off, haven't I ? "

" Plenty of *time*, Miss Abbott. Oodles."

" I'll do that. I'll go at once."

" There's coffee and sandwiches on in the dining-room."

" I don't want them. I'll go now."

" Cold outside. Proper freezer. Need a coat, Miss Abbott, won't you ? "

" It doesn't matter. Oh, very well. Thank you."

She took her coat out of the wardrobe, snatched up her handbag, and hurried out.

" Straight ahead, down the companionway and turn right," he called after her and added : " Don't get lost in the fog, now."

Her manner had been so disturbed that it aroused his curiosity. He went out on the deck and was in time to see her running along the wharf into the fog. " Runs like a man," Dennis thought. " Well, it takes all sorts."

Mr. and Mrs. Cuddy sat on their respective beds and eyed each other with the semi-jocular family air that they reserved for intimate occasions. The blowers on the bulkhead were pouring hot air into the cabin, the porthole was sealed, the luggage was stowed and the Cuddys were cosy.

" All right so far," Mrs. Cuddy said guardedly.

" Satisfied, dear ? "

" Can't complain. Seems clean."

" Our own shower and toilet," he pointed out, jerking his head at a narrow door.

" They've all got that," she said. " I wouldn't fancy sharing."

"What did you make of the crowd, though? Funny lot, I thought."

"R.C. priests."

"Only the one. The other was seeing-off. Do you reckon, R.C.?"

"Looked like it, didn't it?"

Mr. Cuddy smiled. He had a strange thin smile, very broad and knowing. "They look ridiculous to me," he said.

"We're moving in high society, it seems," Mrs. Cuddy remarked. "Notice the furs?"

"And the *perfume*! Phew!"

"I'll have to keep my eye on you, I can see that."

"Could you catch what was said?"

"Quite a bit," Mrs. Cuddy admitted. "She may talk very la-de-dah but her ideas aren't so refined."

"Reely?"

"She's a man-eater."

Mr. Cuddy's smile broadened. "Did you get the flowers?" he asked. "Orchids. Thirty bob each, they are."

"Get on!"

"They are! It's a fact. Very nice, too," Mr. Cuddy said with a curious twist in his voice.

"Did you see what happened with the other lady reading over the elderly chap's shoulder? In the bus?"

"Did I what! Talk about a freezer! Phew!"

"He was reading about those murders. You know. The flower murderer. They make out he leaves flowers all scattered over the breasts of his victims. And sings."

"Before or after?"

"After, isn't it awful?" Mrs. Cuddy asked with enormous relish.

Mr. Cuddy made an indefinite noise.

His wife ruminated: "It gives me the creeps to think about. Wonder what makes him go on so crazy."

" Women."

" That's right. Put it all on the ladies," she said good-naturedly. " Just like a man."

" Well, ask yourself. Was there much in the paper ? "

" I couldn't see properly but I think so. It's on all the placards. They haven't got him, of course."

" Wish we'd got a paper. Can't think how I forgot."

" There might be one in the lounge."

" What a hope ! "

" The old chap left his in the bus. I noticed."

" Did you ? You know," Mr. Cuddy said, " I've got quite a fancy for the evening paper. I might stroll back and see if it's there. The bus doesn't go till eleven. I can just do it."

" Don't be long. You know what I'm like. If you missed the boat——"

" We don't sail till midnight, dear, and it's only ten to eleven now. I won't be more than a few minutes. Think I'd let you go out to sea with all these fascinatin' sailors ? "

" Get along with you ! "

" Won't be half a tick. I've got the fancy for it."

" I know I'm silly," Mrs. Cuddy said, " but whenever you go out—to the Lodge or anything—I always get that *nervous*."

" Silly girl. I'd say come too, but it's not worth it. There's coffee on down below."

" Coffee essence, more like."

" Might as well try it when I get back. Behave yourself now."

He pulled a steel-grey felt hat down almost to his ears, put on a belted raincoat and, looking rather like the film director's idea of a private detective, he went ashore.

Mrs. Cuddy remained, anxious and upright on her bunk.

Aubyn Dale's dearest friend looking through the porthole

said with difficulty : " Darling : it's boiling up for a pea-shuper-souper. I think perhaps we ought to weep ourselves away."

" Darling, are you going to drive ? "

" Naturally."

" You *will* be all right, *won't* you ? "

" Sweetie," she protested, " I'm never safer than when I'm plastered. It just gives me that little something other drivers haven't got."

" How terrifying."

" To show you how completely in control I am, I suggest that it might be better to leave before we're utterly fogged down. Oh, dear ! I fear I am now going into a screaming weep. Where's my hanky ? "

She opened her bag. A coiled mechanical snake leapt out at her, having been secreted there by her lover who had a taste for such drolleries.

This prank, though it was received as routine procedure, a little delayed their parting. Finally, however, it was agreed that the time had come.

" 'Specially," said their dearest male friend, " as we've killed the last bottle. Sorry, old boy. Bad form. Poor show."

" Come on," said their dearest girl friend. " It's been smashing, actually. Darling Auby ! But we ought to go."

They began elaborate leave-takings but Aubyn Dale said he'd walk back to the car with them.

They all went ashore, talking rather loudly, in well-trained voices, about the fog which had grown much heavier.

It was now five past eleven. The bus had gone, the solitary taxi waited in its place. Their car was parked farther along the wharf. They stood round it, still talking, for some minutes. His friends all told Dale many times how much good the voyage would do him, how nice he looked without his celebrated beard, how run down he was and how desperately the programme would sag without him. Finally they drove off waving and trying to make hip-hip-hooray with their horn.

Aubyn Dale waved, shoved his hands down in the pockets of his camel-hair coat and walked back towards the ship. A little damp breeze lifted his hair, eddies of fog drifted past him. He thought how very photogenic the wharves looked. The funnels on some of the ships were lit from below and the effect, blurred and nebulous though it now had become, was exciting. Lights hung like globes in the murk. There were hollow indefinable sounds and a variety of smells. He pictured himself down here doing one of his special features and began to choose atmospheric phrases. He would have looked rather good, he thought, framed in the entrance to the passageway. His hand strayed to his naked chin and he shuddered. He must pull himself together. The whole idea of the voyage was to get away from his job : not to think of it, even. Or of anything else that was at all upsetting. Such as his dearest friend, sweetie though she undoubtedly was. Immediately, he began to think about her. He ought to have given her something before she left. Flowers ? No, no. Not flowers. They had an unpleasant association. He felt himself grow cold and then hot. He clenched his hands and walked into the passage-way.

About two minutes later the ninth and last passenger for the *Cape Farewell* arrived by taxi at the docks. He was Mr. Donald McAngus, an elderly bachelor, who was suffering from a terrible onset of ship-fever. The fog along the Embankment had grown heavier. In the City it had been atrocious. Several times his taxi had come to a stop, twice it had gone off its course and finally, when he was really feeling physically sick with anxiety the driver had announced that this was as far as he cared to go. He indicated shapes, scarcely perceptible, of roofs and walls and the faint glow beyond them. That, he said, was where Mr. McAngus's ship lay. He had merely to make for the glow and he would be aboard. There ensued a terrible complication over the fare, and the tip : first Mr. McAngus undertipped and then, in a frenzy of apprehension he overtipped. The driver adopted a pitying attitude. He put Mr. McAngus's fibre suitcases into their owner's grip and tucked his cardboard box and his brown paper parcel under his arms. Thus burdened Mr. McAngus disappeared at a shambling trot into the fog and the taxi returned to the West End of London.

The time was now eleven-thirty. The taxi from the flower shop was waiting for his fare and P.C. Moir was about to engage him in conversation. The last hatch was covered, the *Cape Farewell* was cleared and Captain Bannerman, Master, awaited his pilot.

At one minute to twelve the siren hooted.

P.C. Moir was now at the police call-box. He had been put through to the C.I.D.

"There's one other thing, sir," he was saying, " beside the flowers. There's a bit of paper clutched in the right hand, sir. It appears to be a fragment of an embarkation notice, like they give passengers. For the *Cape Farewell*."

He listened, turning his head to look across the tops of half-seen roofs at the wraith of a scarlet funnel, with a white band. It slid away and vanished smoothly into the fog.

"I'm afraid I can't board her, sir," he said. "She's sailed."

CHAPTER THREE

Departure

I

At REGULAR two-minute intervals throughout the night, *Cape Farewell* sounded her siren. The passengers who slept were still, at times, conscious of this noise ; as of some monster blowing monstrous raspberries through their dreams. Those who waked listened with varying degrees of nervous exasperation. Aubyn Dale, for instance, tried to count the seconds between blasts, sometimes making them come to as many as one hundred and thirty and at others, by a deliberate tardiness, getting them down to one hundred and fifteen. He then tried counting his pulse but this excited him. His heart behaved with the greatest eccentricity. He began to think of all the things it was better not to think of, including the worst one of all : the awful debacle of the Midsummer Fair at Melton Medbury. This was just the sort of thing that his psychiatrist had sent him on the voyage to forget. He had already taken one of his sleeping-pills. At two o'clock he took another and it was effective.

Mr. Cuddy also was restive. He had recovered Mr. Merryman's *Evening Herald* from the bus. It was in a somewhat dishevelled condition but when he got into bed he read it exhaustively, particularly the pieces about the Flower Murderer. Occasionally he read aloud for Mrs.

Cuddy's entertainment but presently her energetic snores informed him that this exercise was profitless. He let the newspaper fall to the deck and began to listen to the siren. He wondered if his fellow-travellers would exhibit a snobbish attitude towards Mrs. Cuddy and himself. He thought of Mrs. Dillington-Blick's orchids, heaving a little at their superb anchorage, and himself gradually slipped into an uneasy doze.

Mr. Merryman, on the other hand, slept heavily. If he was visited by dreams of a familiar steward or an inquisitive spinster, they were of too deeply unconscious a nature to be recollected. Like many people of an irascible temperament, he seemed to find compensation for his troubles in the profundity of his slumber.

So, too, did Father Jourdain, who on finishing his prayers, getting into bed and putting himself through one or two pretty stiff devotional hoops, fell into a quiet oblivion that lasted until morning.

Mr. Donald McAngus took a little time to recover from the circumstances that attended his late arrival. However he had taken coffee and sandwiches in the dining-room and had eyed his fellow-passengers with circumspection and extreme curiosity. His was the not necessarily malicious but all-absorbing inquisitiveness of the Lowland Scot. He gathered facts about other people as an indiscriminate philatelist gathers stamps : merely for the sake of adding to his collection. He had found himself at the same table as the Cuddys—the passengers had not yet been given their official places—and had already discovered that they lived in Dulwich and that Mr. Cuddy was " in business " though of what nature Mr. McAngus had been unable to divine. He had told them about his trouble with the taxi. Distressed by Mrs. Cuddy's unwavering stare he had tied himself up in a tangle of parentheses and retired unsatisfied to his room and his bed.

There he lay tidily all night in his gay crimson pyjamas, occupied with thoughts so unco-ordinated and feckless that they modulated imperceptibly into dreams and were not at all disturbed by the reiterated booming of the siren.

Miss Abbott had returned from the call box on the wharf, scarcely aware of the fog and with a dull effulgence under her darkish skin. The sailor at the gangway noticed and was afterwards to remember, her air of suppressed excitement. She went to bed and was still wide-awake when the ship sailed. She watched blurred lights slide past the porthole and felt the throb of the engines at dead slow. At about one o'clock in the morning she fell asleep.

Jemima Carmichael hadn't paid much attention to her companions : it took all her determination and fortitude to hold back her tears. She kept telling herself angrily that crying was a voluntary physical process, entirely controllable and in her case absolutely without justification. Lots of other people had their engagements broken off at the last minute and were none the worse for it : most of them without her chance of cutting her losses and bolting to South Africa.

It had been a mistake to peer up at St. Paul's. That particular kind of beauty always got under her emotional guard ; and there she went again with the man in the opposite seat looking into her face as if he'd like to be sorry for her. From then onwards the bus journey had seemed intolerable but the walk through the fog to the ship had been better. It was almost funny that her departure should be attended by such obvious gloom. She had noticed Mrs. Dillington-Blick's high-heeled patent leather shoes tittupping ahead and had heard scraps of the Cuddys' conversation. She had also been conscious of the young man walking just behind her. When they had emerged from the passage-way to the wharf he said :

"Look, do let me carry that suitcase," and had taken it out of her hand before she could expostulate. "My stuff's all on board," he said. "I feel unimportant with nothing in my hand. Don't you hate feeling unimportant ?"

"Well, no," Jemima said, surprised into an unconven-tional reply. "At the moment, I'm not minding it."

"Perhaps it's a change for you."

"Not at all," she said hurriedly.

"Or perhaps women are naturally shrinking creatures, after all. 'Such,' you may be thinking, 'is the essential vanity of the human male.' And you are perfectly right. Did you know that Aubyn Dale is to be a passenger ?"

"Is he ?" Jemima said without much interest. "I would have thought a luxury liner and organised fun would be more his cup-of-tea."

"I understand it's a rest cure. Far away from the madding camera and I bet you anything you like that in no time he'll be missing his spotlights. I'm the doctor, by the way, and this is my first long voyage. My name's Timothy Makepiece. You must be either Miss Katherine Abbott or Miss Jemima Carmichael and I can't help hoping it's the latter."

"You'd be in a bit of a spot if it wasn't," Jemima said.

"I risked everything on the one throw. Rightly, I per-ceive. Is it your first long voyage ?"

"Yes."

"You don't sound as excited as I would have expected. This is the ship, looming up. It's nice to think we shall be meeting again. What is your cabin number ? I'm not being fresh : I just want to put your bag in it."

"It's 4. Thank you very much."

"Not at all," said Dr. Makepiece politely. He led the way to her cabin, put her suitcase into it, made her a rather diffident little bow and went away.

Jemima thought without much interest: "The funny thing is that I don't believe that young man was putting on an act," and at once stopped thinking about him.

Her own predicament came swamping over her again and she began to feel a great desolation of the spirit. She had begged her parents and her friends not to come to the ship, not to see her off at all and already it seemed a long time ago that she had said good-bye to them. She felt very much alone.

The cabin was without personality. Jemima heard voices and the hollow sounds of footsteps on the deck overhead. She smelt the inward rubbery smell of a ship. How was she to support five weeks of the woman with the pin-heels and the couple with Clapham Common voices and that incredibly forbidding spinster ? She unpacked the luggage which was already in her cabin. Dennis looked in and she thought him quite frightful. Then she took herself to task for being bloody-minded and beastly. At that moment she found in her cabin-trunk a parcel from a wonderful shop with a very smart dress in it and a message from her mother and at this discovery she sat down on her bunk and cried like a small girl.

By the time she had got over that and finished her unpacking she was suddenly quite desperately tired and went to bed.

Jemima lay in her bed and listened to the sounds of the ship and the port. Gradually the cabin acquired an air of being her own and somewhere at the back of all the wretchedness there stirred a very slight feeling of anticipation. She heard a pleasant voice saying again : "You don't sound as excited as I would have expected," and then she was so sound asleep that she didn't hear the ship sail and was only very vaguely conscious of the fog signal, booming at two-minute intervals all night.

By half past twelve all the passengers were in bed, even Mrs. Dillington-Blick who had given her face a terrific workout with a new and complicated beauty treatment.

The officers of the watch went about their appointed ways and the *Cape Farewell*, sailing dead slow, moved out of the Thames estuary with a murderer on board.

II

Captain Jasper Bannerman stood on the bridge with the pilot. He would be up all night. Their job was an ancient one and though they had radar and wireless to serve them, their thoughts as they peered into the blank shiftiness of the fog were those of their remote predecessors. An emergency warning had come through with its procession of immemorial names—Dogger, Dungeness, Outer Hebrides, Scapa Flow, Portland Bill and the Goodwin Sands. " She's a corker," said the pilot alluding to the fog. " Proper job, she's making of it."

The voices of invisible shipping, hollow and desolate sounded at uneven distances. Time passed very slowly.

At two-thirty the wireless officer came to the bridge with two messages.

" I thought I'd bring these up myself, sir," he said, referring obliquely to his cadet. " They're in code. Urgent."

Captain Bannerman said : " All right. You might wait, will you," and went into his room. He got out his code book and deciphered the messages. After a considerable interval he called out : " Sparks."

The wireless officer tucked his cap under his arm, entered the captain's cabin and shut the door.

" This is a damned perishing bloody turn-up," Captain

Bannerman said. The wireless officer waited, trying not to look expectant. Captain Bannerman walked over to the starboard porthole and silently re-read the decoded messages. The first was from the Managing Director of the Cape Line Company :

" Very secret. Directors compliments stop confident you will show every courtesy to Superintendent Alleyn boarding you off Portsmouth by pilot cutter stop will travel as passenger stop suggest uses pilots room stop please keep me personally advised all developments stop your company relies on your discretion and judgment stop Cameron stop message ends."

Captain Bannerman made an indeterminate but angry noise and re-read the second message.

" Urgent immediate and confidential stop Superintendent R. Alleyn will board you off Portsmouth by pilot cutter stop he will explain nature of problem stop this department is in communication with your company stop C. A. Majorie-banks Assistant Commissioner Criminal Investigation Department Scotland Yard message ends."

" I'll give you the replies," Captain Bannerman said, glaring at his subordinate. " Same for both ! ' Instructions received and noted Bannerman.' And you'll oblige me, Sparks, by keeping the whole thing under your cap."

" Certainly, sir."

" Dead under."

" Certainly, sir."

" Very well."

" Thank you, sir."

When the wireless officer had gone Captain Bannerman remained in a sort of scandalised trance for half a minute and then returned to the bridge.

Throughout the rest of the night he gave the matter in hand, which was the pilotage of his ship through the worst fog for ten years, his sharpest attention. At the same time

and on a different level, he speculated about his passengers.
He had caught glimpses of them from the bridge. Like
every man who so much as glanced at her, he had received
a very positive impression of Mrs. Dillington-Blick. A
fine woman. He had also noticed Jemima Carmichael who
came under the general heading of Sweet Young Girl and
as they approached the tropics would probably cause a
ferment among his officers. At another level he was aware
of, and disturbed by, the two radiograms. Why the suffering
cats, he angrily wondered, should he have to take in at the last
second, a plain-clothes detective ? His mind ranged through
an assortment of possible reasons. Stowaway ? Escaping
criminal ? Wanted man in the crew ? Perhaps, merely, a
last-minute assignment at Las Palmas but if so, why didn't
the fellow fly ? It would be an infernal bore to have to put
him up : in the pilot's room of all places where one would be
perpetually aware of his presence. At four o'clock, the time
of low vitality, Captain Bannerman was visited by a premoni-
tion that this was going to be an unlucky voyage.

III

All the next morning the fog still hung over the English
Channel. As she waited off Portsmouth the *Farewell* was
insulated in obscurity. Her five male passengers were on
deck with their collars turned up. In the cases of Messrs.
Merryman, McAngus and Cuddy and Father Jourdain,
they wore surprised-looking caps on their heads and
wandered up and down the boat-deck or sat disconsolately
on benches that would probably never be used again
throughout the voyage. Before long Aubyn Dale came back
to his own quarters. He had, in addition to his bedroom,
a little sitting-room : an arrangement known in the company's offices as The Suite. He had asked Mrs. Dillington-
Blick and Dr. Timothy Makepiece to join him there for a

drink before luncheon. Mrs. Dillington-Blick had sumptu-
ously appeared on deck at about eleven o'clock and,
figuratively speaking with one hand tied behind her back,
had achieved this invitation by half past. Dr. Makepiece
had accepted, hoping that Jemima Carmichael, too, had been
invited but Jemima spent the morning walking on the boat-
deck and reading in a chilly but undiscovered little shelter aft
of the centrecastle.

Mr. McAngus, too, remained but a short time on deck and
soon retired to the passengers' drawing-room, where, after
peering doubtfully at the bookcases, he sat in a corner and
fell asleep. Mrs. Cuddy was also there and also asleep.
She had decided in the teeth of the weather forecast that it
was going to be rough and had taken a pill. Miss Abbott
was tramping up and down the narrow lower deck having,
perhaps instinctively, hit upon that part of the ship which,
after the first few hours, is deserted by almost everyone.
In the plan shown to passengers it was called the promenade
deck.

It was Jemima who first noticed the break in the weather.
A kind of thin warmth fell across the page of her book :
she looked up and saw that the curtain of fog had grown
threadbare and that sunlight had weakly filtered through.
At the same moment the *Farewell* gave her noonday hoot
and then Jemima heard the sound of an engine. She went
over to the port side and there, quite close, was the pilot
cutter. She watched it come alongside the rope ladder. A
tall man stood amidships, looking up at the *Farewell*.
Jemima was extremely critical of men's clothes and she
noticed his with absentminded approval. A sailor at the head
of the ladder dropped a line to the cutter and hauled up two
cases. The pilot went off and the tall man climbed the
ladder very handily and was met by the cadet on duty who
took him up to the bridge.

On his way he passed Mr. Merryman and Mr. Cuddy who looked up from their crime novels and were struck by the same vague notion, immediately dismissed, that they had seen the new arrival before. In this they were not altogether mistaken : on the previous evening they had both looked at his heavily distorted photograph in the *Evening Herald*. He was Superintendent R. Alleyn.

IV

Captain Bannerman put his hands in his jacket pockets and surveyed his latest passenger. At the outset Alleyn had irritated Captain Bannerman by not looking like his own conception of a plain-clothes detective and by speaking with what the Captain, who was an inverted snob, considered a bloody posh accent entirely unsuited to a cop. He himself had been at some pains to preserve his own Midland habits of speech.

" Well," he said. " Superintendent A'*leen* is it ?—I take it you'll tell me what all this is in aid of and I don't mind saying I'll be glad to know."

" I suppose, sir," Alleyn said, " you've been cursing ever since you got whatever signals they sent you."

" Well—not to say cursing."

" I know damn' well what a bore this must be. The only excuse I can offer is one of expedience : and I must say of extreme urgency."

Captain Bannerman, deliberately broadening his vowels said : " Sooch a-a-s ? "

" Such as murder. Multiple murder."

" Mooltipul murder ? Here : you don't mean this chap that says it with flowers and sings."

" I do, indeed."

" What the hell's he got to do with my ship ? "

"I've every reason to believe," Alleyn said, "that he's aboard your ship."

"Don't talk daft."

"I dare say it does sound preposterous."

Captain Bannerman took his hands out of his pockets, walked over to a porthole and looked out. The fog had lifted and the *Farewell* was underway. He said, with a change of voice: "There you are! That's the sort of crew they sign on for you these days. Murderers!"

"My bosses," Alleyn said, "don't seem to think he's in the crew."

"The stewards have been in this ship three voyages."

"Nor among the stewards. Unless sailors or stewards carry embarkation notices."

"D'you mean to stand there and tell me we've shipped a murdering passenger?"

"It looks a bit like it at the moment."

"Here!" Captain Bannerman said with a change of voice. "Sit down. Have a drink. I might have known it'd be a passenger."

Alleyn sat down but declined a drink, a circumstance that produced the usual reaction from his companion. "Ah!" Captain Bannerman said with an air of gloomy recognition. "I suppose not. I suppose not."

His manner was so heavy that Alleyn felt impelled to say: "That doesn't mean, by the way, that I'm about to arrest you."

"I doubt if you could, you know. Not while we're at sea. I very much question it."

"Luckily, the problem doesn't at the moment arise."

"I should have to look up the regulations," sighed Captain Bannerman.

"Look here," Alleyn suggested, "may I try and give you the whole story, as far as it affects my joining your ship?"

" That's what I've been waiting for, isn't it ? "

" Yes," Alleyn agreed, " I'm sure it is. Here goes, then ! "

He looked full at Captain Bannerman who seated himself, placed his hands on his knees, raised his eyebrows and waited.

" You know about these cases, of course," Alleyn said, " as far as they're being reported in the papers. During the last thirty days up to about eleven o'clock last night there have been two homicides which we believe to have been committed by the same person, and which may be part of a larger pattern. In each case the victim was a woman and in each case she had been strangled and flowers had been left on the body. I needn't worry you with any other details at the moment. Last night, a few minutes before this ship sailed a third victim was found. She was in a dark side-alley off the passageway between the place where the bus and taxis put down passengers and the actual wharf where you were moored. She was a girl from a flower-shop who was bringing a box of hyacinths to one of your passengers : a Mrs. Dillington-Blick. Her string of false pearls had been broken and the flowers had been scattered, in the usual way, over the victim."

" Any singing ? "

" What ? Oh, that. That's an element that has been very much played up by the Press. It certainly does seem to have occurred on the first occasion. The night of the fifteenth of last month. The victim you may remember was Beryl Cohen who ran a cheapjack stall in Warwick Road and did a bit of the older trade on the side. She was found in her bed-sitting-room in a side street behind Paddington. The lodger in the room above seems to have heard the visitor leaving at about ten o'clock. The lodger says the visitor was singing."

"What a dreadful thing," Captain Bannerman said primly. "What sort of song, for God's sake?"

"The Jewel Song," Alleyn said, "from *Faust*. In an alto voice."

"I'm a bass-baritone, myself," the Captain said absently. "Oratorio," he gloomily added.

"The second victim," Alleyn went on, "was a respectable spinster called Marguerite Slatters, who was found similarly strangled in a street in Fulham on the night of the 25th January. A nightwatchman on duty in a warehouse nearby says he heard someone rendering 'The Honeysuckle and the Bee' in a highish voice at what may have been the appropriate time."

Alleyn paused, but Captain Bannerman merely glowered at him.

"And it appears that the sailor on duty at the head of your gangway last night heard singing in the fog. A funny sort of voice, he said. Might mean anything, of course, or nothing. Drunken seaman. Anything. He didn't recognise the tune."

"Here! About last night. How d'you know the victim was——" Captain Bannerman began and then said: "All right. Go on."

"In her left hand, which was clenched in cadaveric spasm, was a fragment of one of the embarkation notices your company issues to passengers. I believe the actual ticket is usually pinned to this notice and torn off by the officer whose duty it is to collect it. He hands the embarkation notice back to the passenger: it has no particular value but I dare say a great many passengers think it constitutes some kind of authority and stick to it. Unfortunately this fragment only showed part of the word *Farewell* and the date."

"No name?"

"No name."

" Doesn't amount to much, in that case," said Captain Bannerman.

" It suggests that the victim, struggling with her murderer grasped this paper, that it was torn across and that the rest of it may have remained in the murderer's possession or may have been blown somewhere about the wharf."

" The whole thing might have been blowing about the wharf when the victim grabbed it."

" That's a possibility of course."

" Probability, more like. What about the other half, then ? "

" When I left for Portsmouth this morning it hadn't been found."

" There you are ! "

" But if all the others have kept their embarkation notices——"

" Why should they ? "

" May we tackle that one a bit later ? Now, the body was found by the P.C. on that beat, five minutes before you sailed. He's a good chap and kept his head admirably, it seems, but he couldn't do anything about boarding you. You'd sailed. As he talked to me on the dock telephone he saw your funnel slip past into the fog. A party of us from the Yard went down and did the usual things. We got in touch with your Company, who were hellishly anxious that your sailing shouldn't be delayed."

" I'll be bound ! " Captain Bannerman ejaculated.

"——and my bosses came to the conclusion that we hadn't got enough evidence to justify our keeping you back while we held a full-scale inquiry in the ship."

" My Gawd ! "

" So it was decided that I should sail with you and hold it, as well as I can, under the counter."

" And what say," Captain Bannerman asked slowly and

without any particular signs of bad temper, " what say I won't have it ? There you are ! How about that ? "

" Well," Alleyn said, " I hope you don't cut up rough in that particular direction and I'm sure you won't. But suppose you did and suppose I took it quietly, which, by the way, I wouldn't : the odds are you'd have another corpse on your hands before you made your next landfall."

Captain Bannerman leant forward, still keeping his palms on his knees, until his face was within a few inches of Alleyn's. His eyes were of that piercing, incredible blue that landsmen so correctly associate with sailors and his face was the colour of old bricks.

" Do you mean," he asked furiously, " to tell me you think this chap's not had enoof to satisfy him for the voyage ? "

" So far," Alleyn said, " he's been operating at ten-day intervals. That'll carry him, won't it, to somewhere between Las Palmas and Capetown ? "

" I don't believe it. I don't believe he's aboard."

" Don't you ? "

" What sort of a chap is he ? Tell me that."

Alleyn said : " You tell me. You've got just as good a chance of being right."

" Me ! "

" You or anyone else : may I smoke ? "

" Here——" the Captain began and reached for a cigarette box.

"——a pipe, if you don't mind." Alleyn pulled it out and as he talked, filled it.

" These cases," he said, " are the worst of the lot from our point-of-view. We can pick a card-sharp or a con-man or a sneak-thief or a gunman or a dozen other bad lots by certain mannerisms and tricks of behaviour. They develop occupational habits and they generally keep company with their own kind. But not the man who, having never before been in trouble with the police, begins, perhaps latish in

life, to strangle women at ten-day intervals and leave flowers
on their faces. He's a job for the psychiatrist if ever there
was one and he doesn't go in for psychiatry. He's merely
an example. But of what? The result of bad housing
conditions, or a possessive mother or a kick on the head at
football or a bullying schoolmaster or a series of regrettable
grandparents? Again, your guess is as good as mine. He is.
He exists. He may behave with perfect propriety in every
possible aspect of his life but this one. He may be, and
often is, a colourless little fellow who trots to and fro upon
his lawful occasions for, say fifty years, seven months and a
day. On the day after that he trots out and becomes a
murderer. Probably there have been certain eccentricities
of behaviour which he's been at great pains to conceal and
which have suddenly become inadequate. Whatever compulsion it is that hounds him into his appointed crime, it
now takes over. He lets go and becomes a monster."

"Ah!" Captain Bannerman said, "a monster. There's
unnatural things turn up where you'd least expect to find
them in most human souls. That I will agree to. But not
in my ship."

The two men looked at each other, and Alleyn's heart
sank. He knew pigheadedness when he met it.

The ship's engines, now at full speed, drove her, outward
bound, upon her course. There was no more fog: a sunny sea-
scape accepted her as its accident. Her wake opened obedi-
ently behind her and the rhythm of her normal progress
established itself. England was left behind and the *Farewell*,
sailing on her lawful occasions, set her course for Las Palmas.

V

"What," Captain Bannerman asked, "do you want me
to do? The thing's flat-out ridiculous but let's hear what
you want. I can't say fairer than that, can I? Come on."

" No," Alleyn agreed, " that's fair enough and more than I bargained for. First of all, perhaps I ought to tell you what I don't want. Particularly, I don't want to be known for what I am."

" Is that so ? "

" I gather that supercargoes are a bit out-of-date, so I'd better not be a supercargo. Could I be an employee of the company going out to their Durban office ? "

Captain Bannerman stared fixedly at him and then said : " It'd have to be something very senior."

" Why ? On account of age ?——"

" It's nothing to do with age. Or looks. Or rather," Captain Bannerman amended, " it's the general effect."

" I'm afraid I don't quite——"

" You don't look ill, either. Voyage before last, outward bound, we carried a second cousin of the managing director's. Getting over D.T.'s, he was, after taking one of these cures. You're not a bit like him. You're not a bit like a detective either if it comes to that," Captain Bannerman added resentfully.

" I'm sorry."

" Have you always been a 'tec ? "

" Not absolutely."

" I know," Captain Bannerman said, " leave it to me. You're a cousin of the chairman and you're going out to Canberra via Durban to one of these legations or something. There's all sorts of funny jobs going in Canberra. Anybody'll believe anything, almost."

" Will they ? "

" It's a fact."

" Fair enough. Who *is* your chairman ? "

" Sir Graeme Harmond."

" Do you mean a little fat man with pop eyes and a stutter ? "

"Well," said Captain Bannerman, staring at Alleyn, "if you care to put it that way."

"I know him."

"You don't tell me ! "

"He'll do."

"Do ! "

"I'd better not use my own name. There's been something in the papers. How about C. J. Roderick ? "

"Roderick ? "

"It happens to be the first chunk of my own name but it's never appeared in print. When you do this sort of thing you answer more readily to a name you're used to." He thought for a moment. "No," he said. "Let's play safer and make it Broderick."

"Wasn't your picture in last night's *Herald* ? "

"*Was* it ? Hell ! "

"Wait a bit."

The Captain went into his stateroom and came back with a copy of the paper that had so intrigued Mr. Cuddy. He folded it back at the snapshot of piquante Beryl Cohen and Superintendent R. Alleyn (inset).

"Is that like me ? " Alleyn said.

"No."

"Good."

"There may be a very slight resemblance. It looks as if your mouth was full."

"It was."

"I see," said Captain Bannerman heavily.

"We'll have to risk it."

"I suppose you'll want to keep very much to yourself ? "

"On the contrary. I want to mix as much as possible with the passengers."

"Why ? "

Alleyn waited for a moment and then asked : " Have you got a good memory for dates ? "

" *Dates.* "

" Could you, for instance, provide yourself with a cast-iron alibi plus witnesses for the fifteenth of last month between ten and eleven p.m., the twenty-fifth between nine p.m. and midnight and for last night during the half-hour before you sailed ? "

Captain Bannerman breathed stertorously and whispered to himself. At last he said : " Not all three, I couldn't."

" There you are, you see."

Captain Bannerman removed his spectacles and again advanced his now empurpled face to within a short distance of Alleyn's.

" Do I look like a Sex-Monster ? " he furiously demanded.

" Don't ask *me*," Alleyn rejoined mildly. " I don't know what they look like. That's part of the trouble. I thought I'd made it clear."

As Captain Bannerman had nothing to say to this, Alleyn went on. " I've got to try and check those times with all your passengers and—please don't misunderstand me, sir—I can only hope that most of them manage to turn in solider alibis than, on the face of it, yours looks to be."

" Here ! I'm clear for the 15th. We were berthed in Liverpool and I was aboard with visitors till two in the morning."

" If that can be proved we won't pull you in for murder."

Captain Bannerman said profoundly : " That's a queer sort of style to use when you're talking to the Master of the ship."

" I mean no more than I say, and that's not much. After all, you don't come aboard your own ship, clutching an embarkation notice."

Captain Bannerman said : " Not as a rule. No."

Alleyn stood up. " I know," he said, " what a bind this is for you and I really am sorry. I'll keep as quiet as I reasonably may."

" I'll bet you anything you like he hasn't shipped with us. Anything you like ! Now ! "

" If we'd been dead certain we'd have held you up until we got him."

" It's all some perishing mistake."

" It may be."

" Well," Captain Bannerman said grudgingly as he also rose. " I suppose we'll have to make the best of it. No doubt you'd like to see your quarters. This ship carries a pilot's cabin. On the bridge. We can give you that if it suits."

Alleyn said it would suit admirably. " And if I can just be treated as a passenger——"

" I'll tell the Chief Steward." He went to his desk, sat down behind it, pulled a slip of paper towards him and wrote on it, muttering as he did so. " Mr. C. J. Broderick, relative of the chairman, going out to a Commonwealth Relations Office job in Canberra. That it ? "

" That's it. I don't, of course, have to tell you anything about the need for complete secrecy."

" You do not. I've no desire to make a fool of myself, talking daft to my ship's complement."

A fresh breeze had sprung up and was blowing through the starboard porthole. It caught the memorandum that the Captain had just completed. The paper fluttered, turned over and was revealed as a passenger's embarkation notice for the *Cape Farewell*.

Staring fixedly at Alleyn, the Captain said : " I used it yesterday in the offices. For a memo." He produced a curiously uncomfortable laugh. " It's not been torn, anyway," he said.

" No," Alleyn said, " I noticed that."

An irresponsible tinkling on a xylophonic gong announced the first luncheon on board the *Cape Farewell*, outward bound.

CHAPTER FOUR

Hyacinths

I

HAVING WATCHED Alleyn mount the companionway Jemima Carmichael returned to her desolate little veranda aft of the centrecastle and to her book.

She had gone through the morning in a kind of trance, no longer inclined to cry or to think much of her broken engagement and the scenes that had attended it or even of her own unhappiness. It was as if the fact of departure had removed her to a spiritual distance quite out-of-scale with the night's journey down the estuary and along the Channel. She had walked until she was tired, tasted salt on her lips, read a little, heard gulls making their B.B.C. atmospheric noises and watched them fly mysteriously in and out of the fog. Now in the sunshine she fell into a half-doze.

When she opened her eyes it was to find that Doctor Timothy Makepiece stood not far off, leaning over the rail with his back towards her. He had, it struck her, a pleasant nape to his neck : his brown hair grew tidily into it. He was whistling softly to himself. Jemima, still in a strange state of inertia idly watched him. Perhaps he sensed this for he turned and smiled at her.

" Are you all right ? " he asked. " Not sea-sick or any-thing ? "

" Not at all. Only ridiculously sleepy."

" I expect that *is* the sea. They tell me it does have that effect on some people. Did you see the pilot go off and the arrival of the dark and handsome stranger ? "

" Yes, I did. Had he missed the ship last night do you suppose ? "

" I've no idea. Are you going for drinks with Aubyn Dale before lunch ? "

" Not I."

" I hoped you were. Haven't you met him yet ? " He didn't seem to expect an answer to this question but wandered over and looked sideways at Jemima's book.

" Elizabethan Verse ? " he said. " So you don't despise anthologies. Which is your favourite—Bard apart ? "

" Well—Michael Drayton, perhaps, if he wrote ' Since there's no help '."

" I'll back the Bard for that little number every time." He picked up the book, opened it at random and began to chuckle.

" ' *O yes, O yes, if any maid*
Whom leering Cupid hath betrayed,' " he read.
" Isn't *that* a thing, now ? Leering Cupid ! They really were wonderful. Do you—but no," Tim Makepiece said, interrupting himself, " I'm doing the thing I said to myself I wouldn't do."

" What was that ? " Jemima asked, not with any great show of interest.

" Why, forcing my attentions on you to be sure."

" What an Edwardian expression."

" None the worse for that."

" Shouldn't you be going to your party ? "

" I expect so," he agreed moodily. " I don't really like alcohol in the middle of the day and am far from being one of Mr. Aubyn Dale's fans."

" Oh."

" I've yet to meet a man who is."

" All jealous of him, I dare say," Jemima said idly.

" You may be right. And a very sound reason for disliking him. It's the greatest mistake to think that jealousy is necessarily a fault. On the contrary, it may very well sharpen the perception."

" It didn't sharpen Othello's."

" But it did. It was his *interpretation* of what he saw that was at fault. He *saw*, with an immensely sharpened perception."

" I don't agree."

" Because you don't want to."

" Now, look here——" Jemima said, for the first time giving him her full attention.

" He saw Cassio, doing his sophisticated young Venetian act over Desdemona's hand. He saw him at it again after he'd blotted his copy-book. He was pathologically aware of every gallantry that Cassio showed his wife."

" Well," Jemima said, " if you're pathologically aware of every attention Aubyn Dale shows his however-many-they-may-be female fans, I must say I'm sorry for you."

" All right, Smartie," Tim said amiably, " you win."

" After all, it's the interpretation that matters."

" There's great virtue in perception alone. Pure scientific observation that is content to set down observed fact after observed fact——"

" Followed by pure scientific interpretation that adds them all up and makes a nonsense."

" Why should you say that ? " he asked gently. " It's you that's making a nonsense."

" Well, I must say ! "

" To revert to Aubyn Dale. What about his big thing on TV?—' Pack Up Your Troubles.' In other words ' Come to me everybody that's got a bellyache and I'll put you before my public and pay you for it.' If I were a religious man I'd call it blasphemy."

" I don't say I *like* what he does——"

" Still, he does make an ass of himself good and proper, on occasions. Witness the famous Molton Medbury Midsummer Muck-up."

" I never heard exactly what happened."

" He was obviously plastered. He went round televising the Molton Medbury flower show with old Lady Agatha Panthing. You could see he was plastered before he spoke and when he did speak he said the first prize in the competition went to Lady Agatha's umbilicus globular. He meant," Timothy explained, " Agapanthus Umbellatus globosus. I suppose it shattered him because after that a sort of rot set in and at intervals he broke into a recrudescence of Spoonerisms. It went on for weeks. Only the other day he was going all springlike over a display of hyacinths and said that in arranging them all you really needed was a ' turdy stable '."

" Oh, *no* ! Poor chap. How too shaming for him ! "

" So he shaved off his fetching little imperial and I expect he's taking a long sea voyage to forget. He's in pretty poor shape, I fancy."

" Do you ? What sort of poor shape ? "

" Oh, neurosis," Timothy said shortly, " of some sort. I should think."

The xylophonic gong began its inconsequent chiming in the bridge-house.

" Good lord, that's for *eating* ! " Timothy exclaimed.

" What *will* you say to your host ? "

" I'll say I had an urgent case among the greasers. But I'd better just show up. Sorry to have been such a bore. Good-bye, now," said Tim attempting a brogue.

He walked rapidly away.

To her astonishment and slightly to her resentment Jemima found that she was ravenously hungry.

II

The Cape Company is a cargo line. The fact that six of its ships afford accommodation for nine passengers each does not in any way modify the essential function of the company. It merely postulates that in the case of these six ships there shall be certain accommodation. There will also be a Chief Steward without any second string, a bar-and-passengers' steward and an anomalous offsider who may be discovered by the passengers polishing the taps in their cabins at unexpected moments. The business of housing, feeding and, within appropriate limits, entertaining the nine passengers is determined by Head Office and then becomes part of the Captain's many concerns.

On the whole, Captain Bannerman preferred to carry no passengers, and always regarded them as potential trouble-makers. When, however, somebody of Mrs. Dillington-Blick's calibre appeared in his ship, his reaction corres-ponded punctually with that of ninety per cent of all other males whom she encountered. He gave orders that she should be placed at his table (which luckily was all right anyway because she carried V.I.P. letters) and, until Alleyn's arrival, had looked forward to the voyage with the liveliest anticipation of pleasurable interludes. He was, he con-sidered, a young man for his age.

Aubyn Dale he also took at his table because Dale was famous and Captain Bannerman felt that in a way he would be bunching Mrs. Dillington-Blick by presenting her with a No. 1 Personality. Now he decided, obscurely and resentfully, that Alleyn also would be an impressive addition to the table. The rest of the seating he left to his Chief Steward who gave the Cuddys and Mr. Donald McAngus to the First Mate, whom he disliked ; Jemima Carmichael and Dr. Makepiece to the Second Mate and the Wireless

Officer of whom he approved, and Miss Abbott, Father Jourdain and Mr. Merryman to the Chief Engineer towards whom his attitude was neutral.

This, the first luncheon on board, was also the first occasion at which the senior ship's officers with the exception of those on duty were present. At a long table in a corner, sat a number of young men presenting several aspects of adolescence and all looking a trifle sheepish. These were the electrical and engineering junior officers and the cadets.

Alleyn arrived first at the table and was carefully installed by the Captain's steward. The Cuddys, already seated hard-by, settled down to a good long stare and so, more guardedly, did Mr. McAngus. Mrs. Cuddy's burning curiosity manifested itself in a dead-pan glare which was directed intermittently at the objects of her interest. Its mechanics might be said to resemble those of a lighthouse whose different frequencies make its signals recognisable far out at sea.

Mr. Cuddy, on the contrary, kept observation under cover of an absent-minded smile while Mr. McAngus quietly rolled his eyes in the direction of his objective and was careful not to turn his head.

Miss Abbott, at the Chief Engineer's table, gave Alleyn one sharp look and no more. Mr. Merryman rumpled his hair, opened his eyes very wide and then fastened with the fiercest concentration upon the menu. Father Jourdain glanced in a civilised manner at Alleyn and turned with a pleasant smile to his companions.

At this juncture Mrs. Dillington-Blick made her entrance ; rosy with achievement, buzzing with femininity, and followed by the Captain, Aubyn Dale and Timothy Makepiece.

The Captain introduced Alleyn—" Mr. Broderick, who joined us to-day——"

The men made appropriate wary noises at each other. Mrs. Dillington-Blick, who might have been thought to be already in full flower, awarded herself a sort of bonus in effulgence. Everything about her blossomed madly. "Fun!" she seemed to be saying. "This is what I'm really good at. We're all going to like this."

She bathed Alleyn in her personality. Her eyes shone, her lips were moist, her small hands fluttered at the ends of her Rubenesque arms. "But I *watched* you!" she cried. "I watched you with my heart in my mouth! Coming on board! Nipping up that Frightful Thing! Do tell me. Is it as Terrifying as it looks or am I being silly?"

"It's plain murder," Alleyn said, "and you're not being silly at all. I was all of a tremble."

Mrs. Dillington-Blick cascaded with laughter. She raised and lowered her eyebrows at Alleyn and flapped her hands at the Captain. "There now!" she cried. "Just what I supposed. How you dared! If it was a choice of feeding the little fishes or crawling up that ladder I swear I'd pop thankfully into the shark's maw. And don't you look so superior," she chided Captain Bannerman.

This was exactly how he had hoped she would talk. A fine woman who enjoyed a bit of chaff. And troubled though he was, he swelled a little in his uniform.

"We'll have you shinning down it like an old hand," he teased, "when you go ashore at Las Palmas." Aubyn Dale looked quizzically at Alleyn who gave him the shadow of a wink. Mrs. Dillington-Blick was away to a magnificent start. Three men, one a celebrity, two good-looking and all teasing her. Las Palmas? Did they mean . . . ? Would she have to . . . ? Ah no! She didn't believe them.

A number of rococo images chased each other improperly through Alleyn's imagination. "Don't give it another thought," he advised, "you'll make the grade. I understand that if the sea's at all choppy they rig a safety net down below. Same as trapeze artistes have when they lose their nerve."

" I won't listen."

" It's the form, though, I promise you," Alleyn said. " Isn't it, sir ? "

" Certainly."

" Not true ! Mr. Dale, they're being *beastly* to me ! "

Dale said : " I'm on your side." It was a phrase with which he often reassured timid subjects on television. He was already talking to Mrs. Dillington-Blick as if they were lifelong friends and yet with that touch of deference that lent such distinction to his programmes and filled Alleyn, together with eighty per cent of his male viewers, with a vague desire to kick him. There was a great deal of laughter at the Captain's table. Mrs. Cuddy was moved to stare at it so fixedly that at one moment she completely missed her mouth.

A kind of restlessness was engendered in the passengers, a sense of being done out of something and, in two of the women, of resentment. Miss Abbott felt angry with Mrs. Dillington-Blick because she was being silly over three men. Mrs. Cuddy felt angry with her because three men were being silly over her and also because of a certain expression that had crept into Mr. Cuddy's wide smile. Jemima Carmichael wondered how Mrs. Dillington-Blick could be bothered and then took herself to task for being a humbug : the new passenger, she thought, was quite enough to make any girl do her stuff. She found that Dr. Makepiece was looking at her and to her great annoyance she blushed. For the rest of luncheon she made polite conversation with the second mate who was Welsh and bashful and with the Wireless Officer who wore that wild and lonely air common to his species.

After luncheon Alleyn went to see his quarters. The pilot's cabin had a door and porthole opening on to the bridge. He could look down on the bows of the ship, thrust arrow-like into the sea and at the sickle-shaped and watery world beyond. Under other circumstances, he thought, he would have enjoyed this trip. He unpacked his suitcases, winked at a photograph of his wife, went below and carried out a brief inspection of the passengers' quarters. These were at the same level as the drawing-room and gave on to a passage that went through from port to starboard. The doors were all shut with the exception of that opening into the cabin aft of the passage on the port side. This was open and the cabin beyond resembled an over-crowded flower-shop. Here Dennis was discovered, sucking his thumb and lost in contemplation. Alleyn knew that Dennis, of whom this was his first glimpse, might very well become a person of importance. He paused by the door.

"Afternoon," he said. "Are you the steward for the pilot's cabin?"

Evidently Dennis had heard about Alleyn. He hurried to the door, smiled winsomely and said: "Not generally, but I'm going to have the pleasure of looking after *you*, Mr. Broderick."

Alleyn tipped him five pounds. Dennis said: "Oh, you shouldn't sir, really," and pocketed the note. He indicated the flowers and said, "I just can't make up my mind, sir: Mrs. Dillington-Blick said I was to take some into the dining-room and lounge and as soon as I've finished in the bar I'm going to but I *don't* know which to choose. Such an umberance-der-riches! What would you say for the *lounge*, sir? The décor's dirty *pink*."

Alleyn was so long answering that Dennis gave a little giggle. "Isn't it *diffy*!" he sympathised.

Alleyn pointed a long finger. "That," he said. "I should certainly make it that one," and went on his way to the passengers' lounge.

III

It was a modest combination of bar, smoking-room and card-room and in it the passengers were assembled for coffee. Already by the curious mechanism of human attraction and repulsion they had begun to sort themselves into groups. Mr. McAngus having found himself alongside the Cuddys at luncheon was reappropriated by them both and seemed to be not altogether at ease in their company, perhaps because Mrs. Cuddy stared so very fixedly at his hair which, Alleyn noticed, was of an unexpected shade of nutbrown with no parting and a good deal of overhang at the back. He drew a packet of herbal cigarettes from his pocket and lit one, explaining that he suffered from asthma. They began to chat more cosily about diseases. Mr. McAngus confided that he was but recently recovered from an operation and Mr. Cuddy returned this lead with a lively account of a suspected duodenal ulcer.

Father Jourdain and Mr. Merryman had discovered a common taste in crime fiction and smiled quite excitedly at each other over their coffee cups. Of all the men among the passengers, Alleyn thought, Father Jourdain had the most arresting appearance. He wondered what procession of events had led this man to become an Anglo-Catholic celibate priest. There was intelligence and liveliness in the face whose pallor, induced no doubt by the habit of his life, emphasised rather than concealed the opulence of the mouth and watchfulness of the dark eyes. His short white hands were muscular and his hair thick and glossy. He was infinitely more vivid than his companion, whose baby-faced petulance, Alleyn felt, was probably the outward wall of the conventional house-master. He caught himself up. "Conventional?" Was Mr. Merryman the too-familiar pedant who cultivates the eccentric to compensate himself for the deadly boredom of scholastic routine ? A don *manqué* ? Alleyn took himself mildly to task for indulgence in idle speculation and looked elsewhere.

Dr. Timothy Makepiece stood over Jemima Carmichael with the slightly mulish air of a young Englishman in the early stages of an attraction. Alleyn noted the formidable lines of Dr. Makepiece's jaw and mouth and, being at the moment interested in hands, the unusual length of the fingers.

Miss Abbott sat by herself on a settee against the wall. She was reading. The hands that held her neatly-covered book were large and muscular. Her face, he reflected, would have been not unhandsome if it had been only slightly less inflexible and if there had not been the suggestion of— what was it?—harshness ?—about the jaw.

As for Aubyn Dale, there he was, with Mrs. Dillington-Blick who had set herself up with him hard-by the little bar. When she saw Alleyn she beckoned gaily to him. She was busy establishing a coterie. As Alleyn joined them Aubyn Dale laid a large beautifully tended hand over hers and burst into a peal of all-too-infectious laughter. " What a perfectly marvellous person you are ! " he cried boyishly and appealed to Alleyn. " Isn't she wonderful ? "

Alleyn agreed fervently and offered them liqueurs.

" You take the words out of my mouth, dear boy," Dale exclaimed.

" I oughtn't to ! " Mrs. Dillington-Blick protested. " I'm on an *inquisitorial* diet ! " She awarded her opulence a downward glance and Alleyn an upward one. She raised her eyebrows. " My dear ! " she cried. " You can see for yourself. I oughtn't."

" But you're going to," he rejoined and the drinks were served by the ubiquitous Dennis who had appeared behind the bar. Mrs. Dillington-Blick, with a meaning look at Dale, said that if she put on another ounce she would never get into her Jolyon swimsuit and they began to talk about his famous session on commercial television. It appeared that when he visited America and did a specially sponsored half-hour, he had been supported by a great mass of superb models all wearing Jolyon swimsuits. His hands eloquently sketched their curves. He leant towards Mrs. Dillington-Blick and whispered. Alleyn noticed the slight puffiness under his eyes and the blurring weight of flesh beneath the inconsiderable jaw which formally his beard had hidden. " Is this the face," Alleyn asked himself, " that launched a thousand hips ? " and wondered why.

" You haven't forgotten the flowers ? " Mrs. Dillington-Blick asked Dennis and he assured her that he hadn't.

"As soon as I've a spare *sec.* I'll pop away and fetch them," he promised and smiled archly at Alleyn. " They're all chosen and ready."

As Aubyn Dale's conversation with Mrs. Dillington-Blick tended to get more and more confidential Alleyn felt himself at liberty to move away. At the far end of the lounge Mr. Merryman was talking excitedly to Father Jourdain who had begun to look uncomfortable. He caught Alleyn's eye and nodded pleasantly. Alleyn dodged round the Cuddys and Mr. McAngus and by-passed Miss Abbott. There was a settee near the far end but as he made for it Father Jourdain said : " Do come and join us. These chairs are much more comfortable and we'd like to introduce ourselves."

Alleyn said : " I should be delighted," and introductions were made. Mr. Merryman looked sharply at him over the tops of his spectacles and said : " How do you do, sir." He added astonishingly : " I perceived that you were effecting an escape from what was no doubt an excruciating situation."

" I ? " Alleyn said. " I don't quite——"

" The sight," Mr. Merryman continued in none too quiet a voice, " of yonder popinjay ruffling his dubious plumage at the bar is singularly distasteful to me and no doubt intolerable to you."

" Oh, come, now ! " Father Jourdain protested.

Alleyn said : " He's not as bad as all that, is he ? "

" You know who he is, of course."

" Yes, indeed."

" Yes, yes," said Father Jourdain. " We know. Ssh ! "

" Have you witnessed his weekly exhibitions of indecent exposure on the television ? "

" I'm not much of a viewer," Alleyn said.

" Ah ! You show your good judgment. As an underpaid pedagogue it has been my hideous lot to sit on Tuesday evenings among upper middle-class adolescents of low intelligence, ' looking in ' (loathsome phrase) at this man's antics. Let me tell you what he does, sir. He advertises women's bathing clothes and in another programme he incites—arrogant presumption—he incites members of the public to bring their troubles to him ! And the fools do ! Conceive ! " Mr. Merryman invited. " Picture to yourself ! A dupe is discovered. Out of focus, unrecognisable, therefore. Facing this person and us, remorselessly illuminated, and elevated in blasphemous (you will appreciate that in clerical company I use the adjective advisedly) in blasphemous supremacy is or was the countenance you see before you, but garnished with a hirsute growth which lent it a wholly spurious distinction."

Alleyn glanced with amusement at Mr. Merryman and thought what bad luck it was for him that he was unable to give visual expression to his spleen. For all the world he looked like an indignant baby.

" If you will believe me," he continued angrily whispering, " a frightful process known as ' talking it over ' now intervenes. The subject discloses to That Person and to however many thousands of listening observers there may be, some intimate predicament of her (it is, I repeat, usually a woman) private life. *He* then propounds a solution, is thanked, applauded, preens himself and is presented with a fresh sacrifice. Now! What do you think of *that*!" whispered Mr. Merryman.

" I think it all sounds very embarrassing," Alleyn said.

Father Jourdain made a comically despairing face at him. " Let's talk about something else," he suggested. " You were saying Mr. Merryman, that the psychopathic murderer——"

" You heard of course," Mr. Merryman remorselessly interjected, " what an exhibition he made of himself at a later assignment. ' Lady Agatha's umbilicus globular '," he quoted, and broke into a shrill laugh.

" You know," Father Jourdain remarked, " I'm on holiday and honestly *don't* want to start throwing my priestly weight about." Before Mr. Merryman could reply he raised his voice a little and added : " To go back, as somebody, was it Humpty Dumpty ? said, to the last conversation but one : I'm immensely interested in what you were saying about criminals of the Heath type. What was the book you recommended ? By an American psychiatrist, I think you said."

Mr. Merryman muttered huffily : " I don't recollect."

Alleyn asked : " Not, by any chance, *The Show of Violence*, by Frederick Wertham ? "

Father Jourdain turned to him with unconcealed relief. " Ah ! " he said. " You're an addict, too, and a learned one, evidently."

" Not I. The merest amateur. Why, by the way, is everybody so fascinated by crimes of violence ? " He looked at Father Jourdain. " What do you think, sir ? "

Father Jourdain hesitated and Mr. Merryman cut in.

" I am persuaded," he said, " that people read about murder as an alternative to committing it."

" A safety valve ? " Alleyn suggested.

" A conversion. The so-called anti-social urge is fed into a socially acceptable channel : we thus commit our crimes of violence at a safe remove. We are all," Mr. Merryman said tranquilly folding his hands over his stomach, " savages at heart." He seemed to have recovered his good humour.

" Do you agree ? " Alleyn asked Father Jourdain.

" I fancy," he rejoined, " that Mr. Merryman is talking about something I call original sin. If he is, I do of course agree."

An accidental silence had fallen on the little assembly. Into this silence with raised voice, as a stone into a pool, Alleyn dropped his next remark.

" Take for instance, this strangler—the man who ' says it with '—what are they ? Roses ? What, do you suppose, is behind all that ? "

The silence continued for perhaps five seconds.

Miss Abbott said : " Not roses. Hyacinths. Flowers of several kinds."

She had lifted her gaze from her book and fixed it on Mrs. Dillington-Blick. " Hot-house flowers," she said. " It being winter. The first time it was snowdrops, I believe."

" And the second," Mr. Merryman said, " hyacinths."

Aubyn Dale cleared his throat.

" Ah yes ! " Alleyn said. " I remember now. Hyacinths."

" Isn't it awful ? " Mrs. Cuddy gloated.

" Shocking," Mr. Cuddy agreed. " Hyacinths ! Fancy ! "

Mr. McAngus said gently : " Poor things."

Mr. Merryman with the falsely innocent air of a child that knows it's being naughty asked loudly : " Hasn't there been something on television about these flowers ? Something rather ludicrous ? Of what can I be thinking ? "

Everybody avoided looking at Aubyn Dale, but not even Father Jourdain found anything to say.

It was at this juncture that Dennis staggered into the room with a vast basket of flowers which he set down on the central table.

" Hyacinths ! " Mrs. Cuddy shrilly pointed out. " What a coincidence ! "

IV

It was one of those naïve arrangements which can give nothing but pleasure to the person who receives them unless, of course, that person is allergic to scented flowers. The hyacinths were rooted and blooming in a mossy bed. They trembled slightly with the motion of the ship, shook out their incongruous fragrance and filled the smoking-room with reminiscences of the more expensive kinds of shops, restaurants and women.

Dennis fell back a pace to admire them.

" Thank you, Dennis," Mrs. Dillington-Blick said.

" It's a pleasure, Mrs. Dillington-Blick," he rejoined. " Aren't they gorgeous ? "

He retired behind the bar. The passengers stared at the growing flowers and the flowers, quivering, laid upon them a further burden of sweetness.

Mrs. Dillington-Blick explained hurriedly : " There isn't room for all one's flowers in one's cabin. I thought we'd enjoy them together."

Alleyn said : " But what a charming gesture." And was barely supported by a dilatory murmur.

Jemima agreed quickly : " Isn't it ? Thank you so much, they're quite lovely."

Tim Makepiece murmured : " What nice manners you've got, Grandmama."

" I do hope," Mrs. Dillington-Blick said, " that nobody finds the scent too much. Me, I simply wallow in it." She turned to Aubyn Dale. He rejoined : " But of course. You're so wonderfully exotic." Mr. Merryman snorted.

Mrs. Cuddy said loudly : " I'm afraid we're going to be spoilsports : Mr. Cuddy can't stay in the same room with flowers that have a heavy perfume. He's allergic to them."

" Oh, I *am* so sorry," Mrs. Dillington-Blick cried. " Then, of course, they must go." She waved her hands helplessly.

" I'm sure there's no need for that," Mrs. Cuddy announced. " We don't want to make things uncomfortable. We were going to take a turn on deck anyway. Weren't we, dear ? "

Alleyn asked : " Do you suffer from hay-fever, Mr. Cuddy ? "

Mrs. Cuddy answered for her husband. " Not exactly hay-fever, is it, dear ? He just comes over queer."

" Extraordinary," Alleyn murmured.

" Well, it's quite awkward sometimes."

" At weddings and funerals for instance it must be."

" Well on our *silver* wedding some of the gentlemen from Mr. Cuddy's Lodge brought us a gorgeous mixed booky of hothouse flowers and he had to say how much he appreciated it and all the time he was feeling peculiar and when they'd gone he said : ' I'm sorry, Mum, but it's me or the booky ' and we live opposite a hospital so he took them across and had to go for a long walk afterwards to get over it, didn't you, dear ? "

" *Your* silver wedding," Alleyn said, and smiled at Mrs. Cuddy. " You're not going to tell us you've been married twenty-five years ! "

" Twenty-five years and eleven days to be exact. Haven't we, dear ? "

" That's correct, dear."

" He's turning colour," Mrs. Cuddy said, exhibiting her husband with an air of triumph. " Come on, love. Walky-walky."

Mr. Cuddy seemed unable to look away from Mrs. Dillington-Blick. He said : " I don't notice the perfume too heavy. It isn't affecting me."

" That's what *you* say," his wife replied, ominously bluff. " You come into the fresh air, my man." She took his arm and turned him towards the glass doors that gave on to the deck. She opened them. Cold, salt air poured into the heated room and the sound of the sea and of the ship's engines. The Cuddys went out. Mr. Cuddy shut the doors and could be seen looking back into the room. His wife removed him and they walked away, their grey hair lifting in the wind.

" They'll die of cold ! " Jemima exclaimed. " No coats or hats."

" Oh, dear ! " Mrs. Dillington-Blick lamented and appealed in turn to the men. " And I expect it's all my fault." They murmured severally.

Mr. McAngus, who had peeped into the passage confided : " It's all right. They've come in by the side door and I *think* they've gone to their cabin." He sniffed timidly at the flowers, gave a small apologetic laugh and made a little bobbing movement to and from Mrs. Dillington-Blick. " *I* think we're all most awfully lucky," he ventured. He then went out into the passage, putting on his hat as he did so.

" That poor creature dyes its hair," Mr. Merryman observed calmly.

" Oh, come ! " Father Jourdain protested and gave Alleyn a helpless look. " I seem," he said under his breath, " to be saying nothing but ' Oh, come.' A maddening observation."

Mrs. Dillington-Blick blossomed at Mr. Merryman : " Aren't you *naughty* ! " She laughed and appealed to Aubyn Dale : " *Not* true. *Is* it ? "

" I honestly can't see, you know, that if he does dye his

hair, it's anybody's business but his," Dale said, and gave Mr. Merryman his celebrated smile. " Can you ? " he said.

" I entirely agree with you," Mr. Merryman rejoined, grinning like a monkey. " I must apologise. In point of fact I abominate the public elucidation of private foibles."

Dale turned pale and said nothing.

" Let us talk about flowers instead," Mr. Merryman suggested and beamed through his spectacles upon the company.

Mrs. Dillington-Blick at once began to do so. She was supported, unexpectedly, by Miss Abbott. Evidently they were both experienced gardeners. Dale listened with a stationary smile. Alleyn saw him order himself a second double brandy.

" I suppose," Alleyn remarked generally, " everybody has a favourite flower."

Mrs. Dillington-Blick moved into a position from which she could see him. " Hallo, you ! " she exclaimed jollily. " But, of course they have. Mine's magnolias."

" What are yours ? " Tim Makepiece asked Jemima.

" Distressingly obvious—roses."

" Lilies," Father Jourdain smiled, " which may also be obvious."

" Easter ? " Miss Abbott barked.

" Exactly."

" What about you ? " Alleyn asked Tim.

" The hop," he said cheerfully.

Alleyn grinned. " There you are. It's all a matter of association. Mine's lilac and throws back to a pleasant childhood memory. But if beer happened to make you sick or my nanny, whom I detested, had worn lilac in her nankeen bosom or Father Jourdain associated lilies with death, we'd have all hated the sight and smell of these respective flowers."

Mr. Merryman looked with pity at him. " Not," he said,

" a remarkably felicitous exposition of a somewhat elementary proposition, but, as far as it goes, unexceptionable."

Alleyn bowed. " Have you, sir," he asked, " a preference ? "

" None, none. The topic, I confess, does not excite me."

" I think it's a *heavenly* topic," Mrs. Dillington-Blick cried. " But then I adore finding out about people and their preferences." She turned to Dale and at once his smile reprinted itself. " Tell me your taste in flowers," she said, " and I'll tell you your type in ladies. Come clean, now. Your favourite flower ? Or shall I guess ? "

" Agapanthas ? " Mr. Merryman loudly suggested. Dale clapped his glass down on the bar and walked out of the room.

" Now *look* here, Mr. Merryman ! " Father Jourdain said and rose to his feet.

Mr. Merryman opened his eyes very wide and pursed his lips : " What's up ? " he asked.

" You know perfectly well what's up. You're an extremely naughty little man and although it's none of my business I think fit to tell you so."

Far from disconcerting Mr. Merryman this more or less public rebuke appeared to afford him enjoyment. He clapped his hands lightly, slapped them on his knees and broke into elfish laughter.

" If you'll take my advice," Father Jourdain continued, " you will apologise to Mr. Dale."

Mr. Merryman rose, bowed and observed in an extremely high-falutin' manner : " *Consilia formuora sunt de divinis locis.*"

The priest turned red.

Alleyn, who didn't see why Mr. Merryman should be allowed to make a corner in pedantry, racked his own brains for a suitable tag. " ' *Consilium inveniunt multi se docti explicant* ', however," he said.

" Dear me ! " Mr. Merryman observed. " How often one has cause to remark that a platitude sounds none the better for being uttered in an antique tongue. I shall now address myself to my post-prandial nap."

He trotted towards the door, paused for a moment to stare at Mrs. Dillington-Blick's pearls and then went out.

" For pity's sake ! " she ejaculated. " What is all this ! What's happening ? What's the matter with Aubyn Dale ? Why agapanthas ? "

" Can it be possible," Tim Makepiece said, " that you don't know about Lady Agatha's umbilicus globula and the hyacinths on the turdy stable ? " and he retold the story of Aubyn Dale's misfortunes.

" How *frightful* ! " Mrs. Dillington-Blick exclaimed, laughing until she cried. " How too tragically frightful ! And how *naughty* of Mr. Merryman."

Tim Makepiece said : " We don't 'alf look like being a happy family. What will Mr. Chips's form be, one asks oneself, when he enters the Torrid Zone ? "

" He may look like Mr. Chips," Alleyn remarked. " He behaves like Thersites."

Jemima said : " I call it the rock-bottom of him. You could see Aubyn Dale minded most dreadfully. He went as white as his teeth. What could have possessed Mr. Chips ? "

" Schoolmaster," Miss Abbott said, scarcely glancing up from her book. " They often turn sour at his age. It's the life."

She had been quiet for so long they had forgotten her. " That's right," she continued, " isn't it, Father ? "

" It may possibly, I suppose, be a reason. It's certainly not an excuse."

" I think," Mrs. Dillington-Blick lamented, " I'd better throw my lovely hyacinths overboard, don't you ? " She appealed to Father Jourdain. " Wouldn't it be best ? It's not only poor Mr. Dale."

" No," Jemima agreed. " Mr. Cuddy, we must remember, comes over queer at the sight of them."

" Mr. Cuddy," Miss Abbott observed, " came over queer but not, in my opinion, at the sight of the hyacinths." She lowered her book and looked steadily at Mrs. Dillington-Blick.

" My dear ! " Mrs. Dillington-Blick rejoined and began to laugh again.

" Well ! " Father Jourdain said with the air of a man who refuses to recognise his nose before his face. " I think I shall see what it's like on deck."

Mrs. Dillington-Blick stood between him and the double doors and he was quite close to her. She beamed up at him. His back was turned to Alleyn. He was still for a moment and then she moved aside and he went out. There was a brief silence.

Mrs. Dillington-Blick turned to Jemima.

" My dear ! " she confided. " I've *got* that man. He's a reformed rake."

Mr. McAngus re-entered from the passage still wearing his hat. He smiled diffidently at his five fellow passengers.

" All settling down ? " he ventured evidently under a nervous compulsion to make some general remark.

" Like birds in their little nest," Alleyn agreed cheerfully.

" Isn't it delicious," Mr. McAngus said, heartened by this response, " to think that from now on it's going to get warmer and warmer and warmer ? "

" Absolutely enchanting."

Mr. McAngus made the little *chassé* with which they were all to become familiar, before the basket of hyacinths.

" Quite intoxicating," he said. " They are my favourite flowers."

" Are they ! " cried Mrs. Dillington-Blick. " Then do please, *please* have them. Please do. Dennis will take them to your room. Mr. McAngus, I should adore you to have them."

He gazed at her in what seemed to be a flutter of bewildered astonishment. " I ? " Mr. McAngus said. " But why ? I beg your pardon, but it's so very kind, and positively I can't believe you mean it."

" But I do, indeed. Please have them."

Mr. McAngus hesitated and stammered. " I'm quite overcome. Of course I should be delighted." He gave a little giggle and tilted his head over to one side. " Do you know," he said, " this is the first occasion, the *very* first, on which a lady has ever, of her own free will, offered me her flowers ? And my favourites, too. Thank you. Thank you very much indeed."

Alleyn saw that Mrs. Dillington-Blick was touched by this speech. She smiled kindly and unprovocatively at him and Jemima laughed gently.

" I'll carry them myself," Mr. McAngus said. " Of course I will. I shall put them on my little table and they'll be reflected in my looking-glass."

" Lucky man ! " Alleyn said lightly.

" Indeed, yes. May I, really ? " he asked. Mrs. Dillington-Blick nodded gaily and he advanced to the table and grasped the enormous basket with his reddish bony hands. He was an extremely thin man and, Alleyn thought, very much older than his strange nutbrown hair would suggest.

" Let me help you," Alleyn offered.

" No, no ! I'm really very strong, you know. Wiry."

He lifted the basket and staggered on bent legs with it to the door. Here he turned, a strange figure, his felt hat tilted over his nose, blinking above a welter of quivering hyacinths.

" *I* shall think of something to give *you*," he promised Mrs. Dillington-Blick, " after Las Palmas. There must be a reciprocal gesture."

He went groggily away.

" He may dye his hair a screaming magenta if he chooses," Mrs. Dillington-Blick said. " He's a sweetie-pie."

From behind her covered book Miss Abbott remarked in that not very musical voice : " Meanwhile we await his reciprocal gesture. After Las Palmas."

CHAPTER FIVE

Before Las Palmas

I

ALLEYN SAT in the pilot's cabin looking at his file of the case in question. Captain Bannerman was on the bridge outside. At regular intervals he marched past Alleyn's porthole. The weather, as Mr. McAngus had predicted, was getting warmer and in two days *Cape Farewell* would sight Las Palmas. She steamed now through a heavy swell. A tendency to yawn, doze and swap panaceas against seasickness had broken out among the passengers.

"January 15th. 13 Hop Lane. Paddington," Alleyn read. "Beryl Cohen. Jewess. Cheapjack. Part-time prostitute. Showy. Handsome. About 26. 5 feet 6 inches. Full figure. Red (dyed) hair. Black skirt. Red jersey. Artificial necklace (green glass). Found January 16th: 10.5 a.m. by fellow lodger. Estimated time of death: between 10 and 11 p.m. previous night. On floor, face upward. Broken necklace. Flowers (snowdrops) on face and breast. Cause: manual strangulation but necklace probably first. Lodger states she heard visitor leave about 10.45. Singing. Jewel Song, *Faust*. High-pitched male voice."

A detailed description of the room followed. He skipped it and read on.

"January 25th. Alley-way off Ladysmith Crescent, Fulham. Marguerite Slatters, of 36A Stackhouse Street, Fulham. London. Floral worker. Respectable. Quiet. 37. 5 feet 8 inches. Slight. Homely. Dark brown hair. Sallow complexion. Brown dress. Artificial pearls and teeth. Brown beret, gloves and shoes. Returning home from St. Barnabas' Parish Church. Found 11.55 by Stanley Walker, chauffeur. Estimated time of death between 9 and 12 p.m. By doorstep of empty garage. Face upward. Broken necklace. Torn dress. Manual strangulation. Flowers (hyacinths) on face and breast. Had no flowers when last seen alive." Alfred Bates, nightwatchman in warehouse next door, says he heard a light voice singing 'Honeysuckle and the Bee.' Thinks the time was about 10.45.

Alleyn sighed and looked up. Captain Bannerman bobbed past the porthole. The ship was heaved upward and forward, the horizon tilted, rose and sank.

" February 1st. Passageway between sheds, Cape Company's No. 2 wharf Royal Albert Dock. Coralie Kraus of 16 Steep Lane, Hampstead. Assistant at Green Thumb, Knightsbridge. 18. Naturalised Austrian. Lively. Well-conducted. 5 feet 4¾ inches. Fair hair. Pale complexion. Black dress, gloves and shoes. No hat. Pink artificial jewellery. (Ear-rings, bracelet, necklace, clips.) Taking box of hyacinths to Mrs. Dillington-Blick, passenger, *Cape Farewell*. Found 11.48 p.m. by P.C. Martin Moir. Body warm. Death estimated between 11.15 and 11.48 p.m. Face upwards. Stocking torn. Jewellery broken. Ears torn. Manual strangulation. Fragment of embarkation notice for S.S. *Cape Farewell* in right hand. Flowers (hyacinths) on face and breast. Seaman (on duty. *Cape Farewell* gangway) mentioned hearing high male voice singing. Very foggy conditions. All passengers went ashore (ref. above seaman) except Mr. Donald McAngus who arrived last."

Alleyn shook his head, pulled towards him a half-finished letter to his wife and after a moment, continued it.

"——so instead of drearily milling over these grisly, meagre and infuriating bits of information-received I offer them, my darling, to you : together with any developments that may, as Fox says in his more esoteric flights of fancy, accrue. There they are, then, and for the first time you will have the fun, God help you, of following a case as it develops from the casebook. The form, I suppose, is to ask oneself what these three wretched young women had in common and the answer is : very nearly damn' all unless you feel inclined to pay any attention to the fact that in common with ninety per cent of their fellow females, they all wore false jewellery. Otherwise they couldn't physically, racially or morally be less like each other. On the other hand they all met their death in exactly the same fashion and each was left with her broken necklace and ghastly little floral tribute. By the way, I imagine I've spotted one point of resemblance which didn't at first jump to the eye. Wonder if you have ?

" As for the fragment of embarkation notice in Miss Kraus's right hand, that's all I've got to justify my taking this pleasure cruise and if it was blowing about the wharf and she merely happened to clutch it in her death throes, it'll be another case of public money wasted. The Captain, egged on by me, got the steward (a queer little job called Dennis) to collect the embarkation notices as if it was the usual procedure. With this result :

Mrs. Dillington-Blick. Has lost it.

Mr. and Mrs. Cuddy. Joint one. Names written in. Just possible he could have fiddled in ' Mr. and ' when he found he'd lost his own. Room for fiddle. Can check office procedure.

Mr. Merryman. Had it in waistcoat pocket and now accuses steward of pinching it (!).

Father Jourdain. Chucked it overboard.

Mr. McAngus. Can't find it but says he's sure he kept it. Frantic search—fruitless.

Dr. Makepiece. Wasn't given one.

Aubyn Dale. Thinks his sweetie took it. Doesn't know why.

Miss Abbott. Put it in wastepaper basket. (Gone.)

Miss Carmichael. Has got.

So that's not much cop. No torn embarkation notice.

" I've told you about getting the D-B's hyacinths planted
in the lounge. Dazzling reactions from Dale and Cuddy.
Pity it was both. Explanation for Dale's megrim (spoonerism
on TV) very persuasive. Note Cuddys' wedding anniversary
date. Am I or am I not playing fair ? Darling Troy, how
very much, by the way, I love you.

" On a sea voyage, you may remember, human relation-
ships undergo a speeding-up process. People get to know
each other after a fashion very quickly, and often develop a
kind of intimacy. They lose their normal sense of responsibility and become suspended, like the ship, between two
worlds. They succumb to infatuations. Mr. Cuddy is
succumbing to an infatuation for Mrs. D-B and so, in a
vague rarified way, is Mr. McAngus. The Captain belongs
to the well-known nautical group ' middle-aged sea-dog.'
High blood-pressure. Probably soaks in the tropics.
Amorous. (Do you remember your theory about men of a
certain age ?) Has also set his course for Mrs. D-B. Makepiece has got his eye on Jemima Carmichael and so have all
the junior officers. She's a nice child with some sort of
chip on her shoulder. The D-B is a tidy armful and knows
it. Mrs. Cuddy is a network of subfusc complications and
Miss Abbott is unlikely on the face of it, to release the
safety catch in even the most determined sex-monster. But
I suppose I shouldn't generalise. She shaves.

" As for the men : I've told you enough about our
Mr. Merryman to indicate what a cup-of-tea *he* is. It may
help to fill in the picture if I add that he is the product of
St. Chads, Cantor, and Caius, looks a bit like Mr. Pickwick
and much more like Mr. Chips and resembles neither in
character. He's retired from teaching but displays every
possible pedagogic eccentricity from keeping refuse in his

waistcoat pocket to laying down the law in and out of season. He despises policemen, seems to have made a sort of corner in acerbity and will, I bet you, cause a real row before the journey's over.

Aubyn Dale : Education, undivulged. ? Non-U. So like himself on TV that one catches oneself supposing him to be two-dimensional. His line is being a thoroughly nice chap and he drinks about three times as much as is good for him. For all I know, he may be a thoroughly nice chap. He has a distressing predilection for practical jokes and has made a lifelong enemy of Merryman by causing the steward to serve him with a plastic fried egg at breakfast.

Jourdain : Lancing and B.N.C. On a normal voyage would be a pleasant companion. To me, the most interesting of the men but then I always want to find out at what point in an intelligent priest's progress P.C. Faith begins to direct the traffic. I'll swear in this one there's still a smack of the jay-walker.

Cuddy : Methodist School. Draper. Not very delicious. Inquisitive. Conceited. A bit mean. Might be a case for a psychiatrist.

Makepiece : Felsted, New College and St. Thomas's. *Is* a psychiatrist. The Orthodox B.M.A. class. Also M.D. Wants to specialise in criminal psychiatry. Gives the impression of being a sound chap.

McAngus : Scottish High School. Philatelist. Amiable eunuch : but I don't mean literally ; a much-too-facile label. May, for all one knows, be a seething mass of 'thing.' Also very inquisitive. Gets in a tizzy over details. Dyes, as you will have gathered, his hair.

" Well, my dear love, there you are. The night before Las Palmas, with the connivance of Captain Bannerman, who is only joining in because he hopes I'll look silly, I am giving a little party. You have just read the list of guests.

It's by way of being an experiment and may well turn out to be an unproductive bore. But what the hell, after all, am I to do? My instructions are not to dive in, boots and all, declare myself and hold a routine investigation, but to poke and peer and peep about and try to find out if any of these men has *not* got an alibi for one of the three vital occasions. My instructions are also to prevent any further activities, and not antagonise the Master who already turns purple with incredulity and rage at the mere suggestion of our man being aboard his ship. On the face of it the D-B and Miss C. look the likeliest candidates for strangulation, but you never know. Mrs. Cuddy may have a *je ne sais quoi* which has escaped me but I fancy that as a potential victim Miss Abbott is definitely out. However that may be, you can picture me, as we approach the tropics, muscling in on any cosy little party *à deux* that breaks out in the more secluded corners of the boat deck and thus becoming in my own right a likely candidate for throttling. (Not really, so don't agitate yourself.) Because the ladies must be protected. At Las Palmas there should be further reports from headquarters, following Fox's investigations at the Home end. One can only hope they'll cast a little beam. At the moment there's not a twinkle but——"

There was a tap at the door and, on Alleyn's call, the wireless cadet, a wan youth, came in with a radiogram.

" In code, Mr. Broderick," he said

When he had gone Alleyn decoded the message and after an interval continued his letter.

" Pause indicating suspense. Signal from Fox. It appears that a young lady from the hardware department in Woolworth's called Bijou Browne, after thirty days' disastrous hesitation, has coyly informed the Yard that she was half-strangled near Strand-on-the-Green on January 5th. The assailant offered her a bunch of helibore (Christmas roses to you) and told her there was a spider on her neck. He

started in on her rope of beads which, being poppets,
broke ; was interrupted by the approach of a wayfarer and
bolted. It was a dark night and all she can tell Fox about
her assailant is that he too was dark, spoke very nice, and
wore gloves and ever such a full dark beard."

II

Alleyn's suggestion that he should give a dinner party
was made, in the first instance, to Captain Bannerman.

" It may be unorthodox," Alleyn said, " but there's just
a chance that it may give us a lead about these people."

" I can't say I see how you work that out."

" I hope you will, though, in a minute. And, by the by,
I'll want your collaboration, sir, if you'll agree to give it."

" Me ! Now then, now then, what is all this ? "

" Let me explain."

Captain Bannerman listened with an air of moody detach-
ment. When Alleyn had finished the Captain slapped his
palms on his knees and said : " It's a damn' crazy notion
but if it proves once and for all that you're on a wild goose
chase it'll be worth the trouble. I won't say no. Now ! "

Fortified by this authority Alleyn interviewed the Chief
Steward, who expressed astonishment. Any parties that
were given aboard this ship, the Chief Steward explained,
were traditionally cocktail parties for which Dennis, always
helpful, made very dainty little savouries and records were
played over the loudspeaker.

However, before Alleyn's vast prestige as a supposed
V.I.P. and relation of the Managing Director, objections
dissolved. Dennis became flushed with excitement, the
stewards were gracious and the chef, a Portuguese whose
almost moribund interest in his art revived under a whacking
great tip, enthusiastic. Tables were run together and
decorated, wine was chosen and at the appointed hour the

eight passengers, the mate, the chief engineer, Alleyn and Tim Makepiece, having first met for drinks in the lounge, were assembled in the dining-room at a much later hour than was usually observed for dinner at sea.

Alleyn sat at one end of the table with Mrs. Cuddy on his right and Miss Abbott on his left. The Captain sat at the other between Mrs. Dillington-Blick and Jemima : an arrangement that broke down his last resistance to so marked a departure from routine and fortified him against the part he had undertaken to play.

Alleyn was a good host ; his professional knack of getting other people to talk, coupled with the charm to which his wife never alluded without using the adjective indecent, generated an atmosphere of festivity. He was enormously helped by Mrs. Dillington-Blick whose genuine enthusiasm and plunging neckline were, in their separate modes, provocative of jollity. She looked so dazzling that she sounded brilliant. Father Jourdain, who sat next to her was admirable. Aubyn Dale, resplendent in a velvet dinner-jacket, coruscated with bonhomie and regaled his immediate neighbours with stories of practical jokes that he had successfully inflicted upon his chums, as he called them, in the world of admass. These anecdotes met with a gay response in Mrs. Dillington-Blick.

Mr. McAngus wore a hyacinth in his buttonhole. Tim Makepiece was obviously enjoying himself and Jemima had an air of being astonished at her own gaiety. Mr. Merryman positively blossomed or, at any rate, sprouted a little, under the influence of impeccably chosen wines and surprisingly good food while Miss Abbott relaxed and barked quite jovially across the table at Mr. Cuddy. The two officers rapidly eased off their guarded good manners.

The Cuddys were the tricky ones. Mrs. Cuddy looked as if she wasn't going to give herself away if she knew it and Mr. Cuddy's smile suggested that he enjoyed secret information about something slightly discreditable to everyone else. They exchanged looks occasionally.

However as the Montrachet was followed by Pierrier Jouet in a lordly magnum, even the Cuddys shed some of their caginess. Mrs. Cuddy, having assured Alleyn that they never touched anything but a drop of port wine on anniversaries, was persuaded to modify her austerity and did so with abandon. Mr. Cuddy cautiously sipped and asked sharp questions about the wine, pointing out with tedious iteration that it was all above his head, he being a very simple-loving person and not used to posh meals. Alleyn was unable to like Mr. Cuddy very much.

Nevertheless it was he who provided a means of introducing the topic that Alleyn had planned to exploit. There were no flowers on the table. They had been replaced by large bowls of fruit and shaded lamps, in deference, Alleyn pointed out, to Mr. Cuddy's idiosyncrasy. It was an easy step from here to the flower murderer. " Flowers," Alleyn suggested, " must have exactly the opposite effect on him to the one they have on you, Mr. Cuddy. A morbid attraction. Wouldn't you say so, Makepiece ? "

" It might be so," Tim agreed cheerfully. " From the standpoint of clinical psychiatry there is probably an unconscious association——"

He was young enough and had drunk enough good wine to enjoy airing his shop and, it seemed, essentially modest enough to pull himself up after a sentence or two. " But really very little is known about these cases," said he apologetically. " I'm probably talking through my hat."

But he had served Alleyn's purpose, and the talk was now concentrated on the flower murderer. Theories were advanced. Famous cases were quoted. Arguments abounded. Everybody seemed to light up pleasurably on the subject of the death by strangulation of Beryl Cohen and Marguerite

Slatters. Even Mr. Merryman became animated and launched a full-scale attack on the methods of the police who, he said, had obviously made a complete hash of their investigation. He was about to embroider his theme when the Captain withdrew his right hand from under the table-cloth without looking at Mrs. Dillington-Blick, raised his glass of champagne and proposed Alleyn's health. Mrs. Cuddy, shrilly and unexpectedly ejaculated, " Speech, speech ! " and was supported by the Captain, Aubyn Dale, the officers and her husband. Father Jourdain murmured : " By all means, speech." Mr. Merryman looked sardonic and the others, politely apprehensive, tapped the table.

Alleyn stood up. His great height and the circumstances of his face being lit from below like an actor's in the days of footlights, may have given point to the silence that fell upon the room. The stewards had retired into the shadows, there was a distant rattle of crockery. The anonymous throb of the ship's progress re-established itself.

" It's very nice of you," Alleyn said, " but I'm no hand at all at speeches and would make a perfect ass of myself if I tried, particularly in this distinguished company :—The Church ! Television ! Learning ! No, no. I shall just thank you all for making this, I hope I may say, such a good party and sit down." He made as if to do so when to everybody's amazement, and judging by his extraordinary expression, his own as well, Mr. Cuddy suddenly roared out in the voice of a tone-deaf bull : " For—or——"

The sound he made was so destitute of anything remotely resembling any air that for a moment everybody was at a loss to know what ailed him. Indeed it was not until he had got as far as " Jolly Good Fellow," that his intention became clear and an attempt was made by Mrs. Cuddy, the Captain and the officers to support him. Father Jourdain then good-humouredly struck in but even his pleasant tenor could make little headway against the deafening atonalities of Mr.

Cuddy's ground-swell. The tribute ended in confusion and a deadly little silence.

Alleyn hastened to fill it. He said, " Thank you very much," and caught Mr. Merryman's eye.

" You were saying," he prompted, " that the police have made a hash of their investigations : in what respect, exactly ? "

" In every possible respect, my dear sir. What have they done ? No doubt they have followed the procedure they bring to bear upon other cases which they imagine are in the same category. This procedure having failed they are at a loss. I have long suspected that our wonderful police methods so monotonously extolled by a too-complacent public, are in reality, cumbersome, inflexible and utterly without imaginative direction. The murderer has not obliged them by distributing pawn tickets, driving licences or visiting cards about the scenes of his activities and they are left therefore gaping."

" Personally," Alleyn said, " I can't imagine how they even begin to tackle their job. I mean what *do* they do ? "

" You may well ask ! " cried Mr. Merryman now pleasurably uplifted. " No doubt they search the ground for something they call, I understand, occupational dust, in the besotted hope that their man is a bricklayer, knifegrinder or flour-miller. Finding none, they accost numbers of blameless individuals who have been seen in the vicinity and, weeks after the event, ask them to produce alibis. Alibis ! " Mr. Merryman ejaculated and threw up his hands.

Mrs. Dillington-Blick, opening her eyes very wide, said : " What would *you* do, Mr. Merryman, if *you* were the police ? "

There was a fractional pause after which Mr. Merryman said with hauteur that as he was not in fact a detective the question was without interest.

The Captain said : " What's wrong with alibis ? If

a chap's got an alibi he's out of it, isn't he? So far so good."

"Alibis," Mr. Merryman said grandly, "are in the same category as statistics : in the last analysis they prove nothing."

"Oh, come now!" Father Jourdain protested. "If I'm saying compline in Kensington with the rest of my community at the time a crime is committed in Bermondsey, I'm surely incapable of having committed it."

Mr. Merryman had begun to look very put out and Alleyn came to his rescue.

"Surely," he said, "a great many people don't even remember exactly what they were doing on a specific evening at a specific time. I'm jolly certain I don't."

"Suppose, for instance, now—just for the sake of argument," Captain Bannerman said, and was perhaps a trifle too careful not to look at Alleyn, "that all of us had to produce an alibi for one of these crimes. By gum, I wonder if we could do it. I wonder."

Father Jourdain, who had been looking very steadily at Alleyn said : "One might try."

"One might," Alleyn rejoined. "One might even have a bet on it. What do you say, Mr. Merryman ?"

"Normally," Mr. Merryman declared, "I am not a betting man. However : *dissipet Euhius curas edaces :* I would be prepared to wager some trifling sum upon the issue."

"Would you ?" Alleyn asked. "Really ? All right, then. Propose your bet, sir."

Mr. Merryman thought for a moment. "Coom on, now," urged the Captain.

"Very well. Five shillings that the majority, here, will be unable to produce, on the spot, an acceptable alibi for any given date."

"I'll take you !" Aubyn Dale shouted. "It's a bet !"

Alleyn, Captain Bannerman and Tim Makepiece also said they would take Mr. Merryman's bet.

" And if there's any argument about the acceptability of the alibi," the Captain announced, " the non-betters can vote on it. How's that ? "

Mr. Merryman inclined his head.

Alleyn asked what was to be the given date and the Captain held up his hand. " Let's make it," he suggested, " the first of the Flower Murders ? "

There was a general outbreak of conversation through which Mr. Cuddy could be heard smugly asserting that he couldn't understand anybody finding the slightest difficulty over so simple a matter. An argument developed between him and Mr. Merryman and was hotly continued over coffee and liqueurs in the lounge. Gently fanned by Alleyn it spread through the whole party. He felt that the situation had ripened and should be harvested before anybody, particularly the Captain and Aubyn Dale, had anything more to drink.

" What about this bet ? " he asked in a temporary lull. " Dale has taken Mr. Merryman. We've all got to find alibis for the first Flower Murder. I don't even remember when it was. Does anybody remember ? Mr. McAngus ? "

Mr. McAngus at once launched himself upon the uncertain bosom of associated recollections. He was certain, he declared, that he read about it on the morning when his appendix, later to perforate, subjected him to a preliminary twinge. This, he was persuaded, had been on Friday the sixteenth of January. And yet—was it ? His voice sank to a whisper. He began counting on his fingers and wandered disconsolate amidst a litter of parentheses.

Father Jourdain said, " I believe, you know, that it *was* the night of the fifteenth."

"—and only five days afterwards," Mr. McAngus could

be heard, droning pleasurably, " I was whisked into Saint Bartholomew's Hospital where I hung between life and death——"

" Cohen ! " Aubyn Dale shouted. " Her name was Beryl Cohen. Of course ! "

" Hop Lane, Paddington," Tim Makepiece added with a grin. " Between ten and eleven."

The Captain threw an altogether much too conspiratorial glance at Alleyn. " Coom on ! " he said. " There you are ! We're off ! Ladies first."

Mrs. Dillington-Blick and Jemima at once protested that they hadn't a hope of remembering what they did on any night-in-question. Mrs. Cuddy said darkly and confusedly that she preferred to support her husband and refused to try.

" You see ! " Mr. Merryman gleefully ejaculated. " Three failures at once." He turned to Father Jourdain. " And what can the Church produce ? "

Father Jourdain said quietly that he was actually in the neighbourhood of the crime on that night. He had been giving a talk at a boys' club in Paddington. " One of the men there drove me back to the Community. I remember thinking afterwards that we must have been within a stone's throw of Hop Lane."

" Fancy ! " Mrs. Cuddy ejaculated with ridiculous emphasis. " Fred ! Fancy ! "

" Which would, I suppose," Father Jourdain continued, " constitute my alibi, wouldn't it ? " He turned to Alleyn.

" I must say I'd have thought so."

Mr. Merryman, whose view of alibis seemed to be grounded in cantankerousness rather than logic pointed out that it would all have to be proved and that in any case the result would be inconclusive.

" Oh," Father Jourdain said tranquilly, " I could *prove* my alibi quite comfortably. And conclusively," he added.

"More than I could," Alleyn rejoined. "I fancy I was at home that night but I'm blowed if I could prove it."

Captain Bannerman loudly announced that he had been in Liverpool with his ship and could prove it up to the hilt. "Now then!" he exhorted, absent-mindedly seizing Mrs. Dillington-Blick by the elbow, "what's everybody else got to say for themselves? Any murderers present?" He laughed immoderately at this pleasantry and stared at Alleyn who became a prey to further grave misgivings. "What about you, Mr. Cuddy? You, no doubt, *can* account for yourself?"

The passengers' interest had been satisfactorily aroused. If only, Alleyn thought, Captain Bannerman would pipe down, the conversation might go according to plan. Fortunately, at this juncture, Mrs. Dillington-Blick murmured something that caught the Captain's ear. He became absorbed and everybody else turned their attention upon Mr. Cuddy.

Mr. Cuddy adopted an attitude that seemed to be coloured by gratification at finding himself the centre of interest and a suspicion that in some fashion he was being got at by his fellow passengers. He was maddening but in a backhanded sort of way rewarding. The fifteenth of January, he said, consulting a pocketbook and grinning meaninglessly from ear to ear, was a Tuesday and Tuesday was his Lodge night. He gave the address of his Lodge (Tooting) and on being asked by Mr. Merryman if he had, in fact, attended that night, appeared to take umbrage and was silent.

"Mr. Cuddy," his wife said, "hasn't missed for twenty years. They made him an Elder Bison for it and gave him ever such a nice testimonial."

Jemima and Tim Makepiece caught each other's eyes and hurriedly turned aside.

Mr. Merryman who had listened to Mr. Cuddy with every mark of the liveliest impatience began to question him about the time he left his Lodge but Mr. Cuddy grew lofty and said he wasn't feeling quite the thing, which judging by his ghastly colour was true enough. He retired, accompanied by Mrs. Cuddy to the far end of the lounge. Evidently Mr. Merryman looked upon this withdrawal as a personal triumph for himself. He straightened his shoulders and seemed to inflate.

" The discussion," he said, looking about him, " is not without interest. So far we have been presented with two allegedly provable alibis," he made a facetious bob at the Captain and Father Jourdain : " and otherwise, if the ladies are to be counted, with failures."

" Yes, but look here," Tim said, " a little further examination——"

Mr. Merryman blandly and deliberately misunderstood him. " By all means ! " he ejaculated. " Precisely. Let us continue. Miss Abbott——"

" What about yourself ? " Mr. Cuddy suddenly bawled from the far end of the room.

" Ah ! " Mrs. Cuddy rejoined and produced a Rabelaisian laugh : " Ho, ho, ho,". she said, without moving a muscle of her face. " What about yourself, Mr. Merryband ? "

" Steady, Ethel," Mr. Cuddy muttered.

" Good God ! " Tim muttered to Jemima. " She's tiddly ! "

" She was tossing down bumpers at dinner—probably for the first time in her life."

" That's it. Tiddly. How wonderful."

" Ho, ho, ho ! " Mrs. Cuddy repeated. " Where was Merryband when the lights went out ? "

" Eth ! "

" Fair enough," Aubyn Dale exclaimed. " Come along, Mr. Merryman. Alibi, please."

" With all the pleasure in life," Mr. Merryman said. " I have none. I join the majority. On the evening in question," he continued didactically, as if he expected them all to start taking dictation, " I attended a suburban cinema. The Kosy, spelt (abominable vulgarism) with a K. In Bounty Street, Chelsea. By a diverting coincidence the film was *The Lodger*. I am totally unable to prove it," he ended triumphantly.

" Very fishy ! " Tim said, shaking his head owlishly " Oh, very fishy indeed, I fear, sir ! "

Mr. Merryman gave a little crowing laugh.

" I know ! " Mr. McAngus abruptly shouted. " I have it ! Tuesday ! Television ! " And at once added. " No, no, wait a moment. *What* did you say the date was ? "

Alleyn told him and he became silent and depressed.

" What about Miss Abbott, now," Captain Bannerman asked. " Can Miss Abbott find an alibi ? Come along, Miss Abbott. January 15th."

She didn't answer at once but sat, unsmiling and staring straight before her. A silence fell upon the little company.

" I was in my flat," she said at last and gave the address. There was something uncomfortable in her manner. Alleyn thought, " Damn ! The unexpected. In a moment somebody will change the conversation."

Aubyn Dale was saying waggishly : " Not good enough ! Proof, Miss Abbott, proof."

" Did anybody ring up or come in ? " Jemima prompted with a friendly smile for Miss Abbott.

" My friend—the person I share my flat with—came in at ten thirty-five."

" How clever to remember ! " Mrs. Dillington-Blick murmured and managed to suggest that she herself was enchantingly feckless.

" And before that ? " Mr. Merryman demanded.

A faint dull red settled above Miss Abbott's cheekbones. " I watched television," she said.

" Voluntarily ? " Mr. Merryman asked in astonishment.

To everybody's surprise Miss Abbott shuddered. She wetted her lips : " It passed—it—sometimes helped to pass the time——"

Tim Makepiece, Father Jourdain and Jemima, sensing her discomfiture tried to divert Mr. Merryman's attention but he was evidently one of those people who are unable to abandon a conversation before they have triumphed. " ' Pass the time,' " he ejaculated, casting up his eyes. " Was ever there a more damning condemnation of this bastard, this emasculate, this ennervating peepshow. What was the programme?"

Miss Abbott glanced at Aubyn Dale who was looking furiously at Mr. Merryman. " In point of fact——" she began.

Dale waved his hands. " Ah—ah ! I knew it. Alas, I knew it ! Nine to nine-thirty. Every Tuesday night, God help me. I knew." He leant forward and addressed himself to Mr. Merryman. " My session you know. The one you dislike so much. ' Pack Up Your Troubles ' which, oddly enough, appears to create a slightly different reaction in its all-time high viewing audience. Very reprehensible, no doubt, but there it is. They seem quite to like it."

" Hear, hear ! " Mrs. Cuddy shouted vaguely from the far end of the lounge and stamped approval.

" ' Pack Up Your Troubles,' " Mrs. Dillington-Blick ejaculated. " Of *course* ! "

" Madam," Mr. Merryman continued looking severely at Miss Abbott. " Will you be good enough to describe the precise nature of the predicaments that were aired by the— really, I am at a loss for the correct term to describe these people—the protagonist will no doubt enlighten me——"

" The subjects ? " Father Jourdain suggested.

" The victims ? " Tim amended.

" Or the guests ? I like to think of them as my guests," said Aubyn Dale.

Mrs. Cuddy said rather wildly : " That's a lovely *lovely* way of putting it ! "

(" Steady, Eth ! ")

Miss Abbott, who had been twisting her large hands together said : " I remember nothing about the programme. Nothing."

She half rose from her seat and then seemed to change her mind and sank back. " Mr. Merryman, you're not to badger Miss Abbott," Jemima said quickly and turned to Aubyn Dale. " You, at any rate, have got your alibi, it seems."

" Oh, yes ! " he rejoined. He finished his double brandy and, in his turn, slipped his hand under Mrs. Dillington-Blick's forearm. " God, yes ! I've got the entire Commercial TV admass between me and Beryl Cohen. Twenty million viewers can't be wrong ! In spite of Mr. Merryman."

Alleyn said lightly : " But isn't the programme over by nine-thirty ? What about the next half-hour ? "

" Taking off the war-paint, dear boy, and meeting the chums in the jolly old local."

It had been generally agreed that Aubyn Dale's alibi was established when Mr. McAngus said diffidently : " Do you know—I may be quite wrong—but I had a silly notion someone said that particular session was done at another time—I mean—If of course it *was* that programme."

" Ah ? " Mr. Merryman ejaculated pointing at him as if he'd held his hand up. " Explain yourself. Filmed ? Recorded ? "

" Yes. But, of course I may be——"

But Mr. Merryman pounced gleefully on Aubyn Dale. " What do you say, sir ? Was the session recorded ? "

Dale collected everybody else's attention as if he invited them to enjoy Mr. Merryman with him. He opened his arms and enlarged his smile and he patted Mr. McAngus on the head.

D

"Clever boy," he said. "And I thought I'd got away with it. I couldn't resist pulling your leg, Mr. Merryman : you will forgive me won't you ? "

Mr. Merryman did not reply. He merely stared very fixedly at Aubyn Dale and, as Jemima muttered to Tim, may have been restraining himself from saying he would see him in his study after prep.

Dale added to this impression by saying with uneasy boyishness, " I swear, by the way, I was just about to come clean. Naturally."

" Then," Alleyn said, " it was not a live transmission ? "

" Not that one. Usually is but I was meant to be on my way to the States so we filmed it."

" Indeed ? " Mr. Merryman said. " And *were* you on your way to the United States, sir ? "

" Actually, no. One of those things. There was a nonsense made over dates. I flew three days later. Damn' nuisance. It meant I didn't get back till the day before we sailed."

" And your alibi ? " Mr. Merryman continued ominously.

" Well—ah—well—don't look at me, padre. I spent the evening with my popsey. Don't ask me to elaborate, will you ? No names, no pack-drill."

" And no alibi," said Mr. Merryman neatly.

There was a moment's uneasy suspense during which nobody looked at anybody else and then Mr. McAngus unexpectedly surfaced. " I remember it all quite perfectly," he announced. " It *was* the evening before my first hint of trouble and I *did* watch television ! "

" Programme ? " Mr. Merryman snapped. Mr. McAngus smiled timidly at Aubyn Dale. " Oh," he tittered, " I'm no end of a fan, you know."

It turned out that he had, in fact, watched " Pack Up Your Troubles." When asked if he could remember it, he said at once : " Very clearly." Alleyn saw Miss Abbott close her eyes momentarily as if she felt giddy. "There was a lady," Mr. McAngus continued, "asking, I recollect, whether she ought to get married."

"There almost always is," Dale groaned and made a face of comic despair.

"But this was very complicated because, poor thing, she felt she would be deserting her great friend and her great friend didn't know about it and would be dreadfully upset. There ! " Mr. McAngus cried. " I've remembered ! If only one could be sure which evening. The twenty-fifth, I ask myself ? I mean the fifteenth, of course."

Dale said : " I couldn't tell you which programme but, ah, poor darling : I remember her. I think I helped her. I hope I did ! "

"Perhaps," Captain Bannerman suggested, " Miss Abbott remembers now you've mentioned it. That'd fix your alibi for you."

"*Do* you, Miss Abbott ? " Mr. McAngus asked anxiously.

Everybody looked at Miss Abbott and it was at once apparent to everybody but Mr. McAngus that she was greatly upset. Her lips trembled. She covered them with her hand in a rather dreadful parody of cogitation. She shook her head and her eyes overflowed.

" No ? " Mr. McAngus said wistfully oblivious and short-sightedly, blinking, " Do try, Miss Abbott. She was a dark, rather *heavy* lady. I mean, of course, that was the impression one had. Because one doesn't see the face and the back of the head is rather out of focus, isn't it, Mr. Dale ? But she kept saying (and I think they must distort the voice a little, too) that she knew her friend would be dreadfully hurt because apart from herself, she had so few to care for her." He made a little bob at Aubyn Dale. " You were wonderful," he said, " so tactful. About loneliness. I'm sure, if you saw it, Miss Abbott, you must remember. Mr. Dale made such practical and helpful suggestions. I don't remember exactly what they were but——"

Miss Abbott rounded on him and cried out with shocking violence, " For God's sake stop talking. ' Helpful suggestions ' ! What ' suggestions ' can help in that kind of hell ! " She looked round at them all with an expression of evident despair. " For some of us," she said, " there's no escape. We are our own slaves. No escape or release."

" Nonsense ! " Mr. Merryman said sharply. " There is always an escape and a release. It is a matter of courage and resolution."

Miss Abbott gave a harsh sob. " I'm sorry," she muttered. " I'm not myself. I shouldn't have had so much champagne." She turned away.

Father Jourdain said quickly : " You know, Mr. McAngus, I'm afraid you haven't quite convinced us."

" And that's the last alibi gone overboard," said the Captain. " Mr. Merryman wins."

He made a great business of handing over his five shillings. Alleyn, Tim Makepiece and Aubyn Dale followed suit.

They all began to talk at once and with the exception of the Cuddys avoided looking at Miss Abbott. Jemima moved in front of her and screened her from the others. It was tactfully done and Alleyn was confirmed in his view that Jemima was a nice child. Mrs. Dillington-Blick joined her and automatically a group assembled round Mrs. Dillington-Blick. So between Miss Abbott and the rest of the world there was a barrier behind which she trumpeted privately into her handkerchief.

Presently she got up, now mistress of herself, thanked Alleyn for his party and left it.

The Cuddys came forward, clearly agog, eager, by allusion and then by direct reference, to speculate upon Miss Abbott's distress. Nobody supported them. Mr. McAngus merely looked bewildered. Tim talked to Jemima and Captain

Bannerman and Aubyn Dale talked to Mrs. Dillington-Blick. Mr. Merryman looked once at the Cuddys over his spectacles, rumpled his hair and said something about " *Hoc morbido cupiditatis* " in a loud voice to Alleyn and Father Jourdain. Alleyn was suddenly visited by an emotion that is unorthodox in an investigating officer : he felt a liking and warmth for these people. He respected them because they refused to gossip with the Cuddys about Miss Abbott's unhappiness and because they had behaved with decency and compassion when she broke down. He saw Jemima and Mrs. Dillington-Blick speak together and then slip out of the room and he knew they had gone to see if they could help Miss Abbott. He was very much troubled.

Father Jourdain came up to him and said : " Shall we move over here ? " He led Alleyn to the far end of the room.

" That was unfortunate," he said.

" I'm sorry about it."

" You couldn't possibly know it would happen. She is a very unhappy woman. She exhales unhappiness."

" It was the reference to that damn' spiritual striptease session of Dale's," Alleyn said. " I suppose something in the programme had upset her."

" Undoubtedly," Father Jourdain smiled. " That's a good description of it : a spiritual striptease. I suppose you'll think I'm lugging in my cloth but you know I really do think it's better to leave confession to the professional."

" Dale would call himself a professional."

" What he does," Father Jourdain said, with some warmth, " is vulgar, dangerous and altogether odious. But he's not a bad chap, of course. At least I don't think so. Not a bad sort of chap, at all."

Alleyn said : " There's something else you want to say to me, isn't there ? "

" There is, but I hesitate to say it. I am not sure of

myself. Will you laugh at me if I tell you that, by virtue of my training perhaps, and perhaps because of some instinct, I am peculiarly sensitive to—to spiritual atmospheres?"

" I don't know that I——"

Father Jourdain interrupted him.

" I mean that when I feel there is something really out-of-joint, spiritually—I use this word because I'm a priest, you know—with a group of people, I'm usually right."

" And do you feel it now?"

" Very strongly. I suspect it's a sense of unexpressed misery," said Father Jourdain. " But I can't hunt it home."

" Miss Abbott?"

" I don't know. I don't know."

" Even that," Alleyn said, " is not what you want to say."

" You're very perceptive yourself," Father Jourdain looked steadily at him. " When the party breaks up, will you stay behind for a moment?"

" Certainly."

Father Jourdain said so softly that Alleyn could barely hear him, " You *are* Roderick Alleyn, aren't you?"

III

The deserted lounge smelt of dead cigarettes and forgotten drinks. Alleyn opened the doors to the deck outside, the stars were careering in the sky: the ship's mast swung against them and the night sea swept thudding and hissing past her flanks.

" I'm sorry to have kept you waiting," said Father Jourdain behind him.

Alleyn shut the doors again and they sat down.

" Let me assure you at once," Father Jourdain said, " that I shall respect your—I suppose anonymity is not the right word. Your incognito, shall we say?"

"I'm not particularly bothered about the choice of words," Alleyn said dryly.

"Nor need you be bothered about my recognising you. It's by the oddest of coincidences. Your wife may be said to have effected the introduction."

"Really?"

"I have never met her but I admire her painting. Some time ago I went to a one-man show of hers and was very much impressed by a small portrait. It too was anonymous, but a brother-priest, Father Copeland of Winton St. Giles who knows you both, told me it was a portrait of her husband who was the celebrated Inspector Alleyn. I have a very long memory for faces and the likeness was striking. I felt sure I was not mistaken."

"Troy," Alleyn said, "will be enormously gratified."

"And then: that bet of Mr. Merryman's was organised, wasn't it?"

"Lord, lord! I do seem to have made an ass of myself."

"No, no. Not you. You were entirely convincing. It was the Captain."

"His air of spontaneity *was* rather massive, perhaps."

"Exactly." Father Jourdain leant forward and said: "Alleyn: why was that conversation about the Flower Murderer introduced?"

Alleyn said: "For fun. Why else?"

".So you are not going to tell me."

"At least," Alleyn said lightly, "I've got your alibi for January the fifteenth."

"You don't trust me, of course."

"It doesn't arise. As you have discovered, I am a policeman."

"I beg you to trust me. You won't regret it. You can check my alibi, can't you? And the other time: the other poor child who was going to church—when was that? The twenty-fifth. Why, on the twenty-fifth I was at a conference in Paris. You can prove it at once. No doubt you're in touch with your colleagues. Of course you can."

" I expect it can be done."

" Then do it. I urge you to do it. If you are here for the fantastic reason I half-suspect, you will need someone you can trust."

" It never comes amiss."

" These women must not be left alone." Father Jourdain had arisen and was staring through the glass doors. " Look," he said.

Mrs. Dillington-Blick was taking a walk on deck. As she passed the lighted windows above the engine-rooms she paused. Her ear-rings and necklace twinkled, the crimson scarf she had wrapped about her head fluttered in the night breeze. A man emerged from the shadow of the centre-castle and walked towards her. He took her arm. They turned away and were lost to view. He was Aubyn Dale. " You see," Father Jourdain said. " If I'm right, that's the sort of thing we mustn't allow."

Alleyn said: " To-day is the seventh of February. These crimes have occurred at ten-day intervals."

" But there have only been two."

" There was an attempt on January fifth. It was not publicised."

" Indeed ! The fifth, the fifteenth and the twenty-fifth. Why then, ten days have already passed since the last crime. If you are right (and the interval after all may be a coincidence) the danger is acute."

" On the contrary, if there's anything in the ten-day theory, Mrs. Dillington-Blick at the moment is in no danger."

" But——" Father Jourdain stared at him. " Do you mean there's been another of these crimes ? Since we sailed ? Why then——? "

" About half an hour before you sailed and about two

hundred yards away from the ship. On the night of the fourth. He was punctual almost to the minute."

" Dear God ! " said Father Jourdain.

" At the moment, of course, none of the passengers except the classic *one*, knows about this and unless anybody takes the trouble to cable the news to Las Palmas they won't hear about it there."

" The fourteenth," Father Jourdain muttered. " You think we may be safe until the fourteenth."

" One simply hopes so. All the same : shall we take the air before we turn in ? I think we might." Alleyn opened the doors. Father Jourdain moved towards them.

" It occurs to me," he said, " that you may think me a busybody. It's not that. It is, quite simply, that I have a nose for evil and a duty to prevent, if I can, the commission of sin. I am a spiritual policeman, in fact. You may feel that I'm talking professional nonsense."

" I respect the point-of-view," Alleyn said. For a moment they looked at each other. " And, sir, I am disposed to trust you."

" That, at least, is a step forward," said Father Jourdain. " Shall we leave it like that until you have checked my alibis ? "

" If you're content to do so."

" I haven't much choice," Father Jourdain observed. He added, after a moment, " and at any rate it *does* appear that we have an interval. Until February the fourteenth ? "

" Only if the time theory is correct. It may not be correct."

" I suppose—a psychiatrist——? "

" Dr. Makepiece, for instance. He's one. I'm thinking of consulting him."

" But—— "

" Yes ? "

" He had no alibi. He said so."

"They tell us," Alleyn said, "that the guilty man in a case of this sort never says he has no alibi. They say he always produces an alibi. Of some sort. Shall we go out?"

They went out on deck. A light breeze still held but it was no longer cold. The ship, ploughing through the dark, throbbed with her own life and with small orderly noises and yet was compact of a larger quietude. As they moved along the starboard side of the welldeck a bell sounded in four groups of two.

"Midnight," Alleyn said. Sailors passed them, quiet-footed. Mrs. Dillington-Blick and Aubyn Dale appeared on the far side of the hatch, making for the passengers' quarters. They called out good night and disappeared.

Father Jourdain peered at his watch. "And this afternoon we arrive at Las Palmas," he said.

CHAPTER SIX

Broken Doll

I

Las Palmas is known to tourists for its walkie-talkie dolls. They stare out of almost every shop-window, and sit in rows in the street bazaars near the wharves. They vary in size, cost and condition. Some have their garments cynically nailed to their bodies and others wear hand-sewn dresses of elaborate design. Some are bald under their bonnets, others have high Spanish wigs of real hair crowned with real lace mantillas. The most expensive of all are adorned with necklaces, bracelets and even rings and have masses of wonderful petticoats under their flowered and braided skirts. They can be as tall as a child or as short as a woman's hand.

Two things the dolls have in common. If you hold any one of them by the arm it may be induced to jerk its legs to and fro in a parody of walking and as it walks it also jerks its head from side to side and from within its body it ejaculates : " Ma-ma." They all squeak in the same way with voices that are shockingly like those of infants. Nearly everybody who goes to Las Palmas remembers either some little girl who would like a walkie-talkie doll or, however misguidedly, some grown woman who might possibly be amused by one.

The Company placed an open car at the disposal of Captain Bannerman and in it he put Mrs. Dillington-

Blick, looking like a piece of Turkish Delight. They drove about Las Palmas stopping at shops where the driver had a profitable understanding with the proprietor. Mrs. Dillington-Blick bought herself a black lace near-mantilla with a good deal of metal in it, a comb to support it, some Portuguese jewellery and a fan. Captain Bannerman bought her a lot of artificial magnolias because they didn't see any real ones. He felt proud because all the Las Palmanians obviously admired her very much indeed. They came to a shop where a wonderful dress was displayed, a full Spanish dress made of black lace and caught up to display a foam of petticoats, scarlet, underneath. The driver kissed his fingers over and over again and intimated that if Mrs. Dillington-Blick were to put it on she would look like the Queen of Heaven. Mrs. Dillington-Blick examined it with her head on one side.

" Do you know," she said, " allowing for a little Latin exaggeration, I'm inclined to agree with him."

Tim Makepiece and Jemima came along the street and joined them. Jemima said : " *Do* try it on. You'd look absolutely marvellous. Do. For fun."

" Shall I ? Come in with me, then. Make me keep my head."

The Captain said he would go to his agents' offices where he had business to do and return in twenty minutes. Tim, who very much wanted to buy some roses for Jemima, also said he'd come back. Greatly excited, the two ladies entered the shop.

The stifling afternoon wore into evening. Dusk was rapidly succeeded by night, palm trees rattled in an enervated breeze and at nine o'clock, by arrangement, Captain Bannerman and Mrs. Dillington-Blick were to meet Aubyn Dale at the grandest hotel in Las Palmas for dinner.

Mrs. Dillington-Blick had been driven back to the ship where she changed into the wonderful Spanish dress which of course she had bought. She was excitedly assisted by Jemima: "What did I tell you!" Jemima shouted triumphantly. "You ought to be sitting in a box looking at a play by Lope de Vega with smashing caballeros all round you. It's a riot." Mrs. Dillington-Blick, who had never heard of Lope de Vega, half-smiled, opened her eyes very wide, turned and turned again to watch the effect in her looking-glass and said: "Not bad. Really, it's not bad," and pinned one of the Captain's artificial magnolias in her décolletage. She gave Jemima the brilliant look of a woman who knows she is successful.

"All the same," she murmured, "I can't help *rather* wishing it was the G.B. who was taking me out."

"The G.B.?"

"My dear, the Gorgeous Brute. Glamorous Broderick, if you like. I dropped hints like thunder-bolts but no luck, alas."

"Never mind," Jemima said, "you'll have a terrific success, anyway. I promise you."

She ran off to effect her own change. It was when she fastened one of Tim Makepiece's red roses in her dress that it suddenly occurred to Jemima she hadn't thought of her troubles for at least six hours. After all, it *was* rather fun to be dining out in a foreign city on a strange island with a pleasant young man.

It all turned out superbly: an enchanted evening suspended like a dream, between the strange intervals of a sea voyage. The streets they drove through and the food they ate; the music they danced to, the flowers, the extremely romantic lighting and the exotic people were all, Jemima told Tim, "out of this world." They sat at their table on the edge of the dance floor, talked very fast about the things that interested them and were delighted to find how much they liked each other.

At half past nine Mrs. Dillington-Blick arrived with the

Captain and Aubyn Dale. She really was, as Jemima pointed out to Tim, sensational. Everybody looked at her. A kind of religious gravity impregnated the deportment of the head waiter. Opulence and observance enveloped her like an expensive scent. She *was* terrific.

" I admire her," Jemima said, " enormously. Don't you ? "

Jemima's chin rested in the palm of her hand. Her forearm, much less opulent than Mrs. Dillington-Blick's, shone in the candlelight and her eyes were bright.

Tim said : " She's the most suffocatingly feminine job I've ever seen, I think. An all-time-low in inhibitions and an all-time-high in what it takes. If, of course, that happens to be your line of country. It's not mine."

Jemima found this answer satisfactory. " I like her," she said. " She's warm and uncomplicated."

" She's all of that. Hallo ! Look who's here ! "

Alleyn came in with Father Jourdain. They were shown to a table at some distance from Tim's and Jemima's.

" ' Distinguished visitors ' ! " Jemima said, gaily waving to them.

" They are rather grand-looking, aren't they ? I must say I like Broderick. Nice chap, don't you think ? "

" Yes, I do," Jemima said emphatically. " What about Father Jourdain ? "

" I wouldn't know. Interesting face : not typically clerical."

" *Is* there a typically clerical face or are you thinking of comic curates at the Players Theatre Club ? "

" No," said Tim slowly. " I'm not. But look at the mouth and the eyes. He's a celibate, isn't he ? I bet it's been a bit of a hurdle."

" Suppose," Jemima said, " you wanted advice very badly and had to go to one of those two. Which would it be ? "

" Oh, Broderick. Every time. *Do* you by any chance want advice ? "

" No."

" If you did, I'd take it very kindly if you came to me."

" Thank you," said Jemima. " I'll bear it in mind."

" Good. Let's trip a measure."

" Nice young couple," said Father Jourdain as they danced past him and he added : " I do hope you're right in what you say."

" About——? "

" About alibis."

The band crashed and was silent. The floor cleared and two spotlights introduced a pair of tango dancers, very fierce, like game birds. They strutted and stalked, clattered their castinets, and frowned ineffably at each other. " What an angry woo," Tim said.

When they had finished they moved among the tables followed by their spotlight.

" Oh, *no* ! " Father Jourdain exclaimed. " Not *another* doll ! "

It was an enormous and extraordinarily realistic one, carried by the woman dancer. Evidently it was for sale. She flashed brilliant smiles and proudly showed it off, while her escort stood moodily by. " *Senors e Senoras*," announced a voice over the loudspeaker and added, they thought, something about have the honour to present " *La Esmeralda* " which was evidently the name of the doll.

" Curious ! " Alleyn remarked.

" What ? "

" It's dressed exactly like Mrs. D-B."

And so it was—in a flounced black lace dress and a mantilla. It even had a green necklace and ear-rings and lace gloves and its fingers were clamped round the handle of an open fan. It was a woman-doll with a bold, handsome face and a flashing smile like the dancer's. It looked terrifyingly expensive. Alleyn watched with some amusement as it approached the table where Mrs. Dillington-Blick sat with the Captain and Aubyn Dale.

The dancers had of course noticed the resemblance and so had the head waiter. They all smiled and ejaculated and admired as the doll waddled beguilingly towards Mrs. Dillington-Blick.

" Poor old Bannerman," Alleyn said, " he's sunk, I fear. Unless Dale——"

But Aubyn Dale extended his hands in his well-known gesture and with a smile of rueful frankness was obviously saying it was no good them looking at him, while the Captain, ruby-faced, stared in front of him with an expression of acute unconcern. Mrs. Dillington-Blick shook her head and beamed and shook it again. The dancers bowed, smiled and moved on, approaching the next table. The woman stooped and with a kind of savage gaiety, induced the doll to walk. " Ma-ma ! " squeaked the doll. " Ma-ma ! "

" Ladies and Gentlemen," the loudspeaker repeated and continued, this time in English, " we have the honour to present Mees Esmeralda, Queen of Las Palmas."

From somewhere in the shadows at the back of the room a napkin fluttered. The woman snatched up the doll and swept between the tables, followed by her escort. The spotlight settled on them. Heads were turned. One or two people stood up. It was impossible to see the person at the distant table. After a short delay the dancer returned, holding the doll aloft.

" She *hasn't* sold it," Father Jourdain remarked.

" On the contrary," Alleyn rejoined, " I think she has. Look."

The doll was born in triumph to the Captain's table and with a magnificent curtsy, presented to Mrs. Dillington-Blick.

At the other side of the room Tim said : " Look at that, now ! "

" What a triumph ! " Jemima exclaimed delightedly.

" Who's the poor fish, do you suppose ? "

" I can't see. It'll be some superb grandee with flashing eyes and a crimson cummerbund. What *fun* for Mrs. Dillington-Blick."

The dancers were making gestures in the direction of their customer. Mrs. Dillington-Blick, laughing and triumphant holding the doll, strained round to see. The spotlight probed into the distant corner. Somebody stood up.

" Oh, *look* ! " cried Jemima.

" Well, blow me down flat ! " said Tim.

" How very surprising," observed Father Jourdain, " it's Mr. McAngus ! "

" He has made his reciprocal gesture," said Alleyn.

II

The *Cape Farewell* sailed at two in the morning and the passengers were all to be aboard by half past one. Alleyn and Father Jourdain had returned at midnight and Alleyn had gone to his cabin to have another look at his mail. It included a detailed report from the Yard of the attack that had been made upon Miss Bijou Browne on January fifth and a letter from his senior saying nothing had developed that suggested alteration in Alleyn's plan of action. Alleyn had telephoned the Yard from Police Headquarters in Las Palmas and had spoken to Inspector Fox. Following Alleyn's radiogram of the previous night, the Yard had at once tackled the passengers' alibis. Father Jourdain was, Fox said, as good as gold. Mr. Merryman's cinema had in fact shown *The Lodger* on the night in question as the first half of a double bill. The name of Aubyn Dale's sweetie so far eluded the Yard but Fox hoped to get it before long and would, he said, dream up some cock-and-bull story that might give him an excuse to question her about the night of the fifteenth. The rest of Dale's statement had been proved. Fox had got in touch with Mr. Cuddy's Lodge and had told them the Police were making inquiries about a valuable watch. From information received they believed it had been stolen from Mr. Cuddy near the Lodge premises on the night of the fifteenth. A record of attendances showed that Mr. Cuddy had signed in but the secretary remembered that he left very early, feeling unwell. Apart from Mr. McAngus having perforated his appendix four days after the date in question, Fox dryly continued, it would be impossible to check his litter of disjointed reminiscence. They would, however, poke about and see if anything cropped up. An inquiry at Dr. Makepiece's hospital gave conclusive evidence that he had been on duty there until midnight.

Captain Bannerman, it appeared, had certainly been in Liverpool on the night of the fifteenth and a routine check completely cleared the other officers. In any case it was presumed that the ship's complement didn't go aboard clutching passengers' embarkation notices.

The missing portion of the embarkation notice had not been found.

A number of psychiatric authorities had been consulted and all agreed that the ten-day interval would probably be maintained and that the fourteenth February, therefore, might be anticipated as a deadline. One of them added, however, that the subject's homicidal urge might be exacerbated by an untoward event. Which meant, Inspector Fox supposed dryly, that he might cut up for trouble before the fourteenth : if a bit of what he fancied turned up in the meantime and did the trick.

Fox concluded the conversation by inquiring about the weather and on being told it was semi-tropical remarked that some people had all the luck. Alleyn had rejoined that if Fox considered a long voyage with a homicidal maniac (identity unknown and boiling up for trouble) and at least two eminently suitable victims, was a bit of luck, he'd be glad to swap jobs with him. On this note they rang off.

Alleyn had also received a cable from his wife which said : " Lodging petition for desertion do you want anything sent anywhere love darling Troy."

He put his papers away and went down to the well-deck. It was now twenty minutes past midnight but none of the passengers had gone to bed. The Cuddys were in the lounge telling Dennis, with whom they were on informal terms, about their adventures ashore. Mr. Merryman reclined in a deck-chair with his arms folded and his hat over his nose. Mr. McAngus and Father Jourdain leant on the taffrail and stared down at the wharf below. The after-hatch was open and the winch that served it still in operation. The night was oppressively warm.

Alleyn strolled along the deck and looked down into the after-hatch, yawning black, and at the dramatically lit figures that worked it. The rattle of the winch, the occasional voices and the pulse of the engines made a not unattractive accompaniment to the gigantic fishing operation. He had watched and listened for some minutes before he became aware of another and most unexpected sound. Quite close at hand was someone singing in Latin : an austere, strangely measured and sexless chant.

> *Procul recedant somnia*
> *Et noctium phantasmata*
> *Hostemque nostrum comprime*
> *Ne polluantur corpora.*

Alleyn moved across the after end of the deck. In the little veranda, just visible in reflected light sat Miss Abbott, singing. She stopped at once when she saw him. She had under her hands what appeared to be many sheets of paper ; perhaps an immensely long letter.

"That was lovely," Alleyn said, "I wish you hadn't stopped. It was extraordinarily—what ?—tranquil ? "

She said, more it seemed to herself than to him : "Yes. Tranquil and devout. It's music designed against devils."

"What *were* you singing ? "

She roused herself suddenly and became defensive. It seemed incredible that her speaking voice could be so harsh.

"A Vatican plainsong," she said.

"What a fool I was to blunder in and stop you. Would it be—seventh century ? "

"Six-fifty-five. Printed from manuscript in the *Liber Gradualis*, 1883," she barked and got up.

Alleyn said : "Don't move. I'll take myself off."

"I'm going anyway." She walked straight past him. Her eyes were dark with excitement. She strode along the deck to the lighted area where the others were congregated, sat in a deck-chair a little apart from them and began to read her letter.

After a minute or two Alleyn also returned and joined Mr. McAngus. "That was a charming gesture of yours this evening," he said.

Mr. McAngus made a little tittering sound. "I was so lucky ! " he said. "Such a happy coincidence, wasn't it ? And the resemblance, you know, is complete. I *promised* I'd find something and *there* it was. So very appropriate, I felt." He hesitated for a moment and added rather wistfully, "I was invited to join their party but of course, I thought, better to decline. She seemed quite delighted. At the doll, I mean. The doll delighted her."

"I'm sure it did."

"Yes," Mr. McAngus said. "Yes." His voice had trailed away into a murmur. He was no longer aware of Alleyn but looked past him and down towards the wharf.

It was now twenty past one. A taxi had come along the

wharf. Out of it got Jemima Carmichael and Tim Make-piece, talking busily and obviously on the best possible terms with each other and the world at large. They came up the gangway smiling all over their faces. "Oh!" Jemima exclaimed to Alleyn. "Isn't Las Palmas Heaven? We *have* had such fun."

But it was not at Jemima that Mr. McAngus stared so fixedly. An open car had followed the taxi and in it were Mrs. Dillington-Blick, the Captain and Aubyn Dale. They too were gay but with a more ponderous gaiety than Tim's and Jemima's. The men's faces were darkish and their voices heavy. Mrs. Dillington-Blick still looked marvellous. Her smile, if not exactly irrepressible, was full of meaning and if her eyes no longer actually sparkled they were still extremely expressive and the tiny pockets underneath them, scarcely noticeable. The men helped her up the gangway. The Captain went first. He carried the doll and held Mrs. Dillington-Blick's elbow while Aubyn Dale put his hands on her waist and made a great business of assisting her from the rear. There were jokes and a lot of suppressed laughter.

When they arrived on deck the Captain went up to the bridge and Mrs. Dillington-Blick held court. Mr. McAngus was made much of, Father Jourdain appealed to and Alleyn given a great many sidelong glances. The doll was exhibited and the Cuddys came out to see it. Mrs. Cuddy said she supposed the dolls were produced with sweated labour but Mr. Cuddy stared at Mrs. Dillington-Blick and said, with an odd inflection, that there were some things that couldn't be copied. Alleyn was made to walk with the doll and Mrs. Dillington-Blick went behind, imitating its action, jerking her head and squeaking: "Ma-ma!"

Miss Abbott put down her letter and stared at Mrs. Dillington-Blick with a kind of hungry amazement.

"Mr. Merryman!" cried Mrs. Dillington-Blick. "Wake up! Let me introduce my twin sister Donna Esmeralda."

Mr. Merryman removed his hat, gazed at the doll with distaste and then at its owner.

"The resemblance," he said, "is too striking to arouse any emotion but one of profound misgiving."

"Ma-ma!" squeaked Mrs. Dillington-Blick.

Dennis trotted out on deck, plumply smiling, and approached her. "A night-lettergram for *you*, Mrs. Dillington-Blick. It came after you'd gone *ashore*. I've been looking out for you. Oh, mercy!" he added, eyeing the doll, "isn't she *twee*!"

Mr. Merryman contemplated Dennis with something like horror and replaced his hat over his nose.

Mrs. Dillington-Blick gave a sharp ejaculation and fluttered her open night-lettergram.

"My dears!" she shouted. "You'll never credit this! How too frightful and murky! My dears!"

"Darling!" Aubyn Dale exclaimed. "What?"

"It's from a man, a friend of mine. You'll *never* believe it. Listen! 'Sent masses of hyacinths to ship but shop informs me young female taking them latest victim flower murderer stop card returned by police stop what a thing stop have lovely trip Tony'!"

III

Her fellow-passengers were so excited by Mrs. Dillington-Blick's news that they scarcely noticed their ship's sailing. *Cape Farewell* separated herself from Las Palmas with an almost imperceptible gesture and moved away into the dark, taking up the rhythm of her voyage, while Mrs. Dillington-Blick held the stage.

They all gathered round her and Mr. Cuddy managed to get close enough to look sideways at the night-lettergram. Mr. Merryman, with an affectation of stretching his legs, strolled nearer, his head thrown back at an angle that enabled him to stare superciliously from under his hat brim at Mrs. Dillington-Blick. Even Miss Abbott leant forward in her chair, grasping her crumpled letter, her large hands dangling between her knees. Captain Bannerman, who had come down from the bridge, looked much too knowing for Alleyn's peace of mind, and repeatedly attempted to catch his eye. Alleyn avoided him, plunged into the mêlée and was himself loud in ejaculation and comment. There was much speculation as to where and when the girl who brought the flowers could have been murdered. Out of the general conversation Mrs. Cuddy's voice rose shrilly: " And it was hyacinths again, too. Fancy ! What a coincidence."

" My dear madam," Dr. Makepiece testily pointed out, " the flowers are in season. No doubt the shops are full of them. There is no esoteric significance in the circumstance."

" Mr. Cuddy never fancied them," said Mrs. Cuddy. " Did you dear ? "

Mr. Merryman raised his hands in a gesture of despair, turned his back on her and ran slap into Mr. McAngus. There was a clash of spectacles and a loud oath from Mr. Merryman. The two gentlemen began to behave like simultaneous comedians. They stooped, crashed heads, cried out in anguish and rose clutching each other's spectacles, hat and hyacinth.

" I am so very sorry," said Mr. McAngus, holding his head. " I hope you're not hurt."

" I am hurt. That is my hat, sir, and those are my glasses. Broken."

" I do trust you have a second pair."

" The existence of a second pair does not reduce the value of the first which is, I see at a glance, irrevocably shattered," said Mr. Merryman. He flung down Mr. McAngus's hyacinth and returned to his chair.

The others still crowded about Mrs. Dillington-Blick. As they all stood there, so close together that the smell of wine on their breath mingled with Mrs. Dillington-Blick's heavy scent, there was, Alleyn thought, a classic touch, a kind of ghastly neatness in the situation if indeed one of them was the murderer they all so eagerly discussed.

Presently Jemima and Tim moved away and then Father Jourdain walked aft and leant on the rails. Mrs. Cuddy announced that she was going to bed and took Mr. Cuddy's arm. The whole thing, she said, had given her quite a turn. Her husband seemed reluctant to follow her but on Mrs. Dillington-Blick and Aubyn Dale going indoors the whole party broke up and disappeared severally through doors or into shadows.

Captain Bannerman came up to Alleyn. "How about that one?" he said. "Upsets your little game a bit, doesn't it?" and loudly belched. "Pardon me," he added. "It's the fancy muck we had for dinner."

"Eight of them don't know where it happened and they don't know exactly when," Alleyn pointed out. "The ninth knows everything anyway. It doesn't matter all that much."

"It matters damn' all seeing the whole idea's an error." The Captain made a wide gesture. "Well—look at them. I ask you. Look at the way they behave and everything."

"How do you expect him to behave? Go about in a black sombrero making loud animal noises? Heath had very nice manners. Still, you may be right. By the way, Father Jourdain and Makepiece seem to be in the clear. And you, sir. I thought you'd like to know. The Yard's been checking alibis."

"Ta," said the Captain gloomily and began to count on his fingers. "That leaves Cuddy, Merryman, Dale and that funny old bastard what's-'is-name."

"McAngus."

" That's right. Well, I ask you ! I'm turning in," added the Captain. " I'm a wee bit plastered. She's a wonderful woman though. Goodni'."

" Good night, sir."

The Captain moved away, paused and came back.

" I had a signal from the Company," he said. " They don't want any kind of publicity and in my opinion they're right. They reckon it's all my eye. They don't want the passengers upset for nothing and n'more do I. You might 'member that."

" I'll do my best."

" At sea—Master's orders."

" Sir."

" Ver' well." The Captain made a vague gesture and climbed carefully up the companionway to the bridge.

Alleyn walked aft to where Father Jourdain still leaning on the taffrail, his hands loosely folded, stared out into the night.

" I've been wondering," Alleyn said, " if you played Horatio's part just now."

" I ? Horatio ? "

" Observing with the very comment of your soul."

" Oh, that ! If that's to be my role ! I did, certainly, watch the men."

" So did I. How about it ? "

" Nothing. Nothing at all. Unless you count Mr. Merryman keeping his hat over his face or his flying into a temper."

" Or Mr. Cuddy's overt excitement."

" Or Mr. McAngus's queer little trick of dancing backwards and forwards. No ! " Father Jourdain exclaimed strongly. " No ! I can't believe it of any of them. And yet——"

" Do you still smell evil ? "

" I begin to ask myself if I merely imagine it."

"As well you may," Alleyn agreed. "I ask myself continually if we're building a complete fantasy round the fragment of paper clutched in that wretched girl's hand. But then—— You see, you all had your embarkation notices when you came aboard. Or so it seems. Could one of the lost ones—yours, for instance, have blown through the porthole to the dock and into her hand? No. The portholes were all shut as they always are when the ship's tied up. Let's take a turn, shall we?"

They walked together down the well-deck on the port side. When they reached the little veranda aft of the engine house they stopped while Alleyn lit his pipe. The night was still very warm but they had run into a stiff breeze and the ship was alive with it. There was a high thrumming sound in the shrouds.

"Someone singing," Alleyn said.

"Isn't it the wind in those ropes? Shrouds, don't they call them? I wonder why."

"No. Listen. It's clearer now."

"So it is. Someone singing."

It was a high rather sweet voice and seemed to come from the direction of the passengers' quarters.

"' The Broken Doll,' " Alleyn said.

"A strangely old-fashioned choice."

"' *You'll be sorry some day*
You left behind a Broken Doll.' "

The thin commonplace tune evaporated.

"It's stopped, now," said Alleyn.

"Yes. Should these women be warned, then?" Father Jourdain asked as they continued their walk. "Before the deadline approaches?"

"The Shipping Company is all against it and so's the Captain. My bosses tell me, as far as possible to respect their wishes. They think the women should be protected without knowing it, which is all bloody fine for them. Make-piece, by the way, seems O.K. We'll tell him, I think. He'll be delighted to protect Miss Carmichael."

Like the Captain, Father Jourdain said: "That leaves Dale, Merryman, Cuddy and McAngus." But unlike the Captain he added: "I suppose it's possible. I suppose so." He put his hand on Alleyn's arm. "You'll think I'm ridiculously inconsistent: it's only that I've remembered—" He stopped for a moment, and his fingers closed over Alleyn's coatsleeve.

"Yes ?" Alleyn said.

"You see, I'm a priest: an Anglo-Catholic priest. I hear confessions. It's a humbling and an astonishing duty. One never stops being dumbfounded at the un-expectedness of sin."

Alleyn said: "I suppose in a way the same observation might apply to my job."

They walked on in silence, rounded the end of the hatch and returned to the portside. The lights in the lounge were out and great pools of shadow lay about the deck.

"It's an awful thing to say," Father Jourdain observed abruptly, "but do you know, for a moment I almost found myself wishing that rather than go on in such frightful uncertainty, we knew, positively, that this murderer was on board." He turned aside to sit on the hatch. The hatch-coaming cast a very deep shadow along the deck. He seemed to wade into it as if it were a ditch.

"Ma-ma !"

The voice squeaked horridly from under his feet. He gave a stifled ejaculation and lurched against the hatch.

"Good Heavens, what have I done ! " cried Father Jourdain.

"By the sound of it," Alleyn said, "I should say you've trodden on Esmeralda."

He stooped. His hands encountered lace, a hard dead

surface and something else. "Don't move," he said. "Just a moment."

He carried a pencil-thin flashlamp in his pocket. The beam darted out like a replica in miniature of P.C. Moir's torch.

"Have I broken it?" asked Father Jourdain, anxiously.

"It was already broken. Look."

It was indeed broken. The head had been twisted so far and with such violence that Esmeralda now grinned over her left shoulder at a quite impossible angle. The black lace mantilla was wound tightly round the neck and lying on the rigid bosom was a litter of emerald beads and single crushed hyacinth.

"You've got your wish," Alleyn said. "He's on board, all right."

IV

Captain Bannerman pushed his fingers through his sandy hair and rose from his sitting-room table.

"It's half past two," he said, "and for any good the stuff I drank last night does me, I might as well have not taken it. I need a dram and I advise you gentlemen to join me."

He dumped a bottle of whisky and four glasses on the table and was careful not to touch a large object that lay there, covered with a newspaper. "Neat?" he asked. "Water? Or soda?"

Alleyn and Father Jourdain had soda and Tim Makepiece water. The Captain took his neat.

"You know," Tim said. "I can't get myself geared to this situation. Really, it's jolly nearly impossible to believe it."

"I don't," said the Captain. "The doll was a joke. A damn' nasty, spiteful kind of joke, mind. But a joke. I'll be sugared if I think I've shipped a Jack the Ripper. Now!"

"No, no," Father Jourdain muttered. "I'm afraid I can't agree. Alleyn?"

Alleyn said: "I suppose the joke idea's just possible. Given the kind of person and all the talk about these cases and the parallel circumstances."

"There you are!" Captain Bannerman said triumphantly. "And if you ask me, we haven't got far to look for the kind of chap. Dale's a great card for practical jokes. Always at it on his own confession. Bet you what you like——"

"No, no!" Father Jourdain protested, "I can't agree. He'd never perpetrate such an unlovely trick. No."

Alleyn said: "I can't agree either. In my opinion: literally it's no joke."

Tim said slowly: "I suppose you all noticed that—well that Mr. McAngus was wearing a hyacinth in his coat."

Father Jourdain and the Captain exclaimed but Alleyn said: "And that he dropped it when he clashed heads with Mr. Merryman. And that Mr. Merryman picked it up and threw it down on the deck."

"Ah!" said the Captain triumphantly. "There you are! What's the good of that!"

"Where," Tim asked, " did she leave the doll?"

"On the hatch. She put it there when she got her cable and evidently forgot to take it indoors. It was just above the spot where we found it which was about three feet away from the place where Merryman threw down the hyacinth: everything was nice and handy." He turned to Tim. "You and Miss Carmichael were the first to leave the general group. I think you walked over to the starboard side, didn't you?"

Tim, pink in the face, nodded.

"Er—yes."

" Do you mind telling me *exactly* where ? "

" Er—no. No. Naturally not. I was—where was it ?
Well, it was sort of a bit farther along than the doorway
into the passengers' quarters. There's a seat."

" And you were there, would you say—for how long ? "

" Well—er——"

" Until after the group of passengers on deck had dispersed ? "

" O, lord, yes ! Yes."

" Did you notice whether any of them went in or, more
importantly, came out again, by that doorway ? "

" Er—no. No."

" Gentlemen of your vintage," Alleyn said mildly,
" from the point-of-view of evidence are no damn' good
until you fall in love and then you're no damn' good."

" Well, I must say ! "

" Never mind. I think I know how they dispersed.
Mr. Merryman, whose cabin is the first on the left of the
passage on the starboard side and has windows looking aft
and to that side went in at the passengers' doorway near
you. He was followed by Mr. McAngus who has the cabin
opposite his across the passage. The others all moved away
in the opposite direction and presumably went in by the
equivalent passengers' entrance on the portside, with the
exception of Mrs. Dillington-Blick and Aubyn Dale who
used the glass doors into the lounge. Captain Bannerman
and I had a short conversation and he returned to the bridge.
Father Jourdain and I then walked to the after end or back
or rear or whatever you call it of the deck where there's
a veranda and where we could see nothing. It must
have been at that moment somebody returned and garrotted
Esmeralda."

" How d'you remember all that ? " Captain Bannerman
demanded.

" God bless my soul, I'm on duty." Alleyn turned to

Father Jourdain. " The job must have been finished before we walked back along the starboard side."

" Must it ? "

" Don't you remember ? We heard someone singing : ' A Broken Doll.' "

Father Jourdain passed his hand across his eyes. " This is, it really is, quite beastly."

" It appears that he always sings when he's finished."

Tim said suddenly : " We heard it. Jemima and I. It wasn't far off. On the other side. We thought it was a sailor but actually it sounded rather like a choirboy."

" Oh, please ! " Father Jourdain ejaculated and at once added, " Sorry. Silly remark."

" Here ! " the Captain interposed, jabbing a square finger at the newspaper-covered form on the table. " Can't you do any of this funny business with fingerprints ? What about them ? "

Alleyn said he'd try, of course, but he didn't expect there'd be any that mattered as their man was believed to wear gloves. He very gingerly removed the newspaper and there, shockingly large, smirking, with her detached head looking over her shoulder, was Esmeralda. In any case, Alleyn pointed out, the mantilla had been wound so tightly round the neck that any fingerprints would be obliterated. " It's a right-handed job, I think," he said. " But as we've no left-handed passengers that doesn't cast a blinding light on anything." He eased away the black lace, exposing part of the pink plastic neck. " He tried the necklace first but he never has any luck with beads. They break. You can see the dents in the paint."

He dropped the newspaper over the doll and looked at Tim Makepiece.

" This sort of thing's up your street, isn't it ? "

Tim said : " If it wasn't for the immediacy of the problem it'd be damned interesting. It still is. It looks like a classic.

The repetition, the time factor—by the way the doll's out of step in that respect, isn't it ? "

" Yes," Alleyn said. " Dead out. It's six days too soon. Would you say that made the time theory look pretty sick ? "

" On the face of it—no, I don't think I would ; although one shouldn't make those sorts of pronouncements. But I'd think the doll being inanimate might be—well, a kind of extra."

" A *jeu d'esprit* ? "

" Yes. Like a Donald Campbell amusing himself with a toy speedboat. It wouldn't interfere with the normal programme. That'd be my guess. But if one could only get him to talk."

" You can try and get all of 'em to talk," said Captain Bannerman sardonically. " No harm in trying."

" It's a question, isn't it," Alleyn said, " of what we are going to do about it. It seems to me there are three courses open to us. A : We can make the whole situation known to everybody in the ship and hold a routine inquiry, but I'm afraid that won't get us much further. I could ask if there were alibis for the other occasions, of course, but our man would certainly produce one and there would be no immediate means of checking it. We know, by the way, that Cuddy hasn't got one for the other occasion."

" Do we ? " said the Captain woodenly.

" Yes. He went for a walk after leaving his silver-wedding bouquet at a hospital."

" My God ! " Tim said softly.

" On the other hand an inquiry would mean that my man is fully warned and at the cost of whatever anguish to himself goes to earth until the end of the voyage. So I don't make an arrest and at the other side of the world more girls are killed by strangulation. B : We can warn the women privately and I give you two guesses as to what sort of privacy we might hope to preserve after warning Mrs.

Cuddy. C : We can take such of your senior officers as you think fit, into our confidence, form ourselves into a sort of vigilance committee and try by observation and undercover inquiry to get more information before taking action."

" Which is the only course *I'm* prepared to sanction," said Captain Bannerman. " And that's flat."

Alleyn looked thoughtfully at him. " Then it's just as well," he said, " that at the moment it appears to be the only one that's at all practicable."

" That makes four suspects to watch," Tim said after a pause.

" Four ? " Alleyn said. " Everybody says four. You may all be right, of course. I'm almost inclined to reduce the field, tentatively, you know, very tentatively. It seems to me that at least one of your four is in the clear."

They stared at him. " Are we to know which ? " Father Jourdain asked.

Alleyn told him.

" Dear me ! " he said. " How excessively stupid of me. But of course."

" And then, for two of the others," Alleyn said apologetically, " there are certain indications : nothing like certainties, you might object, and yet I'm inclined to accept them as working hypotheses."

" But look here ! " Tim said, " that would mean——"

He was interrupted by Captain Bannerman. " Do you mean to sit there," he roared out, " and tell us you think you know who done—damnation !—who did it ? "

" I'm not sure. Not nearly enough, but I fancy so."

After a long pause Father Jourdain said : " Well—again, are we to know which ? And why ? "

Alleyn waited for a moment. He glanced at the Captain's face, scarlet with incredulity, and then at the other two : dubious, perhaps a little resentful.

" I think perhaps better not," he said.

V

When at last he went to bed, Alleyn was unable to sleep. He listened to the comfortable pulse of the ship's progress and seemed to hear 'beyond it a thin whistle of a voice lamenting a broken doll. If he closed his eyes it was to find Captain Bannerman's face, blown with obstinacy, stupid and intractable, and Esmeralda, smirking over his shoulder. And even as he told himself that this must be the beginning of a dream, he was awake again. He searched for some exercise to discipline his thoughts and remembered Miss Abbott's plainsong chant. Suppose Mr. Merryman had ordered him to do it into English verse ?

> *Dismiss the dreams that sore affright*
> *Phantasmagoria of the night.*
> *Confound our carnal enemy*
> *Let not our flesh corrupted be.*

"No ! *No !* NO !" Mr. Merryman shouted, coming very close and handing him an embarkation notice. "You have completely misinterpreted the poem. My compliments to the Captain and request him to lay on six of the best."

Mr. Merryman then opened his mouth very wide, turned into Mr. Cuddy and jumped overboard. Alleyn began to climb a rope ladder with Mrs. Dillington-Blick on his back and thus burdened, at last fell heavily to sleep.

CHAPTER SEVEN

After Las Palmas

I

THE PASSENGERS always met for coffee in the lounge at eleven o'clock. On the morning after Las Palmas this ceremony marked the first appearance of Mrs. Dillington-Blick and Aubyn Dale, neither of whom had come down for breakfast. It was a day with an enervating faint wind and the coffee was iced.

Alleyn had chosen this moment to present Mrs. Dillington-Blick with the *disjecta membra* of Esmeralda. She had already sent Dennis to find the doll and was as fretful as a good-natured woman can be when he came back empty-handed. Alleyn told her that at a late hour he and Father Jourdain had discovered Esmeralda lying on the deck. He then indicated the newspaper parcel that he had laid out on the end of the table.

He did this at the moment when the men of the party and Miss Abbott were gathered round the coffee. Mrs. Cuddy, Mrs. Dillington-Blick and Jemima always allowed them-selves the little ceremony of being waited upon by the gentlemen. Miss Abbott consistently lined herself up in the queue and none of the men had the temerity to question this procedure.

With the connivance of Father Jourdain and Tim Make-piece, Alleyn unveiled Esmeralda at the moment when

Aubyn Dale, Mr. Merryman, Mr. Cuddy and Mr. McAngus were hard by the table.

" Here she is," he said, " and I'm afraid she presents rather a sorry sight."

He flicked the newspaper away in one jerk. Mrs. Dillington-Blick cried out sharply.

Esmeralda lying on her back with her head twisted over her shoulder and the beads and dead hyacinth in position.

After its owner's one ejaculation the doll's exposure was followed by a dead silence and then by a violent oath from Mr. Merryman.

Almost simultaneously Miss Abbott ejaculated : " Don't ! "

Her cup of iced coffee had tilted and the contents had fallen over Mr. Merryman's hands.

Miss Abbott moistened her lips and said : " You must have jolted my arm, Mr. Merryman."

" My dear Madam, I did nothing of the sort ! " he contradicted and angrily flipped his hands. Particles of iced coffee flew in all directions. One alighted on Mr. Cuddy's nose. He seemed to be quite unaware of it. Half smiling, he stared at Esmeralda and with lightly clasped fingers revolved his thumbs slowly round each other.

Aubyn Dale said loudly : " Why have you done this ! It looks disgusting." He reached out and with a quick movement brushed the dead hyacinth off the doll. The beads fell away with a clatter and rolled about the table. Dale straightened the flashily smiling head.

Mr. McAngus murmured gently : " She looks quite herself again, doesn't she ? Perhaps she can be mended."

" I don't understand all this," Dale said angrily to Alleyn. " Why did you do it ? "

" Do what, exactly ? "

" Lay it out like that. Like—like——"

Mrs. Cuddy said with relish : " Like one of those poor

girls. Flowers and beads and everything: giving us all such a turn."

"The doll," Alleyn said, "is exactly as Father Jourdain and I found it: hyacinth and all. I'm sorry if it's upset anyone."

Mrs. Dillington-Blick had come to the table. It was the first time, Alleyn thought, that he had seen her without so much as a flicker of a smile on her face. "Was it like that?" she asked. "Why? What happened?"

Dale said: "Don't worry, darling Ruby. Somebody must have trodden on it and broken the beads and—and the neck."

"I trod on it," Father Jourdain said. "I'm most awfully sorry, Mrs. Dillington-Blick, but it was lying on the deck in pitch-dark shadow."

"There you are!" Dale exclaimed. He caught Alleyn's eye and recovered something of his professional bonhomie. "Sorry, old boy. I didn't mean to throw a temperament. You gathered the doll up just as it was. No offence, I hope?"

"None in the wide world," Alleyn rejoined politely.

Mrs. Cuddy said: "Yes: but all the same it's funny about the flowers, isn't it, dear?"

"That's right, dear. Funny."

"Being a hyacinth and all. Such a coincidence."

"That's right," smiled Mr. Cuddy. "Funny."

Mr. Merryman, who was still fretfully drying his hands on his handkerchief, suddenly cried out in anguish.

"I was mad enough to suppose," Mr. Merriman lamented, "that in undertaking this voyage I would escape, however briefly, from the egregious, the remorseless ambiguities of the lower school urchin. 'Funny! Funny!' Will you be so kind, my good Cuddy, as to enlighten us? In what respect do you consider droll, entertaining or amusing the discovery of a wilted hyacinth upon the bosom of this

disarticulated puppet ? For my part," Mr. Merryman
added with some violence, " I find the obvious correlation
altogether beastly. And the inescapable conclusion that I
myself was, hypothetically at least, responsible for its
presence, adds to my distaste. ' Funny ! ' " Mr. Merryman
concluded in a fury and flung up his hands.

The Cuddys eyed him with dawning resentment. Mr.
McAngus said brightly : " But of course. I'd *quite* for-
gotten. It was *my* hyacinth. You took it, do you recollect ?
When we had our little collision ? And threw it down."

" I did *not* ' take ' it."

" Accidentally, of course. I meant, accidentally." Mr.
McAngus bent over the doll. His reddish knotted fingers
manipulated the neck. " I'm *sure* she can be mended," he
said.

Mrs. Dillington-Blick said in a constrained voice : " Do
you know—I *hope* you'll forgive me, Mr. McAngus, and I
expect I'm being dreadfully silly—but do you know I don't
somehow think I feel quite the same about Esmeralda.
I don't believe I want her mended, or at any rate not for
me. Perhaps we could think of some little girl—you may
have a niece." Her voice faded into an apologetic murmur.

With a kind of social readiness that consorted very ill
with the look in his eyes, Mr. McAngus said : " But, of
course. I quite understand." His hands were still closed
round the neck of the doll. He looked at them, seemed to
recollect himself, and turned aside. " I quite understand,"
he repeated, and helped himself to a herbal cigarette.

Mrs. Cuddy, relentless as a Greek chorus, said : " All
the same it *does* seem funny." Mr. Merryman gave a strangulated cry but she went on greedily, " The way we were all
talking about those murders. You know. And then the
way Mrs. Blick got that cable from her gentleman-friend
about the girl being murdered who brought the flowers.
And the way hyacinths keep turning up. You'd almost

think it was intentional, really you would." She stared in her unwinking fashion at Mrs. Dillington-Blick. "I don't wonder you feel funny about it with the doll being dressed like you. You know. It might almost *be* you, lying there, mightn't it, Mrs. Blick?"

Miss Abbott struck her big hands together. "For God's sake!" she ejaculated, "do we have to listen to all this. Can't someone take that thing away!"

"Of course," Alleyn said and dropped the newspaper over the doll. "I can."

He gathered up the unwieldy parcel and took it to his cabin.

II

"As usual," he wrote to his wife, "I miss you very much. I miss——" He paused and looked, without seeing them, at the objects in his cabin. He reflected on the old circumstance that although his memory had been trained for a long time to retain with scrupulous accuracy the various items of human faces, it always let him down when he wanted it to show Troy to him. Her photograph was not much good, after all. It merely reminded him of features he knew but couldn't visualise: it was only a map of her face. He put something of this down in his letter, word after careful word, and then began to write about the case-in-hand, setting out in detail everything that had happened since his last letter had been posted in Las Palmas.

"——so you see," he wrote, "the nature of the predicament. I'm miles away from the point where one can even begin to think of making an arrest. All I've been able to do is whittle down the field of possibles. Do you agree? Have you arrived at the predominantly possible one? I'm sure you have. I'm making a mystery about nothing which must be the last infirmity of the police-mind.

" Meanwhile we have laid a plan of action that is purely negative. The First and Second Mates and the Chief Engineer have been put wise by the Captain. They all think with him that the whole idea is completely up the pole and that our man's not on board. But they'll fall in with the general scheme and at this moment are delightedly and vigilantly keeping an eye on the ladies who, by the way, have been told that there have been thefts on board and that they'll be well advised to lock their doors, day and night. It's been made very clear that Dennis, the queer fat steward, you know, is not suspected.

" From almost every point-of-view," Alleyn went on after a pause, " these cases are the worst of the lot. One is always hag-ridden by one's personal conviction that the law is desperately inadequate in its dealings with them. One wonders what sort of frightfulness is at work behind the unremarkable face, the more-or-less unexceptionable behaviour. What *is* the reality ? With a psychiatrist, a priest and a policeman all present we've got the ingredients for a Pirandello play, haven't we ? Jourdain and Makepiece are due here now and no doubt I shall get two completely opposed professional opinions from them. In fact——"

There was a tap on the door. Alleyn hurriedly wrote : "—here they are. *Au revoir*, darling," and called out : " Come in."

Father Jourdain now wore a thin light-coloured suit, a white shirt and a black tie. The change in his appearance was quite startling : it was as if a stranger had walked in.

" I really *don't* feel," he said, " that the mortification of a dog collar in the tropics is required of me. I shall put it on for dinner and, on Sunday, I shall sweat in my decent cassock. The sight of you two in your gents' tropical suitings was too much for me. I bought this in Las Palmas and in happier circumstances would get a great deal of pleasure out of wearing it."

They sat down and looked at Alleyn with an air of expectancy. It occurred to him that however sincerely they might deplore the presence of a homicidal monster as their fellow-traveller they were nevertheless stimulated in a way that was not entirely unpleasurable. They were both, he thought, energetic inquisitive men and each in his own mode had a professional interest in the matter in hand.

" Well," he said, when they were settled, " how do you feel about Operation Esmeralda ? "

They agreed, it appeared, that nothing had happened to contradict Alleyn's theory. The reaction to the doll had been pretty well what he had predicted.

" Though the trouble is," Father Jourdain added, " that when one is looking for peculiar behaviour one seems to see it all over the place. I must confess that I found Dale's outburst, the Cuddys' really almost gloating relish, Merryman's intolerable pedantry and McAngus's manipulations equally disturbing. Of course it doesn't arise," he added after a pause, " but even poor Miss Abbott behaved, or so it seemed to me, with a kind of extravagance. I suppose I lost my eye."

" Why," Alleyn asked, " do you call her ' *poor* Miss Abbott ' ? "

" Oh, my dear Alleyn ! I think you know very well. The problem of the unhappy spinster crops up all along the line in my job."

Tim gave an inarticulate grunt.

" Yes," Alleyn said, " she *is* obviously unhappy." He looked at Tim. " What did that knowledgeable noise mean ? "

Tim said impatiently : " We're not concerned with Miss Abbott, I imagine, but it meant that I too recognise the type though perhaps my diagnosis would not appeal to Father Jourdain."

"Would it not?" Father Jourdain said. "I should like to hear it all the same."

Tim said rapidly: "No, really. I mustn't bore you and at any rate one has no business to go by superficial impressions. It's just that on the face of it she's a textbook example of the woman without sexual attraction who hasn't succeeded in finding a satisfactory adjustment."

Alleyn looked up from his clasped hands. "From your point of view isn't that also true of the sort of homicide we're concerned with?"

"Invariably, I should say. These cases almost always point back to some childish tragedy in which the old gang—fear, frustration and jealousy, have been predominant. This is true of most psychological abnormalities. For instance: as a psychotherapist I would, if I got the chance, try to discover why hyacinths make Mr. Cuddy feel ill and I'd expect to find the answer in some incident that may have been thrust completely into his subconscious and that superficially may seem to have no direct reference to hyacinths. And with Aubyn Dale, I'd be interested to hunt down the basic reason for his love of practical jokes. While if Mr. Merryman were my patient I'd try and find a reason for his chronic irritability."

"Dyspepsia no good?" Alleyn asked. "He's for ever taking sodamints."

"All dyspeptics are not irritable woman-haters. I'd expect to find that his indigestion is associated with some very long-standing psychic disturbance."

"Such as his nurse having snatched away his favourite rattle and given it to his papa?"

"You might not be as far out as you may think you are, at that."

"What about Dale and McAngus?"

"Oh," Tim said, "I wouldn't be surprised if Dale hadn't achieved on the whole, a fairly successful sublimation with his ghastly telly-therapy. He's an exhibitionist who thinks he's made good. That's why his two public blunders upset his applecart and gave him his 'nervous break-down'."

" I didn't know he'd had one," said Father Jourdain.

" He says he has. It's a term psychotherapists don't accept. As for McAngus he really *is* interesting : all that timidity and absent-mindedness and losing his way in his own stories : very characteristic."

" Of what ? " Alleyn asked.

" Of an all-too-familiar type. Completely inhibited. Riddled with anxieties and frustrations. And of course he's quite unconscious of their origins. His giving Mrs. D-B that damn' doll was very suggestive. He's a bachelor."

" Oh dear ! " Father Jourdain murmured and at once added : " Pay no attention to me. Do go on."

" Then," Alleyn said, " the psychiatrist's position in respect of these crimes is that they have all developed out of some profound emotional disturbance that the criminal is quite unaware of and is unable to control ? "

" That's it."

" And does it follow that he may, at the conscious level, loathe what he does, try desperately hard to fight down the compulsion and be filled with horror each time he fails ? "

" Very likely."

" Indeed, yes," Father Jourdain said with great emphasis. " Indeed, indeed ! "

Alleyn turned to him. " Then you agree with Make-piece ? "

Father Jourdain passed a white hand over his dark luxuri-ant hair. " I'm sure," he said, " that Makepiece has des-cribed the secondary cause and its subsequent results very learnedly and accurately."

" The *secondary* cause ! " Tim ejaculated.

" Yes. The repressed fear, or frustration or whatever it

was—I'm afraid," said Father Jourdain with a faint smile,
" I haven't mastered the terminology. But I'm sure you're
right about all that : indeed you *know* it all as a man of
science. But you see I would look upon that early tragedy
and its subsequent manifestations as the—well, as the
modus operandi of an infinitely more terrible agent."

" I don't follow," Tim said. " A more terrible agent ? "

" Yes. The devil."

" I beg your pardon ? "

" I believe that this poor soul is possessed of a devil."

Tim, to Alleyn's amusement, actually blushed scarlet as
if Father Jourdain had committed some frightful social
solecism.

" I see," Father Jourdain observed, " that I have em-
barrassed you."

Tim mumbled something about everybody being entitled
to his opinion.

Alleyn said : " I'm afraid I'm rather stuck for a remark,
too. Forgive me, but you do mean, quite literally, exactly
what you've just said ? Yes, I see you do."

" Quite literally. It is a case of possession. I've seen too
many to be mistaken."

There was a long pause during which Alleyn reminded
himself that there were a great number of not unintelligent
people in the world who managed, with some satisfaction
to themselves, to believe in devils. At last he said :

" I must say, in that case, I very much wish you could
exorcise it."

With perfect seriousness Father Jourdain replied that
there were certain difficulties. " I shall, of course, continue
to pray for him," he said.

Tim shuffled his feet, lit a cigarette and with an air of
striking out rather wildly for some kind of raft, asked
Alleyn for the police view of these kinds of murderers.
" After all," he said, " you must be said to be experts."

" Not at all," Alleyn rejoined. " Very far from it. Our job, God save the mark, is first to protect society and then as a corollary, to catch the criminal. These sorts of criminals are often our worst headache. They have no occupational habits. They resemble each other only in their desire to kill for gratification. In everyday life they may be anything : there are no outward signs. We generally get them but by no means always. The thing one looks for, of course, is a departure from routine. If there's no known routine, if your man is a solitary creature as Jack the Ripper was, your chances lessen considerably." Alleyn paused and then added in a changed voice : " But as to why, fundamentally, he is what he is—we are dumb. Perhaps if we knew we'd find our job intolerable."

Father Jourdain said : " You are, after all, a compassionate man, I see."

Alleyn found this remark embarrassing and inappropriate. He said quickly : " It doesn't arise. An investigating officer examining the bodies of strangled girls who have died on a crescendo of terror and physical agony is not predisposed to feel compassion for the strangler. It's not easy to remember that he may have suffered a complementary agony of the mind. In many cases he hasn't done anything of the sort. He's too far gone."

" Isn't it a question," Tim asked, " of whether something might have been done about him before his obsession reached its climax ? "

" Of course it is," Alleyn agreed, very readily, " that's where you chaps come in."

Tim stood up. " It's three o'clock. I'm due for a game of deck golf," he said. " What's the form ? Watchful diligence ? "

" That's it."

Father Jourdain also rose. " I'm going to do a crossword

with Miss Abbott. She's got the new Penguin. Mr. Merryman is Ximenes standard."

" I'm a *Times* man myself," Alleyn said.

" There's one thing about the afternoons," Father Jourdain sighed, " the ladies do tend to retire to their cabins."

" For the sake of argument only," Tim asked gloomily, " suppose Cuddy was your man. Do you think he'd be at all liable to strangle Mrs. Cuddy ? "

" By thunder," Alleyn said, " if I were in his boots, *I* would. Come on."

In the afternoons there were not very many shady places on deck and a good deal of quiet manœuvring went on among the passengers to secure them. Claims were staked. Mr. Merryman left his air cushion and his Panama on the nicest of the deck-chairs. The Cuddys did a certain amount of edging in and shoving aside when nobody else was about. Mr. McAngus laid his plaid along one of the wooden seats, but as nobody else cared for the seats this procedure aroused no enmity. Aubyn Dale and Mrs. Dillington-Blick used their own luxurious chaise-longues with rubber-foam appointments and had set them up in the little veranda which they pretty well filled. Although they were never occupied till after tea nobody liked to use them in the meantime.

So while Tim, Jemima and two of the junior officers played deck golf, Miss Abbott and five men were grouped in a shady area cast by the centrecastle between the doors into the lounge and the amidships hatch. Mr. Cuddy slept noisily with a *Readers Digest* over his face. Mr. McAngus dozed, Mr. Merryman and Alleyn read, Father Jourdain and Miss Abbott laboured at their crossword. It was a tranquil-looking scene. Desultory sentences and little spurts of observation drifted about with the inconsequence of a conversational poem by Verlaine.

Above their heads Captain Bannerman took his afternoon walk on the bridge, solacing the monotony with pleasurable glances at Jemima, who looked enchanting in jeans and a scarlet shirt. As he had predicted, she was evidently a howling success with his junior officers. And with his medical officer, too, reflected the Captain. Sensible perhaps of his regard, Jemima looked up and gaily waved to him. In addition to being attractive she was also what he called a thoroughly nice, unspoiled little lady ; just a sweet young girl, he thought. Dimly conscious, perhaps, of some not altogether appropriate train of thought aroused by this reflection, the Captain decided to think instead of Mrs. Dillington-Blick : a mental exercise that came very easy to him.

Jemima took a long swipe at her opponent's disc, scuppered her own, shouted " Damn ! " and burst out laughing. The junior officers who had tried very hard to let her win now polished off the game in an expert manner and regretfully returned to duty.

Jemima said : " Oh, Tim, I *am* sorry ! You must get another partner."

" Are you sick of me ? " Tim rejoined. " What shall we do now ? Would you like to have a singles ? "

" Not very much, thank you. I need the support of a kind and forbearing person like yourself. Perhaps some of the others would play. Mr. McAngus for instance. His game is about on a par with mine."

" Mr. McAngus is mercifully dozing and you know jolly well you're talking nonsense."

" Well, who ? " Jemima nervously pushed her hair back and said : " Perhaps it's too hot after all. Don't let's play." She looked at the little group in the shade of the centre-castle. Mr. Merryman had come out of his book and was talking to Alleyn in an admonitory fashion, shaking his finger and evidently speaking with some heat.

" Mr. Chips is at it again," Tim said. " Poor Alleyn ! "

He experienced the sensation of his blood running down into his boots. He thought complicatedly of a number of things at once. Perhaps his predominant emotion was one of incredulity : surely he, Tim Makepiece, a responsible man, a man of science, a psychiatrist, could not have slipped into so feeble, so imbecile an error. Would he have to confess to Alleyn ? How could he recover himself with Jemima ? Her voice recalled him.

" What did you say ? " she asked.

" ' Poor Broderick.' "

" Is he called Allan ? You've got down to Christian names pretty smartly. Very chummy of you."

Tim said after a pause : " I don't to his face. I like him."

" So do I. Awfully. We agreed about it before." Jemima shook her head impatiently. " At any rate," she said, " he's not the guilty one. I'm sure of that."

Tim stood very still and after a moment wetted his lips.

" What do you mean ? " he said. " The guilty one ? "

" Are you all right, Tim ? "

" Perfectly."

" You look peculiar."

" It's the heat. Come back here, do."

He took her arm and led her to the little veranda, pushed her down on the sumptuous footrest belonging to Mrs. Dillington-Blick's chaise-longue and himself sat at the end of Aubyn Dale's. " What guilty one ? " he repeated.

Jemima stared at him. " There's no need, really, to take it so massively," she said. " You may not feel like I do about it."

" About *what* ? "

" The business with the D-B's doll. It seems to me such a beastly thing to have done and I don't care what anyone says, it was done on purpose. Just treading on it wouldn't have produced that result. And then, putting the flower on its chest : a scurvy trick, I call it."

Tim stooped down and made a lengthy business of tying his shoelace. When he straightened up Jemima said : " You *are* all right, aren't you ? You keep changing colour like a chameleon."

" Which am I now ? "

" Fiery red."

" I've been stooping over. I agree with you about the doll. It was a silly unbecoming sort of thing to do. Perhaps it was a drunken sailor."

" There weren't any drunken sailors about. Do you know who I think it was ? "

" Who ? "

" Mr. Cuddy."

" Do you, Jem ? " Tim said. " Why ? "

" He kept smiling and smiling all the time that Mr. Broderick was showing the doll."

" He's got a chronic grin. It never leaves his face."

" All the same——" Jemima looked quickly at Tim and away again. " In my opinion," she muttered, " he's a D.O.M."

" A what ? "

" A dirty old man. I don't mind telling you, I'd simply hate to find myself alone on the boatdeck with him after dark."

Tim hastily said that she'd better make sure she never did. " Take me with you for safety's sake," he said. " I'm eminently trustworthy."

Jemima grinned at him absent-mindedly. She seemed to be in two minds about what she should say next.

" What is it ? " he asked.

" Nothing. Nothing, really. It's just—I don't know— it's ever since Dennis brought Mrs. D-B's hyacinths into the lounge on the second day out. We don't seem to be able to get rid of those awful murders. Everybody talking about them. That alibi discussion the night before Las Palmas and Miss Abbott breaking down. Not that *her* trouble had anything to do with it, poor thing. And then the awful business of the girl that brought Mrs. D-B's flowers being a victim and now the doll being left like that. You'll think I'm completely dotty," Jemima said, " but it's sort of got me down a bit. Do you know, just now I caught myself thinking : ' Wouldn't it be awful if the flower murderer was on board.' "

Tim had put out a warning hand but a man's shadow had already fallen across the deck and across Jemima.

" Dear child ! " said Aubyn Dale, " what a *pathologically* morbid little notion ! "

III

Tim and Jemima got up. Tim said automatically : " I'm afraid we've been trespassing on your footrests," and hoped this would account for any embarrassment they might have displayed.

" My dear old boy ! " Dale cried, " *do* use the whole tatty works ! Whenever you like, as far as I'm concerned. And I'm sure Madame would be enchanted."

He had an armful of cushions and rugs which he began to arrange on the chaise-longues. " Madame tends to emerge for a nice cuppa," he explained. He punched a cushion with all the aplomb of the manservant in *Charley's Aunt* and flung it into position. " There now ! " he said. He straightened up, pulled a pipe out of his pocket, gripped it mannishly between his teeth, contrived to tower over Jemima and became avuncular.

" As for you, young woman," he said, cocking his head quizzically at her, " you've been letting a particularly lively imagination run away with you. What ? "

This was said with such an exact reproduction of his television manner that Tim, in spite of his own agitation, felt momentarily impelled to whistle "Pack Up Your Troubles." However he said quickly: "It wasn't as morbid as it sounded. Jemima and I have been having an argument about the 'Alibi' bet and that led to inevitable conjectures about the flower expert."

"M-m-m," Dale rumbled understandingly, still looking at Jemima. "*I* see." He screwed his face into a whimsical grimace. "You know, Jemima, I've got an idea we've just about had that old topic. After all, it's not the prettiest one in the world, is it? What do you think? Um?"

Pink with embarrassment, Jemima said coldly: "I feel sure you're right."

"Good girl," Aubyn Dale said and patted her shoulder.

Tim muttered that it was tea-time and withdrew Jemima firmly to the starboard side. It was a relief to him to be angry.

"My God, what a frightful fellow," he fulminated. "That egregious nice-chappery! That ineffable decency! That indescribably phoney good-will!"

"Never mind," Jemima said. "I dare say he has to keep in practice. And, after all, little as I relish admitting it, he was in fact right. I suppose I have been letting my imagination run away with me."

Tim stood over her, put his head on one side and achieved a quite creditable imitation of Aubyn Dale. "Good girl," he said unctuously and patted her shoulder.

Jemima made a satisfactory response to this sally and seemed to be a good deal cheered. "Of course," she said, "I didn't *really* think we'd shipped a murderer: it was just one of those things." She looked up into Tim's face.

"Jemima!" he said, and took her hands in his.

"No, don't," she said quickly. "Don't."

"I'm sorry."

"There's nothing to be sorry about. Pay no attention. Let's go and talk to Mr. Chips."

They found Mr. Merryman in full cry. He had discovered Jemima's book, *The Elizabethans*, which she had left on her deck-chair, and seemed to be giving a lecture on it. It was by an authoritative writer but one, evidently, with whom Mr. Merryman found himself in passionate disagreement. It appeared that Alleyn, Father Jourdain and Miss Abbott had all been drawn into the discussion while Mr. McAngus and Mr. Cuddy looked on, the former with admiration and the latter with his characteristic air of uninformed disparagement.

Jemima and Tim sat on the deck and were accepted by Mr. Merryman as if they had come late for class but with valid excuses. Alleyn glanced at them and found time to hope that theirs, by some happy accident, was not merely a shipboard attraction. After all, he thought, he himself had fallen irrevocably in love during a voyage from the Antipodes. He turned his attention back to the matter in hand.

"I honestly *don't* understand," Father Jourdain was saying, "how you can put *The Duchess of Malfi* before *Hamlet* or *Macbeth*."

"Or why," Miss Abbott barked, "you should think *Othello* so much better than any of them."

Mr. Merryman groped in his waistcoat pocket for a soda-mint and remarked insufferably that really it was impossible to discuss criteria of taste where the rudiments of taste were demonstrably absent. He treated his restive audience to a comprehensive de-gumming of *Hamlet* and *Macbeth*. Hamlet, he said, was an inconsistent, deficient and redundant *recl a ffé* of some absurd German melodrama : it was not surprising, Mr. Merryman said, that Hamlet was unable to make up his mind since his creator had himself been the victim of a still greater blight of indecision. Macbeth was merely a muddle-headed blunderer. Strip away the language and what remained? A tediously ignorant expression of defeatism. " ' What's the good of anyfink? Wy nuffink ','" Mr. Merryman quoted in pedantic cockney and tossed his sodamint into his mouth.

"I don't know anything about Shakespeare——"—Mr. Cuddy began and was at once talked down.

"It is at least something," Mr. Merryman said, "that you acknowledge your misfortune. May I advise you not to break your duck with *Macbeth*."

"All the same," Alleyn objected, "there *is* the language."

"I am not aware," Mr. Merryman countered, "that I have suggested that the fellow had no vocabulary." He went on to praise the classic structure of *Othello*, the inevitability of Webster's *The Duchess of Malfi*, and, astoundingly, the admirable directness of *Titus Andronicus*. As an afterthought he conceded that the final scene of *Lear* was " respectable."

Mr. McAngus, who had several times made plaintive little noises, now struck in with unexpected emphasis.

"To me," he said, " *Othello* is almost spoilt by that bit near the end when Desdemona revives and speaks and then, you know, after all, dies. A woman who has been properly strangled would *not* be able to do that. It is quite ridiculous."

"What's the medical opinion?" Alleyn asked Tim.

"Pathological verisimilitude," Mr. Merryman interjected with more than a touch of Pooh-Ba, " is irrelevant. One accepts the convention. It is artistically proper that she should be strangled and speak again. Therefore, she speaks."

"All the same," Alleyn said, " let's have the expert's opinion." He looked at Tim.

"I wouldn't say it was utterly impossible," Tim said. "Of course, her physical condition can't be reproduced by an actress and would be unacceptable if it could. I should think it's just possible that he might not have killed her instantly and that she might momentarily revive and attempt to speak."

"But, Doctor," Mr. McAngus objected diffidently, "I *did* say properly. Properly strangled, you know."

"Doesn't the text," Miss Abbott pointed out, "say she was smothered ? "

"The text ! " Mr. Merryman exclaimed and spread out his hands. "What text, pray ? Which text ? " and launched himself into a general animadversion of Shakespearian editorship. This he followed up with an extremely dogmatic pronouncement upon the presentation of the plays. The only tolerable method, he said, was that followed by the Elizabethans themselves. The bare boards. The boy-players. It appeared that Mr. Merryman himself produced the plays in this manner at his school. He treated them to a lecture upon speechcraft, costume and make-up. His manner was so insufferably cocksure that it robbed his discourse of any interest it might have had for his extremely mixed audience. Mr. McAngus's eyes became glazed. Father Jourdain was resigned and Miss Abbott impatient. Jemima looked at the deck and Tim looked at Jemima. Alleyn, conscious of all this, still managed to preserve the semblance of respectful attention.

He was conscious also of Mr. Cuddy who had the air of a man baulked of his legitimate prey. It was evident throughout the discussion that he had some observation to make. He now raised his voice unmelodiously and made it.

"Isn't it funny," Mr. Cuddy asked generally, "how the conversation seems to get round to the subject of ladies being throttled ? Mrs. Cuddy was remarking on the same thing. Quite a coincidence, she was saying."

Mr. Merryman opened his mouth, shut it, and reopened it when Jemima cried out with some violence :

"I think it's perfectly beastly. I hate it ! "

Tim put his hand over hers. " Well, I'm sorry," Jemima said, " but it *is* beastly. It doesn't matter *how* Desdemona died. Othello isn't a clinical example. Shakespeare wasn't some scruffy existentialist : it's a tragedy of simplicity and —and greatness of heart being destroyed by a common smarty-smarty little placefinder. Well anyway," Jemima mumbled, turning very pink, " that's what I think and I suppose one can try and say what one thinks, can't one ? "

" I should damn' well suppose one can," Alleyn said warmly, " and how right you are, what's more."

Jemima threw him a grateful look.

Mr. Cuddy smiled and smiled. " I'm sure," he said, " I didn't mean to upset anyone."

" Well, you have," Miss Abbott snapped, " and now you know it, don't you ? "

" Thank you very much," said Mr. Cuddy.

Father Jourdain stood up. " It's tea-time," he said. " Shall we go in ? And shall we decide," he smiled at Jemima, "to take the advice of the youngest and wisest among us and keep off this not very delectable subject ? I propose that we do."

Everybody except Mr. Cuddy made affirmative noises and they went in to tea.

" But the curious thing is," Alleyn wrote to his wife that evening, " that however much they may or may not try to avoid the subject of murder, it still crops up. I don't want to go precious about it, but really one might suppose that the presence of this expert on board generates a sort of effluvia. They are unaware of it and yet it infects them. To-night, for instance, after the women had gone to bed, which to my great relief was early, the men got cracking again. Cuddy, Jourdain and Merryman are all avid readers of crime fiction and of the sort of book that calls itself ' Classic Cases of Detection.' As it happens there are two or three of that kind in the ship's little library : among them *The Wain-*

wrights in the admirable Notable Trials series, a very fanciful number on the Yard and an affair called : *The Thing He Loves*. The latter title derives from *The Ballad of Reading Gaol*, of course, and I give you one guess as to the subject matter.

" Well, to-night, Merryman being present, there was automatically a row. Without exception he's the most pugnacious, quarrelsome, arrogant chap I've ever met. It seemed that Cuddy had got *The Thing He Loves*, and was snuffling away at it in the corner of the lounge. Merryman spotted the book and at once said that he himself was already reading it. Cuddy said he'd taken the book from the shelves and that they were free for all. Neither would give in. Finally McAngus announced that he had a copy of *The Trial of Neil Cream* and actually succeeded in placating Merryman with an offer to lend it to him. It appears that Merryman is one of the fanatics who believes the story of Cream's unfinished confession. So peace was in a sense restored though once again we were treated to an interminable discussion on what Cuddy *will* call sex-monstrosity. Dale was full of all kinds of second-hand theories. McAngus joined in with a sort of terrified relish. Makepiece talked from the psychiatric angle and Jourdain from the religious one. Merryman contradicted everybody. Of course, I'm all for these discussions. They give one an unexampled chance to listen to the man one may be going to arrest, propounding the sort of crime with which he will ultimately be charged.

" The reactions go like this :

" McAngus does a great deal of tut-tuttering, protests that the subject is too horrid to dwell upon, is nevertheless quite unable to go away while it's under discussion. He gets all the facts wrong, confuses names and dates so persistently that you'd think it was deliberate and is slapped back perpetually by Merryman.

" Cuddy is utterly absorbed. He goes over the details

and incessantly harks back to Jack the Ripper, describing all the ritualistic horrors and speculating about their possible significance.

"Merryman, of course, is overbearing, didactic and argumentative. He's got a much better brain than any of the others, is conversant with the cases, never muddles the known facts and never loses a chance of blackguarding the police. In his opinion they won't catch their man and he obviously glories in the notion (Hah-hah, did he but know, sneered Hawkshaw, the Detective).

"Dale, like McAngus, puts up a great show of abhorrence but professes an interest in what he calls the 'psychology of sadistic homicide'. He talks like a signed article in one of the less responsible of our dailies and also, of course, like a thoroughly nice chap on television. Poor wretch! is his cry : poor, poor girls, poor everybody. Sad! Sad!

"Meanwhile, being in merry pin, he has had enough misguided energy to sew up Mr. Merryman's pyjamas and put a dummy woman made from one of the D-B's tremendous nightgowns in Mr. McAngus's bed and has thus by virtue of these hilarious pranks graduated as a potential victim himself. Merryman's reaction was to go straight to the Captain and McAngus's to behave as if he was a typical example from Freud's casebook.

"Well, there they are, these four precious favourites in the homicide handicap. I've told you that I fancy one in particular and, in the classic tradition, my dearest, having laid bare the facts I leave you to your deduction ; always bearing in mind that the Captain and his mates may be right and there ain't no flaming murderer on board.

"Good night, darling. Don't miss our next instalment of this absorbing serial."

Alleyn put his letter away, doodled absently on his blotting paper for a few minutes and then thought he'd stretch his legs before turning in.

He went down to the deck below and found it deserted. Having walked six times round it and had a word with the wireless officer who sat lonely as a cloud in his cubby hole on the starboard side, Alleyn thought he would call it a day. He passed Father Jourdain's cabin door on his way through the passengers' quarters and as he did so the handle turned and the door was opened a crack. He heard Father Jourdain's voice.

"But, of course. You must come to me whenever you want to. It's what I'm for, you know."

A woman's voice answered harshly and undistinguishably.

"I think," said Father Jourdain, "you should dismiss all that from your mind and stick to your duties. Perform your penance, come to mass to-morrow, make the special intention I have suggested. Go along, now, and say your prayers. Bless you, my child. Good night."

Alleyn moved quickly down the passage and had reached the stairs before Miss Abbott had time to see him.

CHAPTER EIGHT

Sunday the Tenth

I

THE NEXT day, being Sunday, Father Jourdain with the Captain's permission celebrated Holy Communion in the lounge at seven o'clock. The service was attended among the passengers by Miss Abbott, Jemima, Mr. McAngus and, rather surprisingly, Mr. Merryman. The Third Officer, the Wireless Officer, two of the cadets and Dennis represented the ship's complement. Alleyn, at the back of the room, listened, watched and, not for the first time, felt his own lack of acceptance to be tinged with a faint regret.

When the service was over the little group of passengers went out on deck and presently were joined by Father Jourdain, wearing, as he had promised, his " decent black cassock." He looked remarkably handsome in it with the light breeze lifting his glossy hair. Miss Abbott, standing, characteristically, a little apart from the others, watched him, Alleyn noticed, with a look of stubborn deference. There was a Sunday morning air about the scene. Even Mr. Merryman was quiet and thoughtful while Mr. McAngus who, with Miss Abbott, had carried out the details of Anglo-Catholic observance like an old hand, was quite giddy and uplifted. He congratulated Jemima on her looks and did his little chassé before her with his head on one side. Mr. McAngus's russet-brown hair had grown, of course, even longer at the back and something unfortunate seemed to have happened round the brow and temples. But as he always wore his felt hat out-of-doors and quite often in the lounge, this was not pratically noticeable.

Jemima responded gaily to his blameless compliments and turned to Alleyn.

" I didn't expect to see *you* about so early," she said.

" And why not ? "

" You were up late ! Pacing round the deck. Wrapped in thought ! " teased Jemima.

" That's all very fine," Alleyn rejoined. " But what I might ask were you up to yourself ? From what angle of vantage did you keep all this observation ? "

Jemima blushed. " Oh," she said with a great air of casualness, " I was sitting in the veranda along there. We didn't like to call out as you passed, you looked so solemn and absorbed." She turned an even brighter pink, glanced at the others who were gathered round Father Jourdain and added quickly : " Tim Makepiece and I were talking about Elizabethan literature."

" You were not talking very loudly about it," Alleyn observed mildly.

" Well——" Jemima looked into his face. " I'm not having a shipboard flirtation with Tim. At least—at least, I don't think I am."

" Not a flirtation ? " Alleyn repeated and smiled at her.

" And not anything else. Oh, golly ! " Jemima said impulsively. " I'm in such a muddle."

" Do you want to talk about your muddle ? "

Jemima put her arm through his. " I've arrived at the age," Alleyn reflected, " when charming young ladies take my arm." They walked down the deck together.

" How long," Jemima asked, " have we been at sea ? And, crickey ! " she added, " *what* an appropriate phrase that is ! "

" Six days."

" There you are ! Six days ! The whole thing's ridiculous.

How can anybody possibly know how they feel in six days ? It's out of this world."

Alleyn remarked that he had known how he felt in one. "Shorter even than that," he added. "At once."

"*Really?* And stuck to it ? "

"Like a limpet. She took much longer, though."

"But——? Did you ? "

"We are *very* happily married, thank you."

"How lovely," Jemima sighed.

"However," he added hurriedly, "don't let me raise a finger to urge you into an ill-considered undertaking."

"You don't have to tell me anything about that," she rejoined with feeling. "I've made that sort of ass of myself in quite a big way, once already."

"Really ? "

"Yes, indeed. The night we sailed should have been my wedding night only he chucked me three days before. I've done a bolt from all the *brouhaha*, leaving my wretched parents to cope. Very poor show as you don't need to tell me," said Jemima in a high uneven voice.

"I expect your parents were delighted to get rid of you. Much easier for them, I dare say, if you weren't about : throwing vapours."

They had reached the end of the well-deck and stood, looking aft, near the little veranda. Jemima remarked indistinctly that going to church always made her feel rather light-headed and talkative and she expected that was why she was being so communicative.

"Perhaps the warm weather has something to do with it, as well," Alleyn suggested.

"I dare say. One always hears that people get very unguarded in the tropics. But actually you're to blame. I was saying to Tim the other night that if I was ever in a real jam I'd feel inclined to go bawling to you about it. He quite agreed. And here, fantastically, I am. Bawling away."

" I'm enormously flattered. Are you in a jam ? "

" I suppose not, really. I just need to keep my eye.
And see that he keeps his. Because whatever you say, I
don't see how he can possibly know in six days."

Alleyn said that people saw more of each other in six
days at sea than they did in as many weeks ashore but, he
was careful to add, in rather less realistic circumstances.
Jemima agreed. There was no doubt, she announced owlishly,
that strange things happened to one at sea. Look at her, for
instance, she said with enchanting egoism. She was getting
all sorts of the rummiest notions into her head. After a
little hesitation and then, very much with the air of a child
that screws itself up to confiding a groundless fear, Jemima
said rapidly : " I even started thinking the flower murderer
was on board. Imagine ! "

Among the various items of Alleyn's training as an
investigating officer, the trick of wearing an impassive face
in the teeth of unexpected information was not the least
useful. It stood him in good stead now.

" I wonder," he said, "what in the world could have put
that idea in your head."

Jemima repeated the explanation she had already given
Tim yesterday afternoon. " Of course," she said, " he
thought it as dotty as you do and so did the F.N.C."

" Who," Alleyn asked, " is the F.N.C. ? "

" It's our name for Dale. It stands for Frightfully
Nice Chap only we don't mean it frightfully nicely, I'm
afraid."

" Nevertheless you confided your fantasy to him, did
you ? "

" He overheard me. We were ' squatting ' on his and the
D-B's lush chairs and he came round the corner with
cushions and went all avuncular."

" And now you've brought this bugaboo out into the
light of day it's evaporated ? "

Jemima swung her foot and kicked an infinitesimal object into the scuppers : " Not altogether," she muttered.

" No ? "

" Well, it has, really. Only last night, after I'd gone to bed, something happened. I don't suppose it was anything much but it got me a bit steamed up again. My cabin's on the left hand side of the block. The porthole faces my bed. Well, you know that blissful moment when you're not sure whether you're awake or asleep but kind of floating ? I'd got to that stage. My eyes were shut and I was all airborne and drifting. Then with a jerk I was wide awake and staring at that porthole." Jemima swallowed hard. " It was moonlight outside. Before I'd shut my eyes I'd seen the moon ; looking in and then swinging out of sight and leaving a procession of stars and then swinging back. Lovely ! Well, when I opened my eyes and looked at the porthole—somebody outside was looking in at me."

Alleyn waited for a moment and then said : " You're quite sure, I suppose ? "

" Oh, yes. There he was, blotting out the stars and the moon and filling up my porthole with his head."

" Do you know who it was ? "

" I haven't a notion. Somebody in a hat but I could only see the outline. And it was only for a second. I called out—it was not a startling original remark—' Hallo ! Who's there ? ' and at once it—went down. I mean it sank in a flash. He must have ducked and then bolted. The moon came whooping back and there was I, all-of-a-dither and thinking : ' Suppose the flower murderer is on board and suppose after everyone else has gone to bed, he prowls and prowls around like the hosts of Midian or is it Gideon, in that blissful hymn ? So you see, I haven't quite got over my nonsense, have I ? "

" Have you told Makepiece about this ? "

" I haven't seen him. He doesn't go to church."

" No, of course you haven't. Perhaps," Alleyn said, " it was Aubyn Dale being Puckish."

" I must say I never thought of that. Could he hit quite such an all-time-low for unfunniness, do you suppose ? "

" I would have expected him to follow it up with a dummy spider on your pillow. You do lock your door at night, don't you ? And in the daytime ? "

" Yes. There was that warning about things having been pinched. Oh, lord ! " Jemima ejaculated, " do you suppose that's who it was ? The petty larcener ? Why on earth didn't I remember before ! Hoping he could fish something out through the porthole, would you think ? "

" It wouldn't be the first time," Alleyn said.

The warning gong for breakfast began to tinkle. Jemima remarked cheerfully : " Well, that's *that*, anyway."

Alleyn waited for a moment and then said : " Look. In view of what you've just told me, I'd keep your curtains over your port at night. And as there evidently is a not-too-desirable character in the ship's complement, I don't think, if I were you I'd go out walking after dark by yourself. He might come along and make a bit of a nuisance of himself."

Jemima said : " O.K., but what a *bore*. And, by the way, you'd better hand on that piece of advice to Mrs. D-B. She's the one to go out walking—or dancing, rather—by the light of the moon." Jemima smiled reminiscently. " I do think she's marvellous," she said. " All that *joie-de-vivre* at her age. Superb."

Alleyn found time to wonder how much Mrs. Dillington-Blick would relish this tribute and also how many surprises Jemima was liable to spring on him at one sitting.

He said : " *Does* she dance by the light of the moon ? Who with ? "

" By herself."

" You don't tell me she goes all pixy-wixy on the boat deck ? Carrying that weight ? "

" On the other deck, the bottom one, nearer the sharp end. I've seen her. The weight doesn't seem to matter."

" Do explain yourself."

" Well, I'm afraid you're in for another night-piece—in point of fact the night before last. It was awfully hot : Tim and I had sat up rather late, *not*, I'd have you know again, for amorous dalliance but for a long muddly argument. And when I went to my cabin it was stuffy and I knew I wouldn't sleep for thinking about the argument. So I went along to the windows that look down on the lower deck—it's called the forrard well-deck, isn't it?—and wondered if I could be bothered climbing down and then along and up to the bows where I rather like to go. And while I was wondering and looking down into the forrard well-deck which was full of black shadows, a door opened underneath me and a square patch of light was thrown across the deck."

Jemima's face, vivid and gay with the anticipation of her narrative, clouded a little.

" In point of fact," she said, " for a second or two it was a trifle grizzly. You see, a shadow appeared on the lighted square. And—well—it was exactly as if the doll, Esmeralda, had come to life. Mantilla, fan, wide lace skirt. Everything. I dare say it contributed to my ' thing ' about the Flower Murders. Anyway it gave me quite a jolt."

" It would," Alleyn agreed. " What next ? "

" Well, somebody shut the door and the light patch vanished. And I knew, of course, who it was. There she stood, all by herself. I was looking down on her head. And then it happened. The moon was up and just at that moment it got high enough to shine into the deck. All those lumps of covered machinery cast their inky-black shadows, but there were patches of moonshine and it was exciting to see. She ran out and flirted her fan and did little pirouettes and curtsies and even two or three of those

sliding backsteps like they do with castanets in *The Gondoliers*.
I think she was holding her mantilla across her face. It was
the strangest sight."

"Very rum, indeed. You're sure it was the D-B ?"

"But, of course. Who else ? And, do you know, I found
it rather touching. Don't you agree ? She only stayed for a
few moments and then ran back. The door opened and her
shadow flashed across the patch of light. I heard men's
voices, laughing, and then it was all blanked out. But
wasn't it gay and surprising of Mrs. Dillington-Blick ?
Aren't you astonished ? " asked Jemima.

"Flabbergasted. Although, one does hear, of course, of
elephant dances in the seclusion of the jungle."

Jemima said indignantly : " She's as light as a feather
on her pins. Fat people are, you know. They dance like
fairies. Still, perhaps you'd better warn her not to on
account of the petty larcener. Only please don't say I told
you about her moonlight party. In a funny sort of way I
felt like an interloper."

"I won't," he promised. "And in the meantime don't
take any solitary walks yourself. Tell Makepiece about it,
and see if he doesn't agree with me."

"Oh," Jemima assured him. " He'll agree all right."
And a dimple appeared near the corner of her mouth.

The group round Father Jourdain had moved nearer.
Mr. McAngus called out : " Breakfast ! " and Jemima said
" Coming ! " She joined them, turned, crinkled her eyes
at Alleyn and called out : " You *have* been nice. Thank
you—Allan."

Before he could reply she had made off with the others
in search of breakfast.

II

During breakfast Tim kept trying to catch Alleyn's eye and got but little response for his pains. He was waiting in the passage when Alleyn came out and said with artificial heartiness : " I've found those books I was telling you about : would you like to come along to my room, or shall I bring them up to yours ? "

" Bring them," Alleyn said, " to mine."

He went straight upstairs. In five minutes there was a knock on his door and Tim came in, burdened with un-wanted text-books. " I've got something I think I ought to tell you," he said.

" Jemima Carmichael wonders if the flower-murderer is on board and Aubyn Dale knows she does."

" How the hell did you find out ! " Tim ejaculated.

" She told me."

" Oh."

" And I'm rather wondering why you didn't."

" I didn't get a chance before dinner. I was going to after dinner but you were boxed up with the D-B and Dale in the lounge and later on—well——"

" You were discussing Elizabethan literature on the veranda ? "

" Exactly."

" Very well. At what stage did you inform Miss Carmichael of my name ? "

" Damn it, it's not as bad as you think. Look—did she tell you that too ? "

" She merely called it out before the whole lot of them as we came down to breakfast."

" She thinks it's your christian name—Allan."

" Why ? "

Tim told him. " I really am ashamed of myself," he

said. "It just slipped out. I wouldn't have believed I could be such a *bloody* fool."

"Nor would I. I suppose it comes of all this poodle-faking nonsense. Calling oneself by a false name! Next door to wearing false whiskers, I've always thought, but sometimes it can't be avoided."

"She's not a notion who you are, of course."

"That, at least, is something. And, by the way, she'll be telling you about an incident that occurred last night. I think you'll agree that it's serious. I've suggested the mythical sneak-thief as the culprit. You'd better take the same line."

"But what's happened?"

"A Peeping Tom's happened. She'll tell you. She may also tell you how Mrs. Dillington-Blick goes fey among the derricks by moonlight."

"*What!*"

"I'm going to see the Captain. Father Jourdain's joining me there: you'd better come too, I think. You might as well know about it."

"Of course. If I'm not confined to outer darkness."

"Oh," Alleyn said, "we'll give you another chance."

Tim said: "I'm sorry about my gaffe, Alleyn."

"The name is Broderick."

"I'm sorry."

"She's a nice child. None of my business but I hope you're not making a nonsense. She's had one bad knock and she'd better not be dealt another."

"She seems," Tim observed, "to confide in you a damn' sight more freely than in me."

"Advanced years carry their own compensation."

"For me, this is *it*."

"Certain?"

"Absolutely. I wish I was as certain about her."

"Well—look after her."

" I've every intention of doing so," Tim said, and on that note they found Father Jourdain and went to visit Captain Bannerman.

It was not an easy interview.

Alleyn would have recognised Captain Bannerman for an obstinate man even if he had not been told as much by members of the Cape Line Company before he left. " He's a pig-headed old b.," one of these officials had remarked. " And if you get up against him he'll make things very uncomfortable for you. He drinks pretty hard and is reported to be bloody-minded in his cups. Keep on the right side of him and he'll be O.K."

So far, Alleyn thought, he had managed to follow this suggestion, but when he described the episode of the moonlit figure seen by Jemima on Friday night, he knew he was in for trouble. He gave his own interpretation of this story and he suggested that steps should be taken to ensure that there was no repetition. He met with a flat refusal. He then went on to tell them of the man outside Jemima's porthole. The Captain said at once that he would detail the officer of the watch who would take appropriate steps to ensure that this episode was not repeated. He added that it was of no particular significance and that very often people behaved oddly in the tropics : an observation that Alleyn was getting a little tired of hearing. He attempted to suggest a more serious interpretation and met with blank incredulity.

As for the Dillington-Blick episode, the Captain said he would take no action either to investigate it or prevent a repetition. He treated them to a lecture on the diminishing powers of a ship's master at sea and grew quite hot on the subject. There were limitations. There were unions. Even passengers nowadays had their rights, he added regretfully. What had occurred was in no way an infringement of any of the regulations, he didn't propose to do anything about it and he must request Alleyn to follow suit. And that, he said finally, was flat.

He stood with his hands in his jacket pockets and glared through his porthole at the horizon. Even the back of his neck looked mulish. The other three men exchanged glances.

"The chap's not aboard my ship," the Captain loudly announced without turning his head. "I know that as well as I know you *are*. I've been master under the Cape Company's charter for twenty years and I know as soon as I look at him whether a chap'll blow up for trouble at sea. I had a murderer shipped fireman aboard me, once. Soon as I clapped eyes on him I knew he was no good. Never failed yet. And I've been observing this lot. Observing them closely. There's not a murdering look on one of their faces, not a sign of it." He turned slowly and advanced upon Alleyn. His own face, lobster-red, wore an expression of childish complacency. "You're on a wild goose chase," he said blowing out gusts of whisky. Then with quite astonishing violence he drew his mottled hirsute fist from his pocket and crashed it down on his desk. "That sort of thing," said Captain Bannerman, "doesn't happen in *my ship* !"

"May I say just this ?" Alleyn ventured. "I wouldn't come to you with the suggestion unless I thought it most urgently necessary. You may, indeed, be perfectly right. Our man may not, after all, be aboard. But suppose, sir, that in the teeth of all you feel about it, he *is* in this ship." Alleyn pointed to the Captain's desk calendar. "Sunday the tenth of February," he said. "If he's here we've got four days before his supposed deadline. Shouldn't we take every possible step to prevent him going into action ? I know very well that what I've suggested sounds farfetched, cockeyed and altogether preposterous. It's a precautionary measure against a threat that may not exist. But isn't it better——" He looked at that unyielding front and very nearly threw up his hands. "—Isn't it better, in fact, to be sure than sorry?" said Alleyn in despair. Father Jourdain and Tim murmured agreement but the Captain shouted them down.

"Ah! So it is and it's a remark I often pass myself. But in this case it doesn't apply. What you've suggested is dead against my principles as Master and I won't have it. I don't believe it's necessary and I won't have it."

Father Jourdain said: "If I might just say one word——"

"You may spare yourself the trouble. I'm set."

Alleyn said: "Very good, sir, I hope you're right. Of course we'll respect your wishes."

"I won't have that lady put-about by any interference or—or criticism."

"I wasn't suggesting——"

"It'd look like criticism," the Captain mumbled cryptically and added: "A touch of high spirits never did anyone any harm."

This comment, from Alleyn's point-of-view, was such a masterpiece of meiosis that he could find no answer to it.

He said: "Thank you, sir," in what he hoped was the regulation manner and made for the door. The others followed him.

"Here!" Captain Bannerman ejaculated and they stopped. "Have a drink," said the Captain.

"Not for me at the moment, thank you very much," said Alleyn.

"Why not?"

"Oh, I generally hold off till the sun's over the yard-arm if that's the right way of putting it."

"You don't take overmuch then, I've noticed."

"Well," Alleyn said apologetically, "I'm by the way of being on duty."

"Ah! And nothing to show for it when it's all washed up. Not that I don't appreciate the general idea. You're

following orders I dare say, like all the rest of us, never mind
if it's a waste of time and the public's money."

" That's the general idea."

" Well—what about you two gentlemen ? "

" No, thank you, sir," said Tim.

" Nor I, thank you very much," said Father Jourdain.

" No offence, is there ? "

They hurriedly assured him there was none, waited for a
moment and then went to the door. The last glimpse they
had of the Captain was of a square, slightly wooden figure
making for the corner cupboard where he kept his liquor.

III

The rest of Sunday passed by quietly enough. It was
the hottest day the passengers had experienced and they
were all subdued. Mrs. Dillington-Blick wore white and so
did Aubyn Dale. They lay on their chaise-longues in the
veranda and smiled languidly at passers-by. Sometimes
they were observed to have their hands limply engaged,
occasionally Mrs. Dillington-Blick's rich laughter would
be heard.

Tim and Jemima spent most of the day in or near a canvas
bathing-pool that had been built on the after well-deck.
They were watched closely by the Cuddys who had set
themselves up in a place of vantage at the shady end of the
promenade deck, just under the veranda. Late in the afternoon Mr. Cuddy himself took to the water clad in a rather
grisly little pair of puce-coloured drawers. He developed a
vein of aquatic playfulness that soon drove Jemima out of the
pool and Tim into a state of extreme irritation.

Mr. Merryman sat in his usual place and devoted himself
to Neil Cream and, when that category of horrors had
reached its appointed end, to the revolting fate that met an
assortment of ladies who graced the pages of *The Thing He*

Loves. From time to time he commented unfavourably on the literary style of this work and also on the police methods it described. As Alleyn was the nearest target he found himself at the receiving end of these strictures. Inevitably, Mr. Merryman was moved to enlarge once again on the Flower Murders. Alleyn had the fun of hearing himself described as " some plodding Dogberry drest in a little brief authority. One, Alleyn," Mr. Merryman snorted, " whose photograph was reproduced in the evening news-sheets—a countenance of abysmal foolishness, I thought."

" Really ? "

" Oh, shocking, I assure you," said Mr. Merryman with immense relish. " I imagine, if the unknown criminal saw it, he must have been greatly consoled. I should have been, I promise you."

" Do you believe, then," Alleyn asked, " that there is after all an art ' to find the mind's construction in the face ' ? "

Mr. Merryman shot an almost approving glance at him : " Source ? " he demanded sharply, " and context ? "

" Macbeth, 1, 4. Duncan on Cawdor," Alleyn replied, himself feeling like Alice in Wonderland.

" Very well. You know your way about that essentially second-rate melodrama, I perceive. Yes," Mr. Merryman went on with pedagogic condescension, " unquestionably, there are certain facial evidences which serve as pointers to the informed observer. I will undertake for example to distinguish at first sight a bright boy among a multitude of dullards, and believe me," Mr. Merryman added dryly, " the opportunity does not often present itself."

Alleyn asked him if he would extend this theory to include a general classification. Did Mr. Merryman, for instance, consider that there was such a thing as a criminal type of face ? " I've read somewhere I fancy, that the police say there isn't," he ventured. Mr. Merryman rejoined tartly that for once the police had achieved a glimpse of the obvious. "If you ask me whether there are facial types indicative of brutality and low intelligence I must answer yes. But the sort of person we have been considering," he held up his book, " need not be exhibited in the countenance. The fact that he is possessed by his own particular devil is not written across his face that all who run may read."

"That's an expression that Father Jourdain used in the same context," Alleyn said. "He considers this man must be possessed of a devil."

"Indeed ? " Mr. Merryman remarked: "That is of course the accepted view of the Church. Does he postulate the cloven hoof and toasting-fork ? "

" I have no idea."

A shadow fell across the deck and there was Miss Abbott.

"I believe," she said, " in a personal Devil. Firmly."

She stood above them, her back to the setting-sun, her face dark and miserable. Alleyn began to get up from his deck-chair but she stopped him with a brusque movement of her hand. She jerked herself up on the hatch where she sat bolt upright, her large feet in tennis shoes dangling awkwardly.

"How else," she demanded, " can you explain the cruelties ? God permits the Devil to torment us for His own inscrutable purposes."

"Dear me ! " observed Mr. Merryman, quite mildly for him. "We find ourselves in a positive hive of orthodoxy, do we not ? "

"You're a churchman," Miss Abbott said, " aren't you ? You came to Mass. Why do you laugh at the Devil ? "

Mr. Merryman contemplated her over his spectacles and after a long pause said : "My dear Miss Abbott, if you can persuade me of his existence I assure you I shall not treat the Evil One as a laughing matter. Far from it."

" *I'm* no good," she said impatiently. "Talk to Father

Jourdain. He's full of knowledge and wisdom and will meet you on your own ground. I suppose you think it very uncouth of me to butt in and shove my faith down your throats but when——" she set her dark jaw and went on with a kind of obstinacy, " when I hear people laugh at the Devil it raises him in me. I *know* him."

The others found nothing to say to her. She passed her hand heavily across her eyes. " I'm sorry," she said. " I don't usually throw my weight about like this. It must be the heat."

Aubyn Dale came along the deck, spectacular in sharkskin shorts, crimson pullover and a pair of exotic espadrilles he had bought in Las Palmas. He wore enormous sun-glasses and his hair was handsomely ruffled.

" I'm going to have a dip," he said. " Just time before dinner and the water's absolutely superb. Madame won't hear of it, though. Any takers here ? "

Mr. Merryman merely stared at him. Alleyn said he'd think about it. Miss Abbott got down from the hatch and walked away. Dale looked after her and wagged his head. " Poor soul ! " he said. " I couldn't be sorrier for her. Honestly, life's hell for some women, isn't it ? "

He looked at the other two men. Mr. Merryman ostentatiously picked up his book and Alleyn made a non-committal noise. " I see a lot of that sort of thing," Dale went on, " in my fantastic job. The Lonely Legion, I call them. Only to myself, of course."

" Quite," Alleyn murmured.

" Well, let's face it. What the hell is there for them to do—looking like that ? Religion. Exploring Central Africa ? Or—ask yourself. *I* dunno," said Dale, whimsically philosophical. " One of those things."

He pulled out his pipe, shook his head over it, said " Ah, well ! " and meeting perhaps with less response than he had expected, walked off, trilling a stylish catch.

Mr. Merryman said something quite unprintable into his book and Alleyn went in search of Mrs. Dillington-Blick.

He found her, still reclining on the veranda and fanning herself : enormous but delectable. Alleyn caught himself wondering what Henry Moore would have made of her. She welcomed him with enthusiasm and a helpless flapping gesture to show how hot she was. But her white dress was uncreased. A lace handkerchief protruded crisply from her décolletage and her hair was perfectly in order.

" You look as cool as a cucumber," Alleyn said and sat down on Aubyn Dale's footrest. " What an enchanting dress."

She made comic eyes at him. " My dear ! " she said.

" But then all your clothes are enchanting. You dress quite beautifully, don't you ? "

" How sweet of you to think so," she cried, delightedly.

" Ah ! " Alleyn said, leaning towards her, " you don't know how big a compliment you're being paid. I'm extremely critical of women's clothes."

" *Are* you, indeed. And what do you like about mine, may I ask ? "

" I like them because they are clever enough to express the charm of their wearer," Alleyn said with a mental reservation to tell that one to Troy.

" Now, I do call that a *perfect* remark ! In future I shall dress 'specially for you. There now ! " promised Mrs. Dillington-Blick.

" Will you ? Then I must think about what I should like you to wear. To-night, for instance. Shall I choose that wonderful Spanish dress you bought in Las Palmas. May I ? "

There was quite a long pause during which she looked sideways at him. " I think perhaps that'd be a little too much, don't you ? " she said at last. " Sunday night, remember."

" Well then, to-morrow ? "

" Do you know," she said, " I've gone off that dress. You'll think me a frightful silly-billy but all the rather murky business with poor *sweet* Mr. McAngus's doll has sort of set me against it. Isn't it queer ? "

" *Oh !* Alleyn ejaculated with a great show of disappointment. " *What* a pity ! And what a waste ! "

" I know. All the same, that's how it is. I just *see* Esmeralda looking so like those murdered girls and all I want to do with my lovely, lovely dress is drop it overboard."

" You haven't done that ! "

Mrs. Dillington-Blick gave a little giggle. " No," she said. " I haven't done that."

" Or given it away ? "

" Jemima would swim in it and I can't quite see Miss Abbott or Mrs. Cuddy going all flamenco, can you ? "

Dale came by on his way to the bathing-pool now wearing Palm Beach trunks and looking like a piece of superb publicity for a luxury liner. " *You're* a couple of slackers," he said heartily and shinned nimbly down to the lower deck.

" I shall go and change," sighed Mrs. Dillington-Blick.

" But not into the Spanish dress ? "

" I'm afraid not. Sorry to disappoint you." She held out her luxurious little hands and Alleyn dutifully hauled her up. " It's too sad," he said, " to think we are never to see it."

" Oh, I shouldn't be absolutely sure of that," she said and giggled again. " I may change my mind and get inspired all over again."

" To dance by the light of the moon ? "

She stood quite still for a few seconds and then gave him her most ravishing smile. " You never know, do you ? " said Mrs. Dillington-Blick.

Alleyn watched her stroll along the deck and go through the doors into the lounge.

"—and I expect you will agree," he wrote to his wife that evening, " that in a subsidiary sort of way, this was a thoroughly disquieting bit of information."

IV

Steaming down the west coast of Africa, *Cape Farewell* ran into the sort of weather that is apt to sap the resources of people who are not accustomed to it. The air through which she moved was of the land : enervated and loaded with vague impurities. A thin greyness that resembled dust rather than cloud obscured the sun but scarcely modified its potency. Mr. Merryman got a " touch " of it and looked as if he was running a temperature but refused to do anything about it. Dysentery broke out among the crew and also afflicted Mr. Cuddy who endlessly consulted Tim and, with unattractive candour, anybody else who would listen to him.

Aubyn Dale drank a little more and began to look like it and so, to Alleyn's concern, did Captain Bannerman. The Captain was a heavy, steady drinker, who grew less and less tractable as his potations increased. He now resented any attempt Alleyn might make to discuss the case-in-hand and angrily reiterated his statement that there were no homicidal lunatics on board his ship. He became morose, unapproachable and entirely pig-headed.

Mr. McAngus on the other hand grew increasingly loquacious and continually lost himself in a maze of non sequiturs. " He suffers," Tim said, " from verbal dysentery."

" With Mr. McAngus," Alleyn remarked, " the condition appears to be endemic. We mustn't blame the tropics."

" They seem to have exacerbated it, however," observed

Father Jourdain wearily. " Did you know that he had a row with Merryman last night ? "

" What about ? " Alleyn asked.

" Those filthy medicated cigarettes he smokes. Merryman says the smell makes him feel sick."

" He's got something there," Tim said. " God knows what muck they're made of."

" They stink like a wet haystack."

" Ah, well," Alleyn said, " to our tasks, gentlemen. To our unwelcome tasks."

Since their failure with the Captain they had agreed among themselves upon a plan of campaign. As soon as night fell each of them was to " mark " one of the women passengers. Tim said flatly that he would take Jemima and that arrangement was generally allowed to be only fair. Father Jourdain said he thought perhaps Alleyn had better have Mrs. Dillington-Blick. " She alarms me," he remarked. " I have a feeling that she thinks I'm a wolf in priest's clothing. If I begin following her about after dark she will be sure of it."

Tim grinned at Alleyn : " She's got her eye on you. It'd be quite a thing if you cut the Telly King out."

" Don't confuse me," Alleyn said dryly, and turned to Father Jourdain. " You can handle the double, then," he said. " Mrs. Cuddy never leaves Cuddy for a second and——" He paused.

" And poor Katherine Abbott is not, you feel, in any great danger."

" What do you suppose is the matter with her ? " Alleyn asked and remembered what he had heard her saying as she left Father Jourdain on Saturday night. The priest's eyes were expressionless. " We are not really concerned," he said, " with Miss Abbott's unhappiness, I think."

" Oh," Alleyn said, " it's a sort of reflex action for me to wonder why people behave as they do. When we had the discussion about alibis, her distress over the Aubyn Dale programme of the night of February the fifteenth was illuminating, I thought."

" I thought it damn' puzzling," said Tim. " D'you know, I actually found myself wondering, I can't think why, if she was the victim and not the viewer that night."

" I think she was the viewer."

Father Jourdain looked sharply at Alleyn and then walked over to the porthole and stared out.

" As for the victim——" Alleyn went on, " the woman, do you remember, who told Dale she didn't like to announce her engagement because it would upset her great friend ?—" He broke off and Tim said : " You're not going to suggest that Miss Abbott was the great friend ? "

" At least it would explain her reactions to the programme."

After a short silence Tim said idly : " What does she do ? Has she a job, do you know ? "

Without turning his head Father Jourdain said : " She works for a firm of music publishers. She is quite an authority on early church music, particularly the Gregorian chants."

Tim said involuntarily : " I imagine, with that voice, she doesn't sing them herself."

" On the contrary," Alleyn rejoined, " she does. Very pleasantly. I heard her on the night we sailed from Las Palmas."

" She has a most unusual voice," Father Jourdain said. " If she were a man it would be a counter tenor. She represented her firm at a conference on Church music three weeks ago in Paris. I went over for it and saw her there. She was evidently a person of importance."

" Was she indeed ? " Alleyn murmured and then, briskly : " Well, as you say, we are not immediately concerned with Miss Abbott. The sun's going down. It's time we went on duty."

On the evenings of the eleventh and twelfth, according to plan, Alleyn devoted himself exclusively to Mrs. Dillington-Blick. This manœuvre brought about the evident chagrin of Aubyn Dale, the amusement of Tim, the surprise of Jemima and the greedy observance of Mrs. Cuddy. Mrs. Dillington-Blick was herself delighted. " My dear ! " she wrote to her friend, " I've nobbled the Gorgeous Brute ! My dear, too gratifying ! Nothing, to coin a phrase, *tangible*. As yet ! But *marked* attention ! And with the tropical moon being what it is I feel something *rather* nice may eventuate ? In the meantime I promise you, I've only to wander off after dinner to my so suitable little veranda and he's after me in a flash. A.D., my dear, rapidly becoming peagreen, which is always so gratifying. Aren't I hopeless but what fun ! ! ! "

On the night of the thirteenth, when they were all having coffee, Aubyn Dale suddenly decided to give a supper-party in his private sitting-room. It was equipped with a radiogram on which he proposed to play some of his own records.

" Everybody invited," he said largely, waving his brandy glass. " I won't take no for an answer," and indeed it would have been difficult under the circumstances for anybody to attempt to refuse, though Mr. Merryman and Tim looked as if they would have liked to do so.

The " suite " turned out to be quite a grand affair. There were a great many signed photographs of Aubyn Dale's poppet and of several celebrities and one of Aubyn Dale himself, bowing before the grandest celebrity of all. There was a pigskin writing-case and a pigskin record-carrier. There were actually some monogrammed Turkish cigarettes, a present, Dale explained with boyish ruefulness, from a potentate who was one of his most ardent fans. And almost at once there was a great deal to drink. Mr.

McAngus was given a trick glass that poured his drink over his chin and was not quite as amused as the Captain, the Cuddys and Mrs. Dillington-Blick though he took it quite quietly. Aubyn Dale apologised with the air of a chidden child and did several very accurate imitations of his fellow celebrities in television. Then they listened to four records including one of Dale himself doing an Empire Day talk on how to be Broadminded though British in which he laid a good deal of stress on the National Trait of being able to laugh at ourselves.

" *How* proud we are of it, too," Tim muttered crossly to Jemima.

After the fourth record most of the guests began to be overtaken by the drowsiness of the tropics. Miss Abbott was the first to excuse herself and everybody else except Mrs. Dillington-Blick and the Captain followed her lead. Jemima had developed a headache in the overcrowded room and was glad to get out into the fresh air. She and Tim sat on the starboard side under Mr. McAngus's porthole. There was a small ship's lamp in the deckhead above them.

" Only five minutes," Jemima said. " I'm for bed after that. My head's behaving like a piano accordion."

" Have you got any aspirins ? "

" I can't be bothered hunting them out."

" I'll get you something. Don't move, will you ? " Tim said, noting that the light from Mr. McAngus's porthole and from the ship's lamp fell across her chair. He could hear Mr. McAngus humming to himself in a reedy falsetto as he prepared for bed. " You will stay put," Tim said, " won't you ? "

" Why shouldn't I ? I don't feel at all like shinning up the rigging or going for a strapping walk. Couldn't we have that overhead light off ? Not," Jemima said hurriedly, " in order to create a romantic gloom, I assure you, Tim. It shines in one's eyes, rather ; that's all."

" The switch is down at the other end. I'll turn it off when I come back," he said. " I shan't be half a tick, Jem."

When he had gone, Jemima lay back and shut her eyes. She listened to the ship's engines and to the sound of the sea and to Mr. McAngus's droning. This stopped after a moment and through her closed lids she was aware of a lessening of light. " He's turned his lamp off," she thought gratefully, " and has tucked his poor dithering old self up in his virtuous couch." She opened her eyes and saw the dim light in the deckhead above her.

The next moment it, too, went out.

" That's Tim coming back," she thought. " He *has* been quick."

She was now in almost complete darkness. A faint breeze lifted her hair. She heard no footfall but she was conscious that someone had approached from behind her.

" Tim ? " she said.

Hands came down on her shoulders. She gave a little cry : " Oh, *don't* ! You made me jump."

The hands shifted towards her neck and she felt her chain of pearls move and twist and break. She snatched at the hands and they were not Tim's.

" *No !* " she cried out. " *No ! Tim !* "

There was a rapid thud of retreating feet. Jemima struggled out of her chair and ran down the dark tunnel of the covered deck into someone's arms.

" It's all right," Alleyn said. " You're all right. It's me."

V

A few seconds later, Tim Makepiece came back.

Alleyn still held Jemima in his arms. She quivered and stammered and clutched at him like a frightened child.

" What the hell——" Tim began but Alleyn stopped him.

" Did you turn out the deckhead lights ? "

" No. Jem, darling——"

" Did you meet anyone ? "

" No. Jem——! "

" All right. Take over, will you ? She'll tell you when she's got her second wind."

He disengaged her arms. " You're in clover," he said. " Here's your medical adviser."

She bolted into Tim's arms and Alleyn ran down the deck.

He switched on the overhead lights and followed round the centrecastle. He looked up and down companionways, along hatch combings, behind piles of folded chairs and into recesses. He knew, as he hunted, he was too late. He found nothing but the odd blankness of a ship's decks at night. On the excuse that he had lost his pocket-book with his passport and letters of credit, he knocked up all the men, including Mr. Cuddy. Dale was still dressed and in his sitting-room. The others were in pyjamas and varying degrees of ill-temper. He told Father Jourdain, briefly, what had happened and arranged that they would go, with Tim, to the Captain.

Then he returned to Jemima's chair. Her pearls were scattered on the deck and in the loose seat. He collected them and thought at first that otherwise, he had drawn a blank. But at the last, clinging to the back of the chair, discoloured and crushed, he found a scrap of something which, when he took it to the light, declared itself plainly enough. It was a tiny fragment of a flower petal.

It still retained, very faintly, the scent of hyacinth.

CHAPTER NINE

Thursday the Fourteenth

I

" Now," Alleyn demanded, standing over Captain Bannerman. " *Now*, do you believe this murderer's on board ?
Do you ? "

But as he said it he knew he was up against the unassailable
opponent : the elderly man who has made up his mind
and is temperamentally incapable of admitting he has
made it up the wrong way.

" I'll be damned if I do," said Captain Bannerman.

" I am appalled to hear you say so."

The Captain swallowed the end of his drink and clapped
the glass down on the table. He looked from Alleyn to
Father Jourdain, wiped his mouth with the back of his hand
and said : " You've got this blasted notion into your heads
and every footling little thing that takes place, you make
out is something to do with it. *What* takes place ? Little
Miss Jemima is sitting all alone in her deck-chair. Some
chap comes up and puts his hands on her shoulders. Playful,
like. And what's unnatural in that ? By gum, I wouldn't
blame——" He pulled himself up, turned a darker shade of
brick red and continued : " On your own statement, she's
got ideas into her head about these murders. Natural enough,
I dare say, seeing how the lot of you can't let the matter
alone but never stop talking about it. She's startled-like,
and jumps up and runs away. Again—natural enough.

But you come blustering up here and try to tell me she was nigh-on murdered. You won't get anywhere with me, that road. Someone's got to hang on to his common sense in this ship and, by gum, that's going to be the Master."

Father Jourdain said : " But it's not the one incident, it's the whole sequence, as Alleyn has shown us only too clearly. An embarkation paper in the hand of the girl on the wharf. The incident of the doll. The fact that singing was heard. The peeping Tom at Miss Carmichael's porthole. Now this. What man among us, knowing these crimes are in all our minds, would play such a trick on her ? "

" And what man among you would murder her—tell me that ! "

Tim had been sitting with his head between his hands. He now looked up and said : " Sir, even if you do think there's nothing in it, surely there can be no harm in taking every possible precaution——? "

" What the hell have you all been doing if you haven't been taking precautions ? Haven't I said just that, all along ? Didn't I—" he pointed his stubby finger at Alleyn, —"get them all jabbering about alibis because you asked me to ? Haven't I found out for you that the whole boiling went ashore the night we sailed, never mind if my own deckhand thought I was balmy ? Haven't I given out there's an undesirable character in my ship's company, which there isn't, and ordered the ladies to lock their doors ? What the suffering cats more could I have done ? Tell me that ! "

Alleyn said instantly : " You could, you know, do something to ensure that there's no more wandering about deserted decks at night in Spanish dresses."

" I've told you. I won't have any interference with the rights of the individual in my ship."

" Will you let me say something unofficially about it ? "

" No."

" Will you consider a complete showdown ? Will you tell the passengers who I am and why I'm here ? It'll mean no arrest, of course," Alleyn said, " but with the kind of threat that I believe hangs over this ship I'm prepared to admit defeat. Will you do this ? "

" No."

" You realise that to-morrow is the night when, according to the considered opinion of experts, this man may be expected to go into action again ? "

" He's not aboard my ship."

"—and that Miss Carmichael," Father Jourdain intervened, " naturally will speak of her fears to the other ladies."

Tim said : " No."

" No ? "

" No," Alleyn said. " She's not going to talk about it. She agrees that it might lead to a panic. She's a courageous child."

" She's been given a shock," Tim said angrily to the Captain, " that may very easily have extremely serious results. I can't allow——"

" Doctor Makepiece, you'll be good enough to recollect you have signed on as a member of my ship's company."

" Certainly, sir."

The Captain stared resentfully about him, made a petulant ejaculation and roared out : " Damn it, you can tell her to stay in bed all day to-morrow and the next day too, can't you ? Suffering from shock ? All right. That gets *her* out of the way, doesn't it ? Where is she now ? "

" I've given her a nembutal. She's asleep in bed. The door's locked and I've got the key."

" Well, keep it and let her stay there. The steward can take her meals. Unless you think *he's* the sex monster," said the Captain with an angry laugh.

" Not in the sense you mean," Alleyn said.

" That's enough of that ! " the Captain shouted.

" Where," Father Jourdain asked wearily, " is Mrs. Dillington-Blick ? "

" In bed," the Captain said at once, and added in a hurry : " She left Dale's suite when I did. I saw her to her cabin."

" They do lock their doors, don't they ? "

" She did," said the Captain morosely.

Father Jourdain got up. " If I may be excused," he said. " It's very late. Past midnight."

" Yes," Alleyn said and he also rose. " It's February the fourteenth. Good night, Captain Bannerman."

He had a brief session with Father Jourdain and Tim. The latter was in a rage. " That *bloody* Old Man," he kept saying. " Did you ever know such a *bloody* Old Man ! "

" All right, all right," Alleyn said. " We'll just have to go on under our own steam. The suggestion, by the way, to keep Miss Carmichael in bed for twenty-four hours has its points."

Tim said grandly that he'd consider it. Father Jourdain asked if they were to do anything about the other women. Could they not emphasise that as Jemima had had an unpleasant experience it might be as well if the ladies were particularly careful not to wander about the deck at night without an escort.

Alleyn said : " We've done that already. But think a minute. Suppose one of them chose the wrong escort."

" You know, it's an extraordinary thing," Father Jourdain said after a moment, " but I keep forgetting it's one of us. I almost believe in the legend of the unsavoury deck-hand."

" I think it might be a good idea if you suggest a four of bridge or canasta. Mrs. Dillington-Blick plays both, doesn't she ? Get Mrs. Cuddy and Miss Abbott to come in. Or if Dale and the other men will play you might get two fours going. Makepiece will look after Miss Carmichael."

" What'll you do ? " Tim asked.

" I ? " Alleyn asked. " Look on. Look round. Just look. Of course they may refuse to play. In which case we'll have to use our wits, Heaven help us, and improvise. In the meantime, you probably both want to go to bed."

" And you, no doubt," said Father Jourdain.

" Oh," Alleyn said, " I'm an owl by habit. See you in the morning. Good night."

He was indeed trained to put up with long stretches of sleeplessness and faced the rest of the short night with equanimity. He changed into slacks, a dark shirt and rope-soled shoes and then began a systematic beat. Into the deserted lounge. Out on to the well-deck, past the little veranda where the two chaise-longues stood deserted. Round the hatch, and then to the cabin quarters and their two covered decks.

The portholes were all open. He listened outside each of them. The first, facing aft and to the starboard side, was Mr. Merryman's. It appeared to be in darkness but after a moment he saw that a blue point glowed somewhere inside. It was the little nightlight above the bed. Alleyn stood near the porthole and was just able to make out Mr. Merryman's tousled head on the pillow. Next came the doorway into the passage bisecting the cabin-quarters and then further along on the starboard side was Mr. McAngus who could be heard whistling in his sleep. The Cuddys, in the adjoining, the last on the starboard side, snored anti-phonally. He turned left and moved along the forward face of the block, past Miss Abbott's dark and silent cabin and then on to Father Jourdain's. His light still shone and as the porthole was uncovered Alleyn thought he would have a word with him.

He looked in. Father Jourdain was on his knees before a crucifix, his joined hands pressed edgeways to his lips. Alleyn turned away and walked on to the " suite." Dale's light was still up in his sitting-room. Alleyn stood a little to

one side of the forward porthole. The curtain across it
fluttered and blew out. He caught a brief glimpse of Dale
in brilliant pyjamas with a glass in his hand. He turned
left past Jemima's porthole with its carefully-drawn curtain
and then moved aft to Mrs. Dillington-Blick's cabin. Her
light too was still on. He paused with his back to the bulkhead and close to her porthole and became aware of a
rhythmic slapping noise and a faint whiff of some aromatic
scent. " She's coping with her neckline," he thought.

He moved on past the darkened lounge. He had completed his round and was back at Mr. Merryman's cabin.

He approached the iron ladder leading to the forward
well-deck and climbed down it. When he had reached the
bottom he waited for a moment in the shadow of the centrecastle. On his left was the door through which the figure
in the Spanish dress had come on Friday night. It led into a
narrow passage by the chief steward's quarters. Above him
towered the centrecastle. He knew if he walked out into the
moonlight, the second officer, keeping his watch far above
on the bridge, would see him. He did walk out. His
shadow, black as ink, splayed across the deck and up the
hatch combing.

On the fo'c'sle two bells sounded. Alleyn watched the
seaman who had rung them come down and cross the deck
towards him.

" Good night," he said.

" Good night, sir," the man replied and sounded surprised.

Alleyn said : " I thought I'd go up into the bows and see
if I could find a cap-full of cool air."

" That's right, sir. A bit fresher up there."

The man passed him and disappeared into shadow.
Alleyn climbed up to the fo'c'sle and stood in the bows.
For a moment or two he faced the emptiness of the night.
Beneath him, in a pother of phosphorescence, the waters

were divided. "There is nothing more lonely in the world," he thought, "than a ship at sea."

He turned and looked at the ship, purposeful and throbbing with her own life. Up on the bridge he could see the second officer. He waved with a broad gesture of his arm and after a moment the second officer replied slightly, perhaps ironically.

Alleyn returned to the lower deck. As he climbed down the ladder, a door beneath him, leading into the seamen's quarters in the fo'c'sle, opened and somebody came out. Alleyn looked down over his shoulder. The newcomer, barefooted and clad only in pyjama trousers, moved out, seemed to sense that he was observed and stopped short.

It was Dennis. When he saw Alleyn he made as if to return.

Alleyn said : "You keep late hours, steward."

"Oh, it's *you*, Mr. Broderick. You quite startled me. Yes, *don't* I ? I've been playing poker with the boys," Dennis explained. "Fancy you being up there, sir, at this time of night."

Alleyn completed his descent. "I couldn't sleep," he said. "It's the heat, I suppose."

Dennis giggled. "I *know*. Isn't it terrific ! "

He edged away slightly.

"What's it like in your part of the world ? " Alleyn asked. "Where are your quarters ? "

"I'm in the glory-hole, sir. Down below. It's *frightful*."

"All the same, I fancy it's healthier indoors."

Dennis said nothing.

"You want to be careful what you wear in the tropics. Particularly at night."

Dennis looked at his plump torso and smirked.

Alleyn waited for a moment and then said : "Well, I shall take my own advice and go back to bed. Good night to you."

"Good *morning*, sir," said Dennis pertly.

Alleyn climbed up to the bridge deck. When he got there he looked back. Dennis still stood where he had left him but after a moment turned away and went back into the fo'c'sle.

At intervals, through the rest of the night, Alleyn walked round his beat but he met nobody. When the dawn came up he went to bed and slept until Dennis, pallid, glistening and silent, brought in his morning tea.

II

That day was the hottest the passengers had experienced. For Alleyn it began with a radioed report in code from Inspector Fox who was still sweating away with his checks on alibis. Apart from routine confirmations of Mr. McAngus's appendicular adventure and Aubyn Dale's departure for America, nothing new had come to hand. The Yard, Fox intimated, would await instructions which meant, Alleyn sourly and unfairly reflected, that if he made an arrest before Cape Town, somebody would be flown over with a spare pair of handcuffs or something. He made his way, disgruntled, to continue observation on the passengers.

They were all on the lower deck. Jemima, who was still rather white, had flatly refused to stay in bed and spent most of the day in or near the bathing-pool where an awning had been erected and deck-chairs set out. Here she was joined by Tim and at intervals by one or two of the others. Only Miss Abbott, Mr. McAngus and Mrs. Cuddy refrained from bathing, but they too sat under the awning and looked on.

At noon Mrs. Dillington-Blick took to the water and the appearance was in the nature of a star turn. She wore a sort of bathing-negligee which Aubyn Dale, who escorted her, called a " bewilderment of nonsense." It was all compact of

crisp cotton frills and black ribbons and under it Mrs.
Dillington-Blick was encased in her Jolyon Swimsuit
which belonged to a group advertised as being " for the
Queenly Woman." She had high-heeled thonged sandals
on her feet and had to be supported down the companion-
ladder by Aubyn Dale who carried her towel and sun-
shade. At this juncture only Jemima, Tim, Alleyn and Mr.
Cuddy were bathing. The others were assembled under
the awning and provided an audience for Mrs. Dillington-
Blick. She laughed a great deal and made deprecatory
moues. " My dears ! " she said. " *Look* at me ! "

" You know," Jemima said to Tim, "I really *do* admire her.
She actually cashes in on her size. I call that brilliant."

" It's fascinating," Tim agreed. " Do look ! She's
standing there like a piece of baroque, waiting to be unveiled."

Dale performed this ceremony. Alleyn, who was perched
on the edge of the pool near the steps that led down into it,
watched the reaction. It would have been untrue to say that
anybody gasped when Mrs. Dillington-Blick relinquished
her bathing-robe. Rather, a kind of trance overtook her
fellow-passengers. Mr. Cuddy, who had been frisking in the
waters, grasped the rim of the pool and grinned horridly
through his wet fringe. Mr. Merryman, who wore an old-
fashioned gown and an equally old-fashioned bathing-dress
and whose hair had gone into a damp fuzz like a baby's,
stared over his spectacles, as startled as Mr. Pickwick in the
Maiden Lady's fourposter. Mr. McAngus, who had been
dozing, opened his eyes and his mouth at the same time
and turned dark red in the face. On the bridge, Captain
Bannerman was transfixed. Two deckhands stood idle for
several seconds round a can of red lead and then self-
consciously fell to work with their heads together.

Mrs. Cuddy tried to catch somebody's eye but, failing to
do so, stared in amazement at her infatuated husband.

Miss Abbott looked up from the letter she was writing, blinked twice and looked down again.

Father Jourdain, who had been reading, made a slight movement with his right hand. Alleyn told himself it was absurd to suppose that Father Jourdain had been visited by an impulse to cross himself.

Jemima broke the silence. She called out : " Jolly good ! Come in : it's Heaven."

Mrs. Dillington-Blick put on a bathing cap, removed her sandals, precariously climbed the ladder up to the rim of the pool, avoided looking at Mr. Cuddy and held out her hands to Alleyn.

" Launch me," she invited winningly and at the same moment lost her balance and fell like an avalanche into the brimming pool. The water she displaced surged over the edges. Alleyn, Mr. Cuddy, Jemima and Tim bobbed about like flotsam and jetsam. Aubyn Dale was drenched. Mrs. Dillington-Blick surfaced, gasping and astounded, and struck out for the nearest handhold.

" Ruby ! " Aubyn Dale cried anxiously, as he dashed the sea-water from his face, " what have you done ? "

For the first time in the voyage Mr. Merryman burst into peals of ungovernable laughter.

This incident had a serio-comic sequel. While Mrs. Dillington-Blick floated in a corner of the pool, clinging to the edges, Mr. Cuddy swam slyly alongside and with a quick grab pulled her under. There was a struggle from which she emerged furious and half-suffocated. Her face was streaked with mascara, her nose was running and her bathing cap was askew. She was a terrible sight. Alleyn helped her up the submerged steps. Dale received her on the far side and got her down to deck level.

" That horrible man ! " she choked out. " That horrible man ! "

Mr. McAngus also hurried to her side while Mr. Cuddy leered over the rim of the pool.

A ridiculous and rather alarming scene ensued. Mr. McAngus, in an unrecognisably shrill voice, apostrophised Mr. Cuddy: "You're an unmitigated bounder, sir," he screamed and actually shook his fist in Mr. Cuddy's wet face.

"I must say, Cuddy!" Dale said, all restraint and seemly indignation, "you've got an extraordinary idea of humour."

Mr. Cuddy still leered and blinked. Mrs. Cuddy from her deck-chair, cried anxiously: "Dear! You're forgetting yourself."

"You're an ape, sir!" Mr. McAngus added and he and Dale simultaneously placed an arm round Mrs. Dillington-Blick.

"I'll look after her," said Dale coldly.

"Let me help you," said Mr. McAngus. "Come and sit down."

"Leave her alone. Ruby, darling——"

"Oh, shut up, both of you!" said Mrs. Dillington-Blick. She snatched up her robe and made off: a mountain of defaced femininity.

Mr. Merryman continued to laugh, the other gentlemen separated and Mr. Cuddy swam quietly about the pool by himself.

It was the only incident of note in an otherwise torpid day. After luncheon all the passengers went to their respective cabins and Alleyn allowed himself a couple of hours' sleep. He woke, as he had arranged with himself to wake, at four o'clock and went down to tea. Everybody was limp and disinclined to talk. Dale, Mr. McAngus and Mr. Cuddy had evidently decided to calm down. Mr. Merryman's venture into the pool had brought on his "touch of the sun" again. He looked feverish and anxious and actually didn't seem to have the energy to argue with anyone. Jemima came over to him. She very prettily knelt by his chair, and begged him to let her find Tim and ask him to prescribe. " Or at least take some aspirin," she said. " I'll get some for you. Will you ? " She put her hand on his but he drew it away quickly.

" I think I may have a slight infection," he said in explanation and positively added : " But thank you, my dear."

" You're terribly hot." She went away and returned with the aspirin and water. He consented to take three tablets and said he would lie down for a little while. When he went out they all noticed that he was quite shaky.

" Well," Mr. Cuddy said, " I'm sure I hope it's nothing catching."

" It's not very considerate," Mrs. Cuddy said, " to sit round with everybody if it is. How are you feeling, dear ? "

" Good, thanks, dear. My little trouble," Mr. Cuddy said to everybody, " has cleared up nicely. I'm a box of birds. I really quite enjoy the heat : something a bit intoxicating about the tropics, to my way of thinking."

He himself was not urgently intoxicating. His shirt had unlovely dark areas about it, the insides of his knees were raddled with prickly heat and his enormous hands left wet patches on everything they touched. " I'm a very free perspirer," he said proudly, " and that's a healthy sign, I'm told."

This observation met with a kind of awed silence broken by Mr. McAngus.

" Has everybody seen ? " he asked, turning his back on Mr. Cuddy. " There's going to be a film to-night. They've just put up a notice. On the boat deck, it's going to be."

There was a stir of languid interest. Father Jourdain muttered to Alleyn : " That disposes of our canasta party."

" How lovely ! " Mrs. Dillington-Blick said. " Where do we sit ? "

" I *think*," Mr. McAngus fluted, at once tripping up to her, that we all sit on deck-chairs on the top of the hatch. Such a good idea ! You must lie on your chaise-longue, you know. You'll look quite wonderful," he added with his timid little laugh. " Like Cleopatra in her barge with all her slaves round her. Pagan, almost."

" My dear ! "

" What's the film ? " Dale asked.

" *Othello*. With that large American actor."

" Oh, God ! "

" Mr. Merryman *will* be pleased," said Jemima. " It's his favourite. If he approves, of course."

" Well, *I* don't think he ought to come," Mrs. Cuddy at once objected. " He should consider other people."

" It'll be in the open air," Miss Abbott countered, " and there's no need, I imagine, for you to sit next to Mr. Merryman."

Mrs. Cuddy smiled meaningly at her husband.

Jemima said: " But how exciting ! Orson Welles and everything ! I couldn't be better pleased."

" We'd rather have a nice musical," said Mrs. Cuddy. " But then we're not arty, are we, dear ? "

Mr. Cuddy said nothing. He was looking at Mrs. Dillington-Blick.

III

The film version of *Othello* began to wind up its remarkable course. Mr. Merryman could be heard softly invoking the retribution of the gods upon the head of Mr. Orson Welles.

In the front row Captain Bannerman sighed windily, Mrs. Dillington-Blick's jaw quivered and Dale periodically muttered : " Oh, *no* ! " Alleyn, who was flabbergasted by the film, was able to give it only a fraction of his attention.

Behind the Captain's party sat the rest of the passengers,

while a number of ship's officers were grouped together at one side. Dennis and his fellow-stewards watched from the back.

The sea was perfectly calm, stars glittered with explosive brilliance. The cinema screen, an incongruous accident, with a sterile life of its own, glowed and gestured in the surrounding darkness.

> *Put out the light, and then put out the light.*
> *If I quench thee, thou flaming minister,*
> *I can again thy former light restore,*
> *Should I repent me——*

Jemima caught her breath and Tim reached for her hand. They were moved by a single impulse and by one thought : that it was superbly right for them to listen together to this music.

> *——I know not where is that Promethean heat*
> *That can thy light relume.*

" *Promethean heat*," Father Jourdain murmured appreciatively.

The final movement emerged not entirely obscured by the treatment that had been accorded it. A huge face loomed out of the screen.

> *Kill me to-morrow ; let me live to-night——*
> *——But half an hour !*
> *Being done, there is no pause.*
> *But while I say one prayer !*
> *It is too late.*

A white cloth closed like a shroud about Desdemona's face and tightened horridly.

The screen was no longer there. At their moment of climax Othello and Desdemona were gone and their audience was in darkness. The pulse of the ship's engines emerged and the chief engineer's voice saying that a fuse had blown somewhere. Matches were struck. There was a group of men round the projector. Alleyn produced his torch, slipped out of his seat which was at the end of the row, and walked slowly along the hatch. None of the passengers had stirred but there was a certain amount of movement among the stewards, some of whom, including Dennis, had already left.

"The circuit's gone," a voice near the projector said and another added: "That's the story. Hold everything." One of the figures disentangled itself and hurried away.

"'Put out the light '," a junior officer quoted derisively, "'and then put out the light '." There was a little gust of laughter. Mrs. Cuddy in the middle of the third row, tittered: "He stifles her, doesn't he, dear? Same thing again! We don't seem to be able to get away from it, do we?"

Miss Abbott said furiously: "Oh, for pity's *sake* !"

Alleyn had reached the edge of the hatch. He stood there, watching the backs of the passengers' chairs, now clearly discernible. Immediately in front of him were Tim and Jemima, their hands enlaced, leaning a little towards each other. Jemima was saying: "I don't want to pull it to pieces yet. After all there *are* the words."

A figure rose up from the chair in the middle of the row. It was Mr. Merryman.

"I'm off," he announced.

"Are you all right, Mr. Merryman?" Jemima asked.

"I am nauseated," Mr. Merryman rejoined, "but not for the reason you suppose. I can stomach no more of this. Pray excuse me."

He edged past them and past Father Jourdain, moved round the end of the row and thus approached Alleyn.

"Had enough?" Alleyn asked.

"A bellyful, thank you."

He sat on the edge of the hatch, his back ostentatiously presented to the invisible screen. He was breathing hard. His hand which had brushed against Alleyn's was hot and dry.

" I'm afraid you've still got a touch of your bug, whatever it is," Alleyn said. " Why don't you turn in ? "

But Mr. Merryman was implacable. " I do not believe," he said, " in subjecting myself to the tyranny of indisposition. I do not, like our Scottish acquaintance, surrender to hypochondriacal speculations. On the contrary, I fight back. Besides," he added, " in this Stygian gloom, where is the escape ? There is none. *J'y suis, et j'y reste.*"

And so in fact he remained. The fuse was repaired, the film drew to its close. An anonymous choir roared its anguish and, without benefit of authorship, ended the play. The lights went up and the passengers moved to the lounge for supper. Mr. Merryman alone remained outside, seated in a deck-chair by the open doors and refusing sustenance.

Alleyn, and indeed all of them, were to remember that little gathering very vividly ; Mrs. Dillington-Blick had recovered her usual form and was brilliant. Dressed in black lace, though not that of her Spanish dress, and wreathed in the effulgence of an expensive scent that had by now acquired the authority of a signature tune, she held her customary court. She discussed the film : it had, she said, *really* upset her. " My dear ! That ominous man ! Terrifying ! But all the same—there's *something*. One could quite see why she married him."

" I thought it disgusting," Mrs. Cuddy said. " A black man. She deserved all she got."

Mrs. Dillington-Blick laughed. She and Aubyn Dale, Alleyn noticed, kept catching each other's eye and quickly looking away again. Neither Mr. Cuddy nor Mr. McAngus could remove their gaze from her. The Captain hung over her : even Miss Abbott watched her with a kind of brooding appreciation while Mrs. Cuddy resentfully stared and stared. Only Jemima and Tim, bent on their common voyage of discovery, were unmindful of Mrs. Dillington-Blick.

Presently she yawned, and she even managed to yawn quite fetchingly.

" I'm for my little bed," she announced.

" Not even a stroll round the deck ? " asked the Captain.

" I *don't* think so, really."

" Or a cigarette on the veranda ? " Dale suggested loudly.

" I might."

She laughed and walked over to the open doors. Mr. Merryman struggled up from his deck-chair. She wished him good night, looked back into the lounge and smiled intimately and brilliantly at Mr. McAngus. " Good night," she repeated softly and went out on the deserted deck.

Father Jourdain caught his breath. " All right," Alleyn muttered. " You carry on, here."

Tim glanced at Alleyn and nodded. The Captain had been buttonholed by Mr. McAngus and looked restive. Jemima was talking to Mr. Merryman who half-rose, bestowed on her an old-fashioned bow and sank groggily back into his chair. Aubyn Dale was drinking and Mr. Cuddy was in the grasp of his wife who now removed him.

Alleyn said : " Good night, everybody." He followed the Cuddys into the passageway, turned left and went out to the deck by the portside door. He was just in time to see Mrs. Dillington-Blick disappear round the veranda corner of the engine house. Before he could reach it she returned, paused for a second when she saw him, and then swam gaily towards him.

" Just one gulp of fresh air," she said rather breathlessly. She slipped her arm through his and quite deliberately leant against him.

" Help me negotiate that frightful ladder, will you ? I want to go down to the lower deck."

He glanced back at the lounge. There they all were, lit up like a distant peep show.

" Why the lower deck ? "

" I don't know. A whim." She giggled. " Nobody will find me for one thing."

The companion ladder was close to where they stood. She led him towards it, turned and gave him her hands.

" I'll go backwards. You follow."

He was obliged to do so. When they reached the promenade deck she took his arm again.

" Let's see if there are ghost fires to-night."

She looked over the side still holding him.

Alleyn said : " You're much too dangerous a person for me, you know."

" Do you really think so ? "

" I do indeed. Right out of my class. I'm a dull dog."

" I don't find you so."

" How enchanting of you," Alleyn said. " I must tell my ife. That'll larn her."

" Is she very attractive ? "

Suddenly, in place of the plushy, the abundant, the superbly tended charms now set before him, Alleyn saw his wife's head with its clearly defined planes, its delicate bone and short not very tidy hair.

He said : " I must leave you, I'm afraid. I've got work to do."

" Work ? What sort of work, for heaven's sake ? "

" Business letters. Reports."

" I don't believe you. In mid-ocean ! "

" It's true."

" Look ! There *are* ghost fires."

" And I don't think you'd better stay down here by yourself. Come along. I'll see you to your cabin."

He put his hand over hers. " Come along," he repeated. She stared at him, her lips parted.

" All right ! " she agreed suddenly. " Let's."

They returned by the inside stairway and he took her to her door.

" You're *rather* nice," she whispered.

" Lock your door, won't you ? "

" Oh, good *heavens* ! " said Mrs. Dillington-Blick and bounced into her cabin. He heard her shoot her bolt and he returned quickly to the lounge.

Only Father Jourdain, Tim and Captain Bannerman were there. Miss Abbott came in by the double-doors as Alleyn arrived. Tim furtively signalled " thumbs up," and Father Jourdain said : " Everybody seems to be going to bed early to-night."

" It's not all that early," Captain Bannerman rejoined, staring resentfully at Miss Abbott.

She stopped dead in the middle of the room and with her eyes downcast seemed to take in the measure of her own unwantedness.

" Good night," she said grudgingly and went out.

Father Jourdain followed her to the landing. " By the way," Alleyn heard him say, " I got that word in the Ximenes. It's ' holocaust '."

" How brilliant ! " she said. " That should be a great help."

" I think so. Good night."

" Good night."

Father Jourdain came back : " ' Safely stowed,' " he quoted and smiled at Alleyn.

Alleyn asked sharply, " Where's everybody else ? "

" It's O.K.," Tim rejoined. " The women are all in their cabins : at least I suppose you've accounted for the D-B, haven't you ? "

" And the men ? "

" Does it matter ? Cuddy went off with his wife and

McAngus, very properly, by himself. Merryman toddled off some time after that."

" And Dale ? "

" He left after the Cuddys," Tim said.

" I think," Father Jourdain observed, " that someone must have gone out on deck ? "

" Why ? "

" Only because I thought I heard someone singing." His voice faded and his face blanched. " But there's nothing in that ! " Father Jourdain ejaculated. " We can't panic every time somebody sings."

" I can ! " Alleyn said grimly.

" With the women all in their cabins ? Why ? "

Captain Bannerman interjected, loudly scoffing : " You may well ask why ! Because Mr. Ah-leen's got a bee in his bonnet. That's why ! "

" What had McAngus got to say to you ? " Alleyn asked him.

The Captain glowered at him. " He reckons someone's been interfering with his hyacinths."

" Interfering ? "

" Pinching them."

" Damnation ! " Alleyn said and turned to go out.

Before he could do so, however, he was arrested by the sound of thudding feet.

It came from the deck outside and was accompanied by tortuous breathing. For a moment the brilliant square cast by the light in the lounge was empty. Then into it ran an outlandish figure half-naked, wet, ugly, gasping.

It was Cuddy. When he saw Alleyn he fetched up short, grinning abominably. Water ran from his hair into his open mouth.

" Well ? " Alleyn demanded. " What is it ? "

Cuddy gestured meaninglessly. His arm quivered like a branch.

" What is it ? Speak up ! Quickly."

Cuddy lunged forward. His wet hands closed like clamps on Alleyn's arms.

" Mrs. Dillington-Blick," he stuttered and the syllables dribbled out with the water from his mouth. He nodded two or three times, came close to Alleyn and then threw back his head and broke into sobbing laughter.

" The veranda ? "

" What the bloody hell are you talking about ? " the Captain shouted.

Cuddy nodded and nodded.

Alleyn said : " Captain Bannerman, will you come with me, if you please ? And Dr. Makepiece." He struck up Cuddy's wet arms and thrust him aside. He started off down the deck with them both at his heels.

They had gone only a few paces when a fresh rumpus broke out behind them. Cuddy's hysterical laughter had mounted to a scream.

Father Jourdain shouted : " Doctor Makepiece ! Come back ! "

There was a soft thud and silence.

Captain Bannerman said : " Wait a bit. He's fainted."

" Let him faint."

" But——"

" All right. *All right*."

He strode on down the deck. There was a light in the deckhead over the veranda. Alleyn switched it on.

The Spanish dress was spread out wide, falling in black cascades on both sides of the chaise-longue. Its wearer lay back, luxuriously, each gloved hand trailing on the deck. The head was impossibly twisted over the left shoulder. The face was covered down to the tip of the nose by part of the mantilla which had been dragged down like a blind. The exposed area was livid and patched almost to the colour of the mole at the corner of the mouth. The tongue protruded, the plump throat already was discoloured. Artificial pearls from a broken necklace lay scattered across the décolletage into which had been thrust a white hyacinth.

" All right," Alleyn said without turning. " It's too late, of course, but you'd better see if there's anything you can do."

Tim had come up with Captain Bannerman behind him. Alleyn stood aside. " Only Dr. Makepiece please," he said, " I want as little traffic as possible."

Tim stooped over the body.

In a moment he had straightened up.

" But, look here ! " he said. " It's not—it's—it's——"

" Exactly. But our immediate concern is with the chances of recovery. Are there any ? "

" None."

" Sure ? "

" None."

" Very well. Now, this is what we do——"

IV

Captain Bannerman and Tim Makepiece stood side-by-side exactly where Alleyn had placed them. The light in the deckhead shone down on the area round the chaise-longue. It was dappled with irregular wet patches most of which had been made by large naked feet. Alleyn found that they were overlaid by his own prints and Tim's and by others which he examined closely.

" Espadrilles," he said, " size nine."

The wearer had approached the chaise-longue, stood beside it, turned and made off round the starboard side.

" Running," Alleyn said, following the damp prints. " Running along the deck, then stopping as he got into the light, then turning and stopping by the hatch and then carrying on round the centrecastle to the port side. Not much doubt about that one."

He turned back towards the veranda, pausing by a tall locker near its starboard corner. He shone his torch behind this. " Cigarette ash and a butt."

He collected the butt and found it was monogrammed and Turkish.

" How corny can you get ? " he muttered, showing it to Tim, and returned to the veranda from where he pursued the trace of the wet naked feet. Their owner had come to the port side companion-ladder from the lower deck and the swimming-pool. On the fifth step from the top there was a large wet patch.

He returned to Captain Bannerman.

" In this atmosphere," he said, " I can't afford to wait. I'm going to take photographs. After that we'll have to seal off the veranda. I suggest, sir, that you give orders to that effect."

Captain Bannerman stood louring at him. " This sort of thing," he said at last, " couldn't have been anticipated. It's against common sense."

" On the contrary," Alleyn rejoined, " it's precisely what was to be expected."

CHAPTER TEN

Aftermath

I

THE PASSENGERS sat at one end of the lounge behind shut doors and drawn blinds. Out of force of habit each had gone to his or her accustomed place and the scene thus was given a distorted semblance of normality. Only Mr. Merryman was absent. And, of course, Mrs. Dillington-Blick.

Alleyn himself had visited the unattached men in their cabins. Mr. Merryman had been peacefully and very soundly asleep, his face blank and rosy, his lips parted and his hair ruffled in a cockscomb. Alleyn decided for the moment to leave him undisturbed. Shutting the door quietly, he crossed the passage. Mr. McAngus in vivid pyjamas had been doing something with a small brush to his hair which was parted in the middle and hung in dark elf locks over his ears. He had hastily slammed down the lid of an open box on his dressing-table and turned his back on it. Aubyn Dale, fully dressed, was in his sitting-room. He had a drink in his hand and apparently he had been standing close to his door which was not quite shut. His manner was extraordinary: at once defiant, terrified and expectant. It was obvious also that he was extremely drunk. Alleyn looked at him for a moment and then said :

" What have you been up to ? "

" I ? Have a drink, dear boy ? No ? What d'you mean, up to ? " He swallowed the remains of his drink and poured out another.

" Where have you been since you left the lounge ? "

" What the devil's that got to do with you ? " He lurched towards Alleyn and peered into his face. " Who the bloody hell," he asked indistinctly, " do you think you are ? "

Alleyn took him in the regulation grip : " Come along," he said, " and find out."

He marched Dale into the lounge and deposited him in the nearest chair.

Tim Makepiece had fetched Jemima and Mrs. Cuddy. Mr. Cuddy, recovered from his faint, had been allowed to change into pyjamas and dressing-gown and looked ghastly.

Captain Bannerman, louring and on the defensive, stood beside Alleyn.

He said : " Something's happened to-night that I never thought to see in my ship and a course of action has to be set to deal with it."

He jerked his head at Alleyn. " This gentleman will give the details. He's a Scotland Yard man and his name's A'leen not Broderick and he's got my authority to proceed."

Nobody questioned or exclaimed at this announcement. It was merely accorded a general look of worried bewilderment. The Captain nodded morosely at Alleyn and then sat down and folded his arms.

Alleyn said : " Thank you, sir." He was filled with anger against Captain Bannerman : an anger not unmixed with compassion and no more tolerable for that. At least half the passengers were scarcely less irritating. They were irresponsible, they were helpless, two of them were profoundly silly and one of them was a murderer. He took himself sharply to task and began to talk to them.

He said : " I shan't at the moment elaborate or explain the statement you've just heard. You will, if you please, accept it. I'm a police officer. A murder has been committed and one of the passengers in this ship, almost certainly, is responsible."

Mr. Cuddy's smile, an incredible phenomenon, was stamped across his face like a postmark. His lips moved. He said with a kind of terrified and incredulous jocosity : " Oh, go on ! " His fellow passengers looked appalled but Mrs. Cuddy dreadfully and incredibly tossed her head and said : " Mrs. Blick, isn't it ? I suppose it's a remark I shouldn't pass but I must say that with that type of behaviour——"

" No ! " Father Jourdain interposed very strongly. " You must stop. Be quiet, Mrs. Cuddy ! "

" Well, I must say ! " she gasped and turned to her husband. " It *is* Mrs. Blick, Fred, isn't it ? "

" Yes, dear."

Alleyn said : " It will become quite apparent before we've gone very much further who it is. The victim was found a few minutes ago by Mr. Cuddy. I am going to take statements from most of you. I'm sorry I can't confine the whole business to the men only and I hope to do so before long. Possibly it's less distressing for the ladies who are obviously not under suspicion to hear the preliminary examination than it would be for them to be kept completely in the dark."

He glanced at Jemima, white and quiet, sitting by Tim and looking very young in a cotton dressing-gown and with her hair tied back. Tim had fetched her from her cabin. He had said : " Jem : something rather bad has happened to somebody in the ship. It's going to shock you, my dear."

She had answered : " You're using the doctor's voice that means somebody has died." And after looking into his face for a moment, " Tim——? *Tim*, can it be the thing I've been afraid of ? Is it that ? "

He told her that it was and that he was not able just then to say anything more. " I've promised not," he had said. " But don't be frightened. It's not as bad as you'll think at first. You'll know all about it in a few minutes and— I'm here, Jem."

So he had taken her to join the others and she sat beside him, watching and listening to Alleyn.

He turned to her now. " Perhaps," he said, " Miss Carmichael will tell me at once when she went to her cabin."

" Yes, of course," she said. " It was just after you left. I went straight to bed."

" I saw her to her door," Tim said, " and heard her lock it. It was still locked when I returned just now."

" Did you hear or see anything that seemed out of the way ? " Alleyn asked her.

" I heard—I heard voices in here and—somebody laughed and then screamed, and there were other voices shouting. Nothing else."

" Would you like to go back to your cabin now ? You may if you'd rather."

She looked at Tim. " I think I'd rather be here."

" Then stay. Miss Abbott, I remember that you came in here from outside, on your way to your cabin. Where had you been ? "

" I walked once round the deck," she said, " and then I leant over the rails on the, I think, starboard side. Then I came in for a few minutes."

" Did you meet or see or hear anyone ? "

" Nobody."

" Was there anything at all, however slight, that you noticed ? "

" I think not. Except——"

"Yes."

"When I'd passed the veranda and turned, I thought I smelt cigarette smoke. Turkish. But there was nobody about."

"Thank you. When you left here I think Father Jourdain walked to your door with you?"

"Yes. He saw me go in, I suppose. Didn't you, Father?"

"I did," said Father Jourdain. "And I heard you lock it. It's the same story, I imagine."

"Yes, and I'd rather stay here, too," said Miss Abbott.

"Are you sure?" Father Jourdain asked. "It's not going to be very pleasant, you know. I can't help feeling, Alleyn, that the ladies——"

"It would be much less pleasant for the ladies," Miss Abbott said grimly, "to swelter in their cabins in a state of terrified ignorance." Alleyn gave her an appreciative look.

"Very well," he said. "Now, Mrs. Cuddy, if you please. Your cabin faces forward and to the starboard side and is next to Mr. McAngus's. You and your husband went to it together. Is that right?" Mrs. Cuddy who, unlike her husband, never smiled, turned her customary fixed stare upon Alleyn. "I don't see that it matters," she said, "but I retired with Mr. Cuddy, didn't I, dear?"

"That's right, dear."

"And went to bed?"

"I did," she said in an affronted voice.

"But your husband evidently did not go to bed?"

Mrs. Cuddy said after a pause and with some constraint: "He fancied a dip."

"That's right. I fancied it. The prickly heat was troubling me."

"I told you," Mrs. Cuddy said without looking at him, "it's unwholesome in the night air and now see what's happened. Fainting. I wouldn't be surprised if you hadn't caught an internal chill and with the trouble you've been having——"

Alleyn said : " So you changed into bathing trunks ? "

" I don't usually go in fully dressed," Mr. Cuddy rejoined. His wife laughed shortly and they both looked triumphant.

" Which way did you go to the pool ? "

" Downstairs, from here, and along the lower deck."

" On the starboard side ? "

" I don't know what they call it," Mr. Cuddy said contemptuously. " Same side as our cabin."

" Did you see anything of Miss Abbott ? "

" I did not," Mr. Cuddy said and managed to suggest that there might be something fishy about it.

Miss Abbott raised her hand.

" Yes, Miss Abbott ? "

" I'm sorry, but I do remember now that I noticed someone was in the pool. That was when I walked round the deck. It's a good way off and down below : I didn't see who it was. I'd forgotten."

" Never mind. Mr. Cuddy, did you go straight into the pool ? "

" It's what I was there for, isn't it ? "

" You must have come out almost at once."

There was a long pause. Mr. Cuddy said : " That's right. Just a cooler and out."

" Please tell me exactly what happened next."

He ran the tip of his tongue round his lips. " I want to know where I stand. I've had a shock. I don't want to go letting myself in for unpleasantness."

" Mr. Cuddy's very sensitive."

" There's been things said here that I don't fancy. I know what the police are like. I'm not going to talk regardless. Pretending you was a cousin of the Company's ! "

Alleyn said : " Did you commit this crime ? "

" There you are ! Asking me a thing like that."

Mrs. Cuddy said : " The idea ! "

" Because if you didn't you'll do well to speak frankly and truthfully."

" I've got nothing to conceal."

" Very well, then," Alleyn said patiently, " don't behave as if you had. You found the body. After a fashion you reported your discovery. Now, I want the details. I suppose you've heard of the usual warning. If I was thinking of charging you I'd be obliged to give it."

" Don't be a fool, man," Captain Bannerman suddenly roared out. " Behave yourself and speak up."

" I'm ill. I've had a shock."

" My dear Cuddy," Father Jourdain said, " I'm sure we all realise that you've had a shock. Why not get your story over and free yourself of responsibility ? "

" That's right, dear. Tell them and get it over. It's all they deserve," said Mrs. Cuddy mysteriously.

" Come along," Alleyn said. " You left the pool and you started back. Presumably you didn't return by the lower deck but by one of the two companion-ladders up to this deck. Which one ? "

" Left hand."

" Port side," the Captain muttered irritably.

" That would bring you to within a few feet of the veranda and a little to one side of it. Now, Mr. Cuddy, do go on like a sensible man and tell me what followed."

But Mr. Cuddy was reluctant and evasive. He reiterated that he had had a shock, wasn't sure if he could exactly recall the sequence of events and knew better than to let himself in for a grilling. His was the sort of behaviour that is a commonplace in the experience of any investigating officer but in this instance, Alleyn was persuaded, it arose from a specific cause. He thought that Mr. Cuddy hedged, not because he mistrusted the police on general grounds but because there was something he urgently wished to conceal. It became increasingly obvious that Mrs. Cuddy, too, was prickly with misgivings.

"All right," Alleyn said. "You are on the ladder. You climb up it and your head is above the level of the upper deck. To your right, quite close and facing you is the veranda. Can you see into the veranda?"

Mr. Cuddy shook his head.

"Not at all?"

He shook his head.

"It was in darkness? Right, you stay there for some time. Long enough to leave quite a large wet patch on the steps. It was still there some minutes later when I looked at them. I think you actually may have sat down on a higher step which would bring your head below the level of the upper deck. Did you do this?"

A strange and unlovely look had crept into Mr. Cuddy's face, a look at once furtive and—the word flashed up in Alleyn's thoughts—salacious.

"I do hope," Alleyn went on, "that you will tell me if this is in fact what happened. Surely there can be no reason why you shouldn't."

"Go on, Fred," Mrs. Cuddy urged. "They'll only get thinking things."

"Exactly," Alleyn agreed and she looked furious.

"All right, then," Mr. Cuddy said angrily. "I did. Now!"

"Why? Was it because of something you saw? No? Or heard?"

"Heard's more like it," he said and actually, after a fashion, began to smile again.

"Voices?"

"Sort of."

"What the hell," Captain Bannerman broke out, "do you mean, sort of! You heard someone talking or you didn't."

" Not to say talking."

" Well, what *were* they doing. Singing ? " Captain Bannerman demanded and then looked horrified.

" That," said Mr. Cuddy, " came later."

There was a deadly little silence.

Alleyn said : " The first time was it one voice ? Or two ? "

" Sounded to me like one. Sounded to me——" He looked sidelong at his wife, " like hers. You know. Mrs. Blick." He squeezed his hands together and added : " I thought at the time it was, well—just a bit of fun."

Mrs. Cuddy said : " Disgusting. Absolutely disgusting."

" Steady, Ethel."

Father Jourdain made a small sound of distress. Jemima thought : " This is the worst thing yet," and couldn't look at the Cuddys. But Miss Abbott watched them with hatred and Mr. McAngus, who had not uttered a word since he was summoned, murmured : " Must we ! Oh, must we ! "

" I *so* agree," Aubyn Dale began with an alcoholic travesty of his noblest manner. " Indeed, *indeed* must we ? "

Alleyn lifted a hand and said, " The answer, I'm afraid, is that indeed, indeed, we must. Without interruption, if possible." He waited for a moment and then turned again to Cuddy. " So you sat on the steps and listened. For how long ? "

" I don't know how long. Until I heard the other thing."

" The singing ? "

He nodded. " It sort of faded out. In the distance. So I knew he'd gone."

" Did you form any idea," Alleyn asked him, " who it was ? "

They had all sat quietly enough until now. But at this moment, as if all their small unnoticeable movements had been disciplined under some imperative stricture, an excessive stillness fell upon them.

Mr. Cuddy said loudly : " Yes. I did."

" Well ? "

" Well, it was what he was singing. You know. The chune," said Mr. Cuddy.

" What was it ? "

He turned his head and looked at Aubyn Dale. Like automata the other repeated this movement. Dale got slowly to his feet.

" You couldn't fail to pick it. It's an old favourite. ' Pack Up Your Troubles.' After all," Cuddy said grinning mirthlessly at Aubyn Dale, " it *is* your theme song, Mr. Dale, isn't it ? "

II

There was no outcry from any of the onlookers : not even from Aubyn Dale himself. He merely stared at Cuddy as if at some unidentifiable monster. He then turned slowly, looked at Alleyn and wetted his lips.

" You can't pay any attention to this," he said with difficulty, running his words together. " It's pure fantasy. I went to my cabin—didn't go out on deck." He passed his hand across his eyes. " I don't know that I can prove it. I—can't think of anything. But it's true, all the same. Must be some way of proving it. Because it's true."

Alleyn said : " Shall we tackle that one a bit later ? Mr. Cuddy hasn't finished his statement. I should like to know, Mr. Cuddy, what you did next. At once, without evasions, if you please. What did you do ? "

Cuddy gave his wife one of his sidelong glances, and then slid his gaze over to Alleyn. " I haven't got anything to conceal," he said. " I went up and I thought—I mean it seemed kind of quiet. I mean—you don't want to get fanciful, Eth—I got the idea I'd see if she was O.K. So I—so I went into that place and she didn't move. So I put out my hand in the dark. And she didn't move and I touched *her* hand. She had gloves on. When I touched it, it sort of slid sideways like it wasn't anything belonging to anybody and I heard it thump on the deck. And I thought she's fainted. So, in the dark, I felt around and I touched her face and—and—then I knew and—Gawd, Eth, it was ghastly!"

"Never mind, Fred."

"I don't know what I did. I got out of it. I suppose I ran round the side. I wasn't myself. Next thing I knew I was in the doorway there and—well, I come over faint and I passed out. That's all. I never did anything else, I swear I didn't. Gawd's my judge, I didn't."

Alleyn looked thoughtfully at him for a moment and said: "That, then, is an account of the discovery by the man who made it. So far, of course, there's no way of checking, but in the meantime we shall use it as a working hypothesis. Now. Mr. McAngus."

Mr. McAngus sat in a corner. The skirts of his dressing-gown, an unsuitably heavy one, were pulled tight over his legs and clenched between his knees. His arms were crossed over his chest and his hands buried in his arm-pits. He seemed to be trying to protect himself from anything anybody might feel inclined to say to him. He gazed dolorously at Alleyn as the likeliest source of assault.

"Mr. McAngus," Alleyn began, "when did you leave this room?"

"I don't remember."

"You were still here when I left. That was after Mrs. Dillington-Blick had gone. Did you leave before or after Mr. and Mrs. Cuddy?" He added: "I would rather Mr. McAngus was not prompted." Several of Mr. McAngus's fellow passengers who had opened their mouths, shut them again.

Mr. McAngus did not embark on his usual round of

periphases. He blinked twice at Alleyn and said : " I am too upset to remember. If I tried I should only muddle myself and you. A dreadful tragedy has happened : I cannot begin to think of anything else."

Alleyn, his hands in his coat pockets, said dryly : " Perhaps, after all, a little help is called for. May we go back to a complaint you made to Captain Bannerman before you went to bed. You said, I think, that somebody has been taking the hyacinths that Mrs. Dillington-Blick gave you."

" Oh, *yes*. Two. I noticed the second had gone this morning. I was *very* much distressed. And now—of course —even more so."

" The hyacinths are growing, aren't they, in a basket which I think is underneath your porthole ? "

" I keep them there for the fresh air."

" Have you any idea who was responsible ? "

Mr. McAngus drew down his upper lip. " I am very much averse," he said, " to making unwarranted accusations but I confess I *have* wondered about the steward. He is always admiring them. Or, then again he might have knocked one off by accident. But he denies it, you see. He denies it."

" What colour was it ? "

" White, a handsome spike. I believe the name is Virgin Queen."

Alleyn withdrew his hand from his pocket, extended and opened it. His handkerchief was folded about an irregular object. He laid it on the table and opened it. A white hyacinth, scarcely wilted, was disclosed.

Mr. McAngus gave a stifled cry, Jemima felt Tim's hand close on hers. She saw again in an instantaneous muddle, the mangled doll, the paragraphs in the newspapers and the basket of hyacinths that Dennis had brought in on their first morning at sea. She heard Miss Abbott say : " I *beg* you not to speak, Mrs. Cuddy," and Mrs. Cuddy's inevitable cry of : " Hyacinths ! Fred ! " And then she saw Mr. McAngus rise, holding his lower lip between his thumb and forefinger.

" Is that it ? " Alleyn asked.

Mr. McAngus moved slowly to the table and stopped.

" Don't touch it, if you please."

" It—it looks like it."

Mrs. Cuddy shrilly ejaculated : " Wherever did you find it ? "

Mr. Cuddy said : " Never mind, Eth," but Mrs. Cuddy's deductive capacity was under a hard drive. She stared, entranced, at the hyacinth. Everyone knew what she was about to say, no one was able to forestall it.

" My Gawd ! " said Mrs. Cuddy, " you never found it on the corpse ! My Gawd, Fred, it's the Flower Killer's done it. He's on the ship, Fred, and we can't get orf ! "

Miss Abbott raised her large hands and brought them down heavily on her knees. " We've been asked to keep quiet," she cried out. " Can't you, for pity's sake, hold your tongue ! "

" Gently, my child," Father Jourdain murmured.

" I'm not feeling gentle."

Alleyn said : " It will be obvious to all of you before long that this crime has been committed by the so-called Flower Murderer. At the moment, however, that's a matter which need not concern us. Now, Mr. McAngus. You left this room, immediately after Mr. and Mrs. Cuddy. Did you go straight to your cabin ? "

After a great deal of painstaking elucidation it was at last collected from Mr. McAngus that he had strayed out through the double doors of the lounge to the deck, had walked round the passengers' block to the port side, had gazed into the heavens for a few addled minutes and had re-entered by the door into the interior passageway and thus arrived at his own quarters. " My thoughts," he said,

" were occupied by the film. I found it *very* moving. Not, perhaps, what one would have expected but nevertheless *exceedingly* disturbing."

As he had not been seen by anybody else after he had left the lounge, his statement could only be set down for what it was worth and left to simmer.

Alleyn turned to Aubyn Dale.

Dale was slumped in his chair. He presented a sort of travesty of the splendid figure they had grown accustomed to. His white dinner-jacket was unbuttoned. His tie was crooked, his rope-soled shoes were unlatched, his hair was disordered and his eyes were imperfectly focused. His face was deadly pale.

Alleyn said : " Now, Mr. Dale, are you capable of giving me an account of yourself ? "

Dale crossed his legs and with some difficulty joined the tips of his fingers. It was a sketch of his customary position before the cameras.

" Captain Bannerman," he said, " I think you realise I'm ver' close friend of the General Manager of y'r Company. He's going to hear juss how I've been treated in this ship and he's *not* going to be pleased about it."

Captain Bannerman said : " You won't get anywhere that road, Mr. Dale. Not with me nor with anyone else."

Dale threw up his hands in an unco-ordinated gesture. " *All* right. On y'own head ! "

Alleyn crossed the room and stood over him. " You're drunk," he said, " and I'd very much rather you were sober. I'm going to ask you a question that may have a direct bearing on a charge of murder. This is not a threat : it is a statement of fact. In your own interest you'd better pull yourself together if you can and answer me. Can you do that ? "

Dale said : " I know I'm plastered. It's not fair. Doc', I'm plastered, aren't I ? "

Alleyn looked at Tim. " Can you do anything ? "

" I can give him something, yes. It'll take a little time."

" I don't want anything," Dale said. He pressed the palms of his hands against his eyes, held them there for some seconds and then shook his head sharply. " I'll be O.K.," he muttered and actually did seem to have taken some sort of hold over himself. " Go on," he added with an air of heroic fortitude. " I can take it."

" Very well. After you left this room to-night you went out on deck. You went to the veranda. You stood beside the chaise-longue where the body was found. What were you doing there ? "

Dale's face softened as if it had been struck. He said : " You don't know what you're talking about."

" Do you deny that you were there ? "

" Refuse to answer."

Alleyn glanced at Tim who went out.

" If you're capable of thinking," Alleyn said, " you must know where that attitude will take you. I'll give you a minute."

" Tell you, I refuse."

Dale looked from one of his fellow passengers to the other : the Cuddys, Jemima, Miss Abbott, Father Jourdain, Mr. McAngus ; and he found no comfort anywhere.

" You'll be saying presently," he said with a sort of laugh, " that I had something to do with it."

" I'm saying now that I've found indisputable evidence that you stood beside the body. In your own interest don't you think you'd be well advised to tell me why you didn't at once report what you saw ? "

" Suppose I deny it ? "

" In your boots," Alleyn said dryly, " I wouldn't." He pointed to Dale's rope-soled shoes. " They're still damp," he said.

Dale drew his feet back as if he'd scorched them.

" Well, Mr. Dale ? "

" I—I didn't know—I didn't know there was anything the matter. I didn't know he—I mean she—was dead."

" Really ? Did you not say anything ? Did you just stand there meekly and then run away ? "

He didn't answer.

" I suggest that you had come into the veranda from the starboard side : the side opposite to that used by Mr. Cuddy. I also suggest that you had been hiding by the end of the locker near the veranda corner."

Unexpectedly Dale behaved in a manner that was incongruously, almost embarrassingly theatrical. He crossed his wrists, palms outward, before his face and then made a violent gesture of dismissal. " No ! " he protested, " you don't understand. You frighten me. No ! "

The door opened and Tim Makepiece returned. He stood, keeping it open and looking at Alleyn.

Alleyn nodded and Tim, turning his head to the passage, also nodded.

A familiar scent drifted into the stifled room. There was a tap of high heels in the passage. Through the door, dressed in a wonderful negligee, came Mrs. Dillington-Blick.

Mrs. Cuddy made a noise that was not loud but strangulated. Her husband and McAngus got to their feet, the latter looking as if he had seen a phantom and the former as if he was going to faint again. But if, in fact, they were about to say or do anything more they were forestalled. Jemima gave a shout of astonishment and relief and gratitude. She ran across the room and took Mrs. Dillington-Blick's hands in hers and kissed her. She was half-crying, half-laughing. " It wasn't you ! " she stammered. " You're all right. I'm so glad. I'm so terribly glad."

Mrs. Dillington-Blick gazed at her in amazement.

" You don't even know what's happened, do you ? "

Jemima went on. "Something quite dreadful but——"
She stopped short. Tim had come to her and put his arm
round her. "Wait a moment, my darling," he said and she
turned to him.

"Wait a moment," he repeated and drew her away.

Mrs. Dillington-Blick looked in bewilderment at Aubyn
Dale.

"What's all the fuss ? " she asked. "Have they found
out ? "

He floundered across the room and seized Mrs. Dillington-
Blick by the arms, shaking and threatening her.

"Ruby, don't speak ! " he said. "Don't say anything.
Don't tell them. Don't you dare ! "

"Has everybody gone mad ? " asked Mrs. Dillington-
Blick. She wrenched herself out of Dale's grip. "Don't ! "
she said and pushed away the hand that he actually tried to
lay across her mouth. "What's happened ? *Have* they
found out ? " And after a moment, with a change of voice :
"Where's Dennis ? "

"Dennis," Alleyn said, " has been murdered."

III

It was, apparently, Mr. Cuddy who was most disturbed
by the news of Dennis's death but his was an inarticulate
agitation. He merely stopped smiling, opened his mouth,
developed a slight tremor of the hands and continued to gape
incredulously at Mrs. Dillington-Blick. His wife, always
predictable, put her hand over his and was heard to say that
someone was trying to be funny. Mr. McAngus kept
repeating : "Thank God. I thank God ! " in an unnatural
voice. Miss Abbott said loudly : "Why have we been
misled ! An abominable trick ! " While Aubyn Dale
crumpled back into his chair and buried his face in his
hands.

"Mrs. Dillington-Blick herself," Alleyn thought, "was bewildered and frightened." She looked once at Aubyn Dale and away again, quickly. She turned helplessly towards Captain Bannerman who went to her and patted her shoulder.

"Never you fret," he said and glared uneasily at Alleyn. "You ought to have had it broken to you decently, not sprung on you without a word of warning. Never mind. No need to upset yourself."

She turned from him to Alleyn and held out her hands. "You make me nervous," she said, "It's not true, is it? Why are you behaving like this? You're angry, aren't you? Why have you brought me here?"

"If you'll sit down," he said, "I'll tell you." She tried to take his hands. "No, just sit down, please, and listen."

Father Jourdain went to her. "Come along," he said and led her to a chair.

"He's a plain-clothes detective, Mrs. Blick," Mrs. Cuddy announced with a kind of angry triumph. "We've all been spied upon and made mock of and put in danger of our lives and now there's a murderer loose in the ship and he says it's one of us. In my opinion——"

"Mrs. Cuddy," Alleyn said, "I must ask you for the moment to be quiet."

Mr. Cuddy automatically and for the last time on the voyage said: "Steady, Ethel."

"Indeed," Alleyn went on, "I must ask you all to be quiet and to listen carefully. You will understand that a state of emergency exists and that I have the authority to deal with it. The steward, Dennis, has been killed in the manner you have all discussed so often. He was clad in the Spanish dress Mrs. Dillington-Blick bought in Las Palmas and the inference is that he was killed in mistake for her. He was lying in the chair in the unlit veranda. The upper part of his face was veiled and it was much too dark to see the mole at the corner of his mouth. In the hearing of all of the men in this room Mrs. Dillington-Blick had said she was going to the veranda. She did go there. I met her there and went with her to the lower deck and from thence to her cabin door. She was wearing a black lace dress, not unlike the Spanish one. I returned here and almost immediately Mr. Cuddy arrived announcing that he had discovered her and that she was dead. Apparently he had been deceived by the dress. Dr. Makepiece examined the body and says death had occurred no more than a few minutes before he did so. For reasons which I shall give you when we have time for them, there can be no question of his having been murdered by some member of the ship's complement. His death is the fourth in the series that you have so often discussed and one of the passengers is, in my opinion, undoubtedly responsible for all of them. For the moment you'll have to accept that."

He waited. Aubyn Dale raised his head and suddenly demanded : " Where's Merryman ? "

There were excited ejaculations from the Cuddys.

" That's right ! " Mr. Cuddy said. " Where is he ! All this humbugging the rest of us about. Insinuations here and questions there ! And Mister Know-all Merryman mustn't be troubled, I suppose ! "

" Personally," Mrs. Cuddy added, " I wouldn't trust him. I've always said there was something. Haven't I, dear ? "

" Mr. Merryman," Alleyn said, " is asleep in bed. He's been very unwell and I decided to leave him there until we actually needed him as, of course, we shall. I have not forgotten him."

" He was well enough to go to the pictures," Mrs. Cuddy pointed out. " I think the whole thing looks very funny. Very funny indeed."

Jemima suddenly found herself exclaiming indignantly :
" Why do you say it looks ' funny ' ? Mr. Merryman has
already pointed out what a maddeningly incorrect expression
it is and he *is* ill and he only came to the pictures because
he's naughty and obstinate and I think he's a poppet and
certainly not a murderer and I'm sorry to interrupt but I
do."

Alleyn said, almost as Father Jourdain might have said :
" All right, my child. All right," and Tim put his arm
round Jemima.

" It will be obvious to you all," Alleyn went on exactly
as if there had been no interruption, " that I must find out
why the steward was there and why he was dressed in this
manner. It is here that you, Mrs. Dillington-Blick, can
help us."

" Ruby ! " Dale whispered, but she was not looking at
him.

" It was only a joke," she said. " We did it for a joke.
How could we possibly know——? "

" We ? You mean you and Mr. Dale, don't you ? "

" And Dennis. Yes. It's no good, Aubyn. I can't not
say."

" Did you give Dennis the dress ? "

" Yes."

" After Las Palmas ? "

" Yes. He'd been awfully obliging and he said—you
know what an odd little creature he was—he admired it
awfully and I, I told you, I took against it after the doll
business. So I gave it to him. He said he wanted to dress up
for a joke at some sort of birthday party the stewards were
having."

" On Friday night ? "

" Yes. He wanted me not to say anything. That was why,
when you asked me about the dress I didn't tell you. I
wondered if you knew. Did you ? "

Alleyn was careful not to look at Captain Bannerman. " It doesn't arise at the moment," he said.

The Captain made an indeterminate rumbling noise that culminated in utterance.

" Yes, it does ! " he roared. " Fair's fair and little though I may fancy the idea, I'm not a man to shirk my responsibilities." He jerked his head at Alleyn. " The superintendent," he said, " came to me and told me somebody had been seen fooling about the forrard well-deck in that damned dress. He said he hadn't seen it himself and whoever did see it reckoned it was Mrs. Dillington-Blick. And why not, I thought ? Her dress, and why wouldn't she be wearing it ? He asked me to make inquiries and stop a repetition. I didn't see my way to interfering and I wouldn't give my consent to him doing it on his own. All my time as Master, I've observed a certain attitude towards my passengers. I didn't see fit to change it. I was wrong. I didn't believe I'd shipped a murderer. Wrong again. Dead wrong. I don't want it overlooked or made light of. I was wrong."

Alleyn said : " That's a very generous statement," and thought it best to carry on. " I had not seen the figure in the Spanish dress," he said. " I had been told it was Mrs. Dillington-Blick and there was no reason that anybody would accept to suppose it wasn't. I merely had a notion, unsupported by evidence, that the behaviour as reported was uncharacteristic."

Jemima said : " It was I who told about it. Mr. Alleyn asked me if I was sure it was Mrs. Dillington-Blick and I said I was."

Mrs. Dillington-Blick said : " Dennis told me what he'd done. He said he'd always wanted to be a dancer." She looked at Alleyn. " When you asked me if I would wear the dress to dance by the light of the moon, I thought you'd seen him and mistaken him for me. I didn't tell you. I pretended it *was* me, because——" her face crumpled and she began to cry, " because we were planning the joke."

" Well," Alleyn said, " there it was. And now I shall tell you what I think happened. I think, Mr. Dale, that with your fondness for practical jokes, you suggested that it would be amusing to get the steward to dress up to-night and go to the veranda and that you arranged with Mrs. Dillington-Blick to let it be understood that she herself was going to be there. Is that right ? "

Aubyn Dale had sobered up considerably. Something of his old air of conventional decency had reappeared. He exhibited all the troubled concern of a good chap who is overwhelmed with self-reproach.

" Of course," he said, " I'll never forgive myself for this. It's going to haunt me for the rest of my life. But how could I know ? How *could* I know ! We—I mean, I—I take the whole responsibility," he threw a glance, perhaps slightly reproachful, at Mrs. Dillington-Blick. "—I just thought it would be rather amusing to do it. The idea was that this poor little devil should——" He hesitated and stole a look at Mr. McAngus and Mr. Cuddy. "—well, should go to the veranda as you say and, if anybody turned up he was just to sort of string them along a bit. I mean, putting it like that in cold blood after what's happened, it may sound rather poor but——"

He stopped and waved his hands.

Miss Abbott broke her self-imposed silence. She said : " It sounds common, cheap and detestable."

" I resent that, Miss Abbott."

" You can resent it till you're purple in the face but the fact remains. To plot with the steward ! To make a vulgar practical joke out of what may have been the wretched little creature's tragedy—his own private, inexorable weakness—his devil ! "

" My child ! " Father Jourdain said. " You must stop."

H

But she pointed wildly and clumsily at Cuddy. "To trick that man ! To use his idiotic, hopeless infatuation ! And the other——"

"No, no. Please ! " Mr. McAngus cried out. "It doesn't matter. Please ! "

Miss Abbott looked at him with what might have been a kind of compassion and turned on Mrs. Dillington-Blick. "And you," she said, "with your beauty and fascination, with everything that unhappy women long for : to lend yourself to such a thing ! To give him your lovely dress, to allow him to so much as touch it ! What were you thinking of ! " She ground her heavy hands together. "Beauty is sacred ! " she said. "It is sacred in its own right : you have committed sacrilege."

"Katherine, you must come away. As your priest, I insist. You will do yourself irreparable harm. Come with me."

For the first time she seemed to hear him. The familiar look of mulish withdrawal returned and she got up.

"Alleyn ? " Father Jourdain asked.

"Yes, of course."

"Come along," he said and Miss Abbott let him take her away.

IV

"That woman's upset me," Mrs. Dillington-Blick said, angrily sobbing. "I don't feel at all well. I feel awful."

"Ruby, darling ! "

"No ! No, Aubyn, don't paw me. We shouldn't have done it. You shouldn't have started it. I feel ghastly."

Captain Bannerman squared his shoulders and approached her. "Nor you ! " she said, and, perhaps for the first time in her adult life she appealed to someone of her own sex. "Jemima ! " she said. "Tell me I needn't feel like this. It's not fair. I'm hating it."

Jemima went to her. "I can't tell you you needn't," she said, "but we all know you do and that's much better than not minding at all. At least—" She appealed to Alleyn. "—isn't it ?"

"Of course it is."

Mr. McAngus, tying himself up in a sort of agonised knot of sympathy, said : "You mustn't think about it. You mustn't reproach yourself. You are goodness itself. Oh, don't !"

Mrs. Cuddy sniffed piercingly.

"It's this awful heat," Mrs. Dillington-Blick moaned. "One can't *think*." She had, in fact, gone very white. "I—I feel faint."

Alleyn opened the double doors. "I was going to suggest," he said, "that we let a little air in." Jemima put her arm round Mrs. Dillington-Blick and Tim went over to her. "Can you manage ?" he asked. "Come outside."

They helped her through the doors. Alleyn moved Mr. Merryman's chair so that its back was turned to the lounge and Mrs. Dillington-Blick sank out of sight. "Will you stay here ?" Alleyn asked. "When you feel more like it I should be glad of another word with you. I'll ask Dr. Makepiece to come and see how you are. Perhaps, Miss Carmichael, you'd stay with Mrs. Dillington-Blick. Would you ?"

"Yes, of course."

"All right ?" Tim asked her.

"Perfectly."

Alleyn had a further word with Tim and then the two men went back into the room.

Alleyn said : "I'm afraid I must press on. I shall need all the men but if you, Mrs. Cuddy, would rather go to your cabin, you may."

"I prefer to stay with Mr. Cuddy, thank you."

Mr. Cuddy moistened his lips and said : " Look, Eth, you toddle off. It's not suitable for ladies."

" I wouldn't fancy being there by myself."

" You'll be O.K., dear."

" What about you, though ? "

He didn't look at her. " I'll be O.K.," he said.

She was staring at him : expressionless as always. It was odd to see that her eyes were masked in tears.

" Oh, Fred," Mrs. Cuddy said, " why did you do it ? "

CHAPTER ELEVEN

Arrest

I

THE FOUR men in the lounge behaved exactly as if Mrs.
Cuddy had uttered an indecency. They looked anywhere
but at the Cuddys, they said nothing and then after a moment
eyed Alleyn surreptitiously as if they expected him to take
drastic action.

His voice broke across the little void of silence.

" Why did he do what, Mrs. Cuddy ? "

" Eth," Mr. Cuddy said, " for God's sake choose your
words. They'll be thinking things, Eth. Be careful."

She didn't take her eyes off him and though she seemed
to disregard completely what he had said to her, Alleyn
thought that she was scarcely aware of anybody else in the
room. Mr. Cuddy returned her gaze with a look of terror.

" You know how I feel about it," she said, " and yet you
go on. Making an exhibition of yourself. I blame her, mind,
more than I do you : she's a wicked woman, Fred. She's
poking fun at you. I've seen her laughing behind your back
with the others. I don't care," Mrs. Cuddy went on,
raising her voice and indicating the inarticulate back of
Mrs. Dillington-Blick's deck-chair, " if she hears what I
say. What's happened is her fault : she's as good as responsible for it. And you had to go and chase after her and get
yourself mixed up with a corpse. I hope it'll be a lesson to

you." A kind of spasm twitched at her mouth and her eyes overflowed. She ended as she had begun. "Oh, Fred," Mrs. Cuddy said again, "why did you do it!"

"I'm sorry, dear. It was just a bit of fun."

"Fun!" Her voice broke. She went up to him and made a curious gesture, a travesty of playfulness, shaking her fist at him. "You old fool!" she said and without a word to anyone else bolted out of the room.

Mr. Cuddy made a slight move as if to follow her but found himself confronted by Alleyn. He stood in the middle of the room, half-smiling, scanning the faces of the other men.

"You don't want to misunderstand Mrs. Cuddy," he ventured. "I'm not a violent man. I'm quiet."

Captain Bannerman cleared his throat. "It looks to me," he said, "as if you'll have to prove that." He glanced at the open doors to the deck, at the back of Mrs. Dillington-Blick's chair and at Jemima who sat on the edge of the hatch with her chin in her hands.

"This is a man's job," he said to Alleyn. "For God's sake, keep the women out of it," and with some emphasis, shut the doors.

Alleyn had been speaking to Tim. He said: "Very well. For the moment."

The Captain pulled chairs up to the biggest table in the room, motioning Alleyn to sit at one end and himself taking the other. "I like to see things done shipshape," he muttered and his longing for a boardroom could be sensed. Aubyn Dale and Mr. McAngus at once took chairs. Tim, after a moment's hesitation, followed suit. Mr. Cuddy hung off, winding the cord of his dressing-gown round his spatulate fingers. Mr. McAngus, with trembling fingers, lit one of his medicated cigarettes.

Father Jourdain came back and in response to a gesture from the Captain, also sat at the table.

"That's more like it," sighed Captain Bannerman and made a clumsy ducking movement at Alleyn.

"Carry on, if you please, Mr. A'leen," he said.

But Aubyn Dale who for some time had been casting fretful glances at the bar cut in. "Look, I need a drink. Is there anything against my ringing for the steward?"

"Which steward?" Captain Bannerman asked, and Dale said: "God, I forgot."

"We'll do our drinking," the Captain pronounced, "later. Mr. Cuddy, I'll thank you to take a seat."

Mr. Cuddy said: "That's all right, Captain. Don't rush us. I'd still like to know why we don't send for Merryman," and he pulled out his chair, sat back in it with an affectation of ease, and stared, nervously impertinent, at Alleyn.

Aubyn Dale said: "I must say, seeing this gets more like a board-meeting every second, I don't see why Merryman should have leave-of-absence. Unless——" He paused and the others stirred, suddenly alert and eager. "Unless——"

Alleyn walked to the head of the table and surveyed its occupants. "If this were a normal investigation," he said, "I would see each of you separately while the others were kept under observation. In these circumstances I can't do that: I am taking each of your statements now in the presence of you all. That being done I shall send for Mr. Merryman."

"Why the hell should he be the king pin?" Dale demanded and then took the plunge. "Unless, by God, he did it."

"Mr. Merryman," Alleyn rejoined, "sat in the deck-chair now occupied by Mrs. Dillington-Blick. He was still there when the men left this room. He commanded a view of the deck: each side of it. He could see both approaches to the veranda. He is, therefore, the key witness. His temperament is not complaisant. If he were here he'd try to run the whole show. I therefore prefer to let you account for yourselves now and bring him in a little later."

"That's all very well," Mr. Cuddy said. "But suppose he did it. Suppose he's the Flower Murderer. How about that ? "

"In that case, being ignorant of what you have all told me, he may offer a statement that one of you can disprove."

"So it'll be our word," Dale said, "against his ? "

"With this reservation. That he was in a position to see you all and none of you, it seems, was able to see him or each other. He can speak about you all, I hope. Each of you can only speak for himself."

Mr. McAngus said : "I don't know why you all want him : he makes *me* feel uncomfortable and silly."

"Ah, for God's sake ! " Dale ejaculated. "Can't we get on with it ! "

Alleyn still standing, put his hands on the back of his chair and said : "By all means. This is the position as far as we've gone. I suggest that you consider it."

They were at once silent and uneasily attentive.

"Three of you," Alleyn said, "have given me statements about your movements during the crucial time—the time, a matter of perhaps eight minutes, between the moment when Mrs. Dillington-Blick left this room and the moment when Mr. Cuddy came back with an account of his discovery of the body. During those eight minutes the steward Dennis was strangled, I believe in mistake for Mrs. Dillington-Blick. None of the three statements corroborates either of the other two. We have a picture of three individuals all moving about, out there in the semi-dark, without catching sight of each other. For myself, I was the first to go. I met Mrs. Dillington-Blick by the veranda to which she went (I'm sorry to put it like this but there's no time for polite evasions) as a decoy. No doubt she assured herself that Dennis was there and she was about to take cover when I appeared. To get rid of me she asked me to help her down the port-side companion-ladder to the lower deck. I did so and then saw her to her cabin and returned here. Mr. Cuddy, in the meantime, had changed, gone below and then to the pool by way of the starboard side on the lower deck. Miss Abbott, who left after he did, walked round this deck and stood for some minutes on the starboard side. She remembers that she saw somebody in the pool.

" Mr. McAngus says he left by these double doors, stood for a time by the passengers' quarters on the port side and then went to his cabin and to bed. Nobody appeared to have noticed him.

" Mr. Dale, I imagine, will now admit that his first statement to the effect that he went straight to his cabin, was untrue. On the contrary, he was on deck. He hid behind a locker on the starboard side near the veranda corner hoping to overhear some cruelly ludicrous scene of mistaken identity. He afterwards went into the veranda, presumably discovered the body, returned to his cabin and drank himself into the state from which he has at least partially recovered."

" I resent the tone——" Dale began.

" You'll have to lump the tone, I'm afraid. I now want to know what, if anything, you heard from your hiding-place and exactly what you did and saw when you went into the veranda. Do you propose to tell me ? "

" Captain Bannerman——"

" No good coming at me," said the Captain. " You're in a tight spot, Mr. Dale, and truth had better be your master."

Dale smacked the palm of his hand down on the table. " *All right !* Turn on me. The whole gang of you and much good may it do you. You badger and threaten and get a man tied up in knots until he doesn't know what he's saying. I'm as anxious as anyone for this bloody murderer to be caught. If I could tell you anything that'd bring him to book I would. All right. I did what you say. I sat behind the locker. I heard Miss Abbott go past. Tramp, tramp. She walks like a man. I couldn't see her but I knew it was Miss Abbott because she was humming a churchy tune. I've heard her before. And then, it was quiet. And then, after a bit, somebody else went by. Going towards the veranda. Tip-toe. Furtive. I heard him turn the corner and I heard somebody—Dennis I suppose—it was rather high-pitched—make a little sound. And then——" He wiped his hand across his mouth. " Then there were other sounds. The chair legs scraped. Somebody cried out. Only once and it was cut short. Then there was another sort of bumping and scraping. Then nothing. I don't know for how long. Then the tip-toe footsteps passed again. A bit faster but not running and somebody singing, like Cuddy said. "Pack Up Your Troubles." In a head-voice. Falsetto. Only a phrase of it and then nothing."

" In tune ? " Alleyn asked.

" I beg your pardon ? "

" Was the voice in tune ? "

Dale said : " Well really ! Oh, yes. Yes. Perfectly in tune," and gave a half-laugh.

" Thank you. Go on. What did you do next ? "

" I was going to come out but I heard another voice."

He screwed round in his chair and jerked his head at Cuddy. " You," he said. " It was your voice. Unmistakably. You said : ' All alone ? ' " He aped a mellifluous, arch inquiry. " I heard you go in. Wet feet on the deck. And then, after a pause, you made a sort of retching noise and you ran out, and I suppose you bolted down the deck."

" I've explained everything," Mr. Cuddy said. " I've told them. I've concealed nothing."

" Very well," Alleyn said. " Keep quiet. And then, Mr. Dale ? "

" I waited. Then I thought I'd just go round and ask what had happened. I must have had some sort of idea there was something wrong : I realise that now. It was— it was so deadly quiet."

" Yes ? "

" So I did. I went in. I said something, I don't remember what and there was no answer. So I—I got out my cigarette lighter and flashed it on—Oh, God, God !"

" Well ? "

" I couldn't see much at first. It seemed funny he didn't say anything. I put the flame nearer and then I saw. It was hell. Like that doll. Broken. And the flowers. The deck was wet and slippery. I thought : ' I've done this : it's my fault. I arranged it and she'll say I did. Let some-body else discover it ! ' Something like that. I'd had one or two drinks over the eight and I suppose that's why I panicked. I ran out and round the deck, past the locker. I heard Cuddy's voice and I saw him by the doors here. I ducked down behind the hatch and heard him tell you. Then I heard you walk past on the other side and I knew that you'd gone to look. I thought ' It's too late for me to tell them. I'm here. I'll be involved.' So I made for the forward end of the deck."

" Father Jourdain," Alleyn said, " I think you must at that time have been by the entrance to this room looking after Mr. Cuddy, who had fainted. Did you see Mr. Dale ? "

" No. But, as you say I was stooping over Mr. Cuddy. I think my back was turned to the hatch."

" Yes," Dale said. " Yes, it was. I watched you. I don't remember much else except—my God, yes ! "

" What have you remembered ? "

Dale had been staring at his hands clasped before him on the table. He now raised his head. Mr. McAngus sat opposite him. They seemed to be moved by some common resentment.

" Go on," Alleyn said.

" It was when I'd gone round the passengers' block to the port side. I wanted a drink damn' badly, and I wanted to be by myself. I'd got as far as the entrance into the passage and waited for a bit to make sure nobody was about. Ruby —Mrs. Dillington-Blick, was in her cabin. I could hear her slapping her face. I wondered if I'd tell her and then— then I smelt it."

" Smelt what ? "

Dale pointed at Mr. McAngus. " That. One of those filthy things he smokes. It was quite close."

Mr. McAngus said : " I have already stated that I waited for a little on deck before I went to my cabin. I have said so."

" Yes. But *where* ? *Where* were you ? I couldn't see you and yet you must have been quite close. I actually saw the smoke."

" Well, Mr. McAngus ? " Alleyn asked.

" I—don't exactly remember where I stood. Why should I ? " He ground out his cigarette. A little malodorous spiral rose from the butt.

Dale said excitedly : " But the deck's open and there was the light from her porthole. Why couldn't I see him ? "

" The door giving on the passage opens back on the out-side bulkhead," Alleyn said. " Close to Mrs. Dillington-Blick's porthole. Were you standing behind that door, Mr. McAngus ? "

" Hiding behind it, more like," Mr. Cuddy eagerly exclaimed.

" Well, Mr. McAngus ? "

The long indeterminate face under the dyed hair was unevenly pallid. " I admit nothing," said Mr. McAngus. " Nothing."

" Are you sure ? "

" Nothing."

" Do you think he might have been there, Mr. Dale ? "

" Yes. Yes, I do. You see, I thought he must be in the passage and I waited and then I thought : ' I've *had* this ! ' And I looked and there was nobody there. So I went straight in. My door's just on the left. I had a Scotch neat and I dare say it was a snorter. Then I had another. I was all anyhow. My nerves are shot to pieces. I've had a breakdown. I'm supposed," Dale said in a trembling voice, " to be on a rest cure. This has set me all back to hell."

" Mr. McAngus, did you hear Mr. Cuddy when he came and told us of his discovery ? He was hysterical and made a great noise. Did you hear him ? "

Mr. McAngus said : " I heard something. It didn't matter."

" Didn't matter ? "

" I knew where she was."

" Mrs. Dillington-Blick ? "

" I cannot answer you, sir."

" You have yourself told us that you left this room by the deck doors, walked round the centrecastle block and then waited for some time on the port side. Do you stick to that statement ? "

Mr. McAngus, holding to the edge of the table as if for support, did not take his eyes off Alleyn. He had compressed his mouth so ruthlessly that drops of saliva oozed out of the corners. He inclined his head slightly.

" Very well then——"

" No ! No, no ! " Mr. McAngus suddenly shouted. " I refuse ! What I have done, I have done under compulsion. I cannot discuss it. Never ! "

" In that case," Alleyn said, " we have reached an impasse. Dr. Makepiece, will you be so kind as to ask Mr. Merryman if he will join us ? "

II

Mr. Merryman could be heard coming down the passage. His sharp voice was raised to its familiar pitch of indignation.

"I should have been informed of this," he was saying, "at once. Immediately. I demand an explanation. *Who* did you say the man is?"

An indistinguishable murmur from Tim.

"Indeed? *Indeed!* Then he has no doubt enjoyed the salutary experience popularly assigned to eavesdroppers. This is an opportunity," the voice continued as its owner drew nearer, "that I have long wished for. If I had been consulted at the outset, the typical, the all-too-familiar, pattern of official ineptitude might have—nay, would have been anticipated. But, of course, that was too much to hope for. I——"

The door was opened by Tim who came in, pulled an eloquent grimace at Alleyn and stood aside.

Mr. Merryman made a not ineffective entrance. He was girded into his dressing-gown. His cockscomb was erect and his eyes glittered with the light of battle. He surveyed the party round the table with a Napoleonic eye.

Captain Bannerman half rose and said: "Come in, Mr. Merryman. Hope you're feeling well enough to join us. Take a chair." He indicated the only vacant chair which faced the glass doors leading to the deck. Mr. Merryman made a slight acknowledgement but no move. He was glaring at Alleyn. "I dare say," the Captain went on, "that it's in order, under the circumstances, for me to make an introduction. This gentleman is in charge of the meeting. Superintendent A'leen."

"The name," Mr. Merryman said at once, "is Alleyn. *All*eyn, my good sir. Al-*lane* is permissible. A'leen, never. It is, presumably, too much to expect that you should have so much as heard of the founder of Dulwich College: an Elizabethan actor who was unsurpassed in his day : Edward Alleyn. Or, less acceptably in my poor opinion, Al-*lain*. Good evening, sir," Mr. Merryman concluded, nodding angrily at Alleyn.

"Over to you," the Captain muttered woodenly, "Mr. Allan."

"*No !*" Mr. Merryman objected on a rising inflexion.

"It's of no consequence," Alleyn hastily intervened. "Will you sit down, Mr. Merryman ? "

"Why not ? " Mr. Merryman said and did so.

"I believe," Alleyn went on, "that Dr. Makepiece has told you what has happened."

"I have been informed in the baldest manner conceivable, that a felony has been committed. I assume that I am about to be introduced to the insupportable *longeurs* of a police investigation."

"I'm afraid so," Alleyn said cheerfully.

"Then perhaps you will be good enough to advise me of the nature of the crime and the circumstances under which it was committed and discovered. Unless, of course," Mr. Merryman added, throwing back his head and glaring at Alleyn from under his spectacles, "you regard me as a suspect in which case you will no doubt attempt some elephantine piece of finesse. *Do* you, in fact, regard me as a suspect ? "

"Yes," Alleyn said coolly. "Together with sundry others. I do. Why not ? "

"Upon my word ! " he said after a pause. "It does not astonish me. And pray what am I supposed to have done ? And to whom ? And where ? Enlighten me, I beg you."

"You are supposed at this juncture to answer questions, and not to ask them. You will be good enough not to be troublesome, Mr. Merryman. No," Alleyn said as Mr. Merryman opened his mouth, "I really can't do with any more tantrums. This case is in the hands of the police. I am a policeman. Whatever you may think of the procedure you've no choice but to put up with it. And we'll all get along a great deal faster if you can contrive to do so gracefully. Behave yourself, Mr. Merryman."

Mr. Merryman put on an expression of mild astonishment. He appeared to take thought. He folded his arms, flung himself back in his chair and stared at the ceiling. "Very well," he said. "Let us plumb the depths. Continue."

Alleyn did so. Without giving any indication whatever of the nature or locale of the crime, an omission which at once appeared to throw Mr. Merryman into an extremity of annoyance, he merely asked for an account in detail of anything Mr. Merryman may have seen from his vantage point in the deck-chair, facing the hatch.

"*May* I ask ?" Mr. Merryman said, still looking superciliously at the ceiling, "*why* you adopt this insufferable attitude ? *Why* you elect to withhold the nature of your little problem ? Do I detect a note of professional jealousy ? "

"Let us assume that you do," said Alleyn with perfect good nature.

"Ah ! You are afraid——"

"I am afraid that if you were told what has happened you would try and run the show and I don't choose to let you. What did you see from your deck-chair, Mr. Merryman ? "

A faint, an ineffably complaisant smile played about Mr. Merryman's lips. He closed his eyes.

"What did I see ? " he ruminated and, as if they had joined the tips of their fingers and thumbs round the table, his listeners were involved in a current of heightened tension. Alleyn saw Aubyn Dale wet his lips. Cuddy yawned nervously and McAngus again hid his hands in his armpits. Captain Bannerman was glassy-eyed. Father Jourdain's head was inclined as if to hear a confession. Only Tim

Makepiece kept his eyes on Alleyn rather than on Mr. Merryman.

"What did I see?" Mr. Merryman repeated. He hummed a meditative air and looked slyly round the table and said loudly: "Nothing. Nothing at all."

"Nothing?"

"For a very good reason. I was sound asleep."

He broke into a triumphant cackle of laughter. Alleyn nodded to Tim who again went out.

McAngus, rather shockingly, joined in Mr. Merryman's laughter: "The key witness!" he choked out, hugging himself. "The one who was to prove us all right or wrong. Fast asleep! What a farce!"

"It doesn't affect you," Dale pointed out. "He wouldn't have seen you anyway. You've still got to account for yourself."

"That's right. That's dead right," Mr. Cuddy cried out.

"Mr. Merryman," Alleyn said, "when did you wake up and go to your room?"

"I have no idea."

"Which way did you go?"

"The direct way. To the entrance on the starboard side."

"Who was in the lounge at that time?"

"I didn't look."

"Did you meet anyone?"

"No."

"May I just remind you of your position out there?"

Alleyn went to the double doors. He jerked the spring blinds and they flew up with a sharp rattle.

The lights were out on deck. In the glass doors only the reflexion of the room and of the occupants appeared: faint, hollow-eyed and cadaverous as phantoms their own faces stared back at them.

From a region of darkness there emerged through these

images, another. It moved towards the doors, gaining substance. Mrs. Dillington-Blick was outside. Her hands were pressed against the glass. She looked in.

Mr. Merryman screamed like a ferret in a trap.

His chair overturned. He was round the table before anyone could stop him. His hands scrabbled at the glass pane.

" No. No ! Go away. Go away ! Don't speak. If you speak I'll do it again. I'll kill you if you speak."

Alleyn held him. It was quite clear to everybody that Mr. Merryman's hands, scrabbling against the glass like fish in an aquarium, were ravenous for Mrs. Dillington-Blick's throat.

CHAPTER TWELVE

Cape Town

I

CAPE FAREWELL steamed into Table Bay at dawn and hove-to awaiting the arrival of her pilot cutter and the police launch from Cape Town. Like all ships coming in to port she had begun to withdraw into herself, conserving her personality against the assaults that would be made upon it. She had been prepared. Her derricks were uncovered, her decks broken by orderly litter. Her servants, at their appointed stations, were ready to support her.

Alleyn looked across neatly scalloped waters at the butt-end of a continent and thought how unlikely it was that he would ever take such another voyage. At Captain Bannerman's invitation, he was on the bridge. Down on the dismantled boat-deck eight of the nine passengers were already assembled. They wore their shore-going clothes because *Cape Farewell* was to be at anchor for two days. Their deck-chairs had been stowed away, the hatch was uncovered and there was nowhere for them to sit. Sea-gulls, always a little too true to type, squawked and dived, squabbled and swooped about the bilgewater of which *Cape Farewell* blandly relieved herself.

Two black accents appeared distantly on the surface of the Bay.

" There we are," Captain Bannerman said, handing Alleyn his binoculars.

Alleyn said : " If you don't mind I'm going to ask for the passengers to be sent to their sitting-room."

" Do you expect any trouble ? "

" None."

" He won't——" Captain Bannerman began and hesitated. " You don't reckon he'll cut up rough ? "

" He is longing," Alleyn said, " to be taken away."

" Bloody monster," the Captain muttered uneasily. He took a turn round the bridge, and came back to Alleyn.

" There's something I ought to say to you," he said. " It doesn't come easy and for that reason, I suppose, I haven't managed to get it out. But it's got to be said. I'm responsible for that boy's death. I know it. I should have let you act like you wanted."

" I might just as easily have been wrong."

" Ah ! But you weren't, and there's the trouble." The Captain fixed his gaze on the approaching black accents. " Whisky," he said, " affects different men in different ways. Some, it makes affable, some it makes glum. Me, it makes pig-headed. When I'm on the whisky I can't stomach any man's notions but my own. How do you reckon we'd better handle this job ? "

" Could we get it over before the pilot comes on board ? My colleague from the Yard has flown here and will be with the Cape police. They'll take charge for the time being."

" I'll have a signal sent."

" Thank you, sir," Alleyn said and went below.

A seaman was on guard outside the little hospital. When he saw Alleyn he unlocked the door and Alleyn went in.

Sitting on the unmade-up bed with its sharp mattress and smartly folded blankets, Mr. Merryman had adopted an attitude quite unlike the one to which his fellow passengers had become accustomed. His spine curved forward and his head depended from it as if his whole structure had wilted. Only the hands, firmly padded and sinewed, clasped between the knees, retained their eloquence. When Alleyn came in, Mr. Merryman looked up at him over the tops of his spectacles but said nothing.

"The police-launch," Alleyn said, "is sighted. I've come to tell you that I have packed your cases and will have the things you need sent with you. I shall not be coming in the launch but will see you later to-day. You will be given every opportunity to take legal advice in Cape Town or to cable instructions to your solicitors. You will return to England as soon as transport is available : probably by air. If you have changed your mind and wish to make a statement——"

Alleyn stopped. The lips had moved. After a moment, the voice, remotely tinged with arrogance, said : "—not in the habit of rescinding decisions—tedium of repetition. No."

"Very well."

He turned to go and was arrested by the voice.

"—a few observations. Now. No witnesses and without prejudice. Now."

Alleyn said : "I must warn you : the absence of witnesses doesn't mean that what you may tell me will not be given in evidence. It may be given in evidence. You understand that," he added, as Mr. Merryman raised his head and stared blankly at him, "don't you ?" He took out his notebook and opened it. "You see, I shall write down anything that you say."

Mr. Merryman said with a vigour that a moment ago would have seemed impossible : "Esmeralda. Ruby. Beryl. Bijou. Coralie. Marguerite."

He was still feverishly repeating these names when Inspector Fox from the Yard, with members of the Cape Town police force, came to take him off.

II

For a little while Alleyn watched the police launch dip and buck across the Bay. Soon the group of figures aboard her lost definition and she herself became no more than a receding dot. The pilot cutter was already alongside. He turned away and for the last time opened the familiar doors into the sitting-room.

They were all there, looking strange in their shore-going clothes.

Alleyn said : " In about ten minutes we shall be alongside. I'm afraid I shall have to ask you all to come to the nearest police-station to make your depositions. Later on you will no doubt be summoned to give evidence and if that means an earlier return, arrangements will be made for transport. I'm sorry but that's how it is. In the meantime I feel that I owe you an explanation, and perhaps something of an apology." He paused for a moment.

Jemima said : " It seems to me the boot's on the other foot."

" And to me," said Tim.

" I'm not so sure," Mrs. Cuddy remarked. " We've been treated in a very peculiar manner."

Alleyn said : " When I boarded this ship at Portsmouth I did so on the strength of as slight a piece of information as ever sent an investigating officer to sea. It consisted of the fragment of an embarkation notice for this ship and it was clutched in the hand of the girl who was killed on the wharf the night you sailed. It was at least arguable that this paper had been blown ashore or dropped or had come by some irrelevant means into the girl's hand. I didn't think so, your statements didn't suggest it, but it was quite possible. My superior officers ordered me to conceal my identity, to make what inquiries I could, entirely under cover, to take no action that did not meet with the Captain's approval and to prevent any further catastrophe. This last, of course, I have failed to do. If you consider them, these conditions may help to explain the events that followed. If the Flower Murderer was aboard, the obvious procedure was to discover which of you had an acceptable alibi for any of the times when these crimes were committed. I took the occasion of the fifteenth of January when Beryl Cohen was murdered. With Captain Bannerman's assistance I staged the alibi conversation."

" Good lord ! " Miss Abbott ejaculated. She turned dark red and added : " Go on. Sorry."

" The results were sent by radio to London and my colleagues there were able to confirm the alibis of Father Jourdain and Dr. Makepiece. Mr. Cuddy's and Mr. McAngus's were unconfirmed but in the course of the conversation it transpired that Mr. McAngus had been operated upon for a perforated appendix on the nineteenth of January which made him incapable of committing the crime of the twenty-fifth when Marguerite Slatters was murdered. If, of course, he was speaking the truth. Mr. Cuddy, unless he was foxing, appeared to be unable to sing in tune and one of the few things we did know about our man was his ability to sing."

Mrs. Cuddy, who was holding her husband's hand, said : " Well really, Mr. Cuddy would be the last to pretend he was a performer ! Wouldn't you, dear ? "

" That's right, dear."

" Mr. Dale," Alleyn went on, " had no alibi for the fifteenth but it turned out that on the twenty-fifth he was in New York. That disposed of him as a suspect."

" Then why the hell," Dale demanded, " couldn't you tell me what was up ? "

" I'm afraid it was because I formed the opinion that you were not to be relied upon. You're a heavy drinker and you have been suffering from nervous strain. It would, I felt, be unsafe to trust to your discretion."

" I must say ! " Dale began angrily but Alleyn went on.

" It has never been supposed that a woman was responsible for these crimes but," he smiled at Miss Abbott, " one of the ladies, at least, had an alibi. She was in Paris on the twenty-fifth, at the same conference, incidentally, as Father Jourdain who was thus doubly cleared. Until I could hear that the remaining alibis were proved I couldn't take any of the passengers except Father Jourdain and Dr. Makepiece into my confidence. I should like to say, now, that they have given me every possible help and I'm grateful as can be to both of them."

Father Jourdain who was very pale and withdrawn, raised his hand and let it fall again. Tim said they both felt they had failed at the crucial time. " We were sceptical," he said, " about Mr. Alleyn's interpretation of Jem's glimpse of the figure in the Spanish dress. We thought it must have been Mrs. Dillington-Blick. We thought that with all the women accounted for, there was nothing to worry about."

" I saw it," Jemima said, "and I told Mr. Alleyn I was sure it was Mrs. Dillington-Blick. That was my blunder."

" I even heard the singing," Father Jourdain said. " How could I have been so tragically stupid ! "

" I gave Dennis the dress and pretended I didn't," Mrs. Dillington-Blick lamented.

Aubyn Dale looked with something like horror at Mr. Cuddy. " And you and I, Cuddy," he pointed out, " listened to a murder and did nothing about it."

Mr. Cuddy, for once, was not smiling. He turned to his wife and said : " Eth, I'm sorry. I'm cured, Eth. It won't occur again."

Everybody tried to look as if they didn't know what he was talking about, especially Mrs. Dillington-Blick.

"O.K., dear," said Mrs. Cuddy, and herself, actually smiled.

Mr. McAngus leant forward and said very earnestly: "I can, of course, see that I have not behaved at all helpfully. Indeed, now I come to think of it I almost ask myself if I haven't been suffering from some complaint." He looked wistfully at Mrs. Dillington-Blick. "A touch of the sun perhaps," he murmured and made a little bob at her. "It is," he added after a moment's added reflection, "very fussing to consider how one's actions go on and on having the most distressing results. For instance, when I ventured to buy the doll I never intended——"

A steamer hooted and there, outside, was a funnel sliding past and beyond it a confusion of shipping and the wharves themselves.

"I never intended," Mr. McAngus repeated but he had lost the attention of his audience and did not complete his sentence.

Miss Abbott said in her harsh way: "It's no good any of us bemoaning our intentions. I dare say we've all behaved stupidly one way or another. I know I have. I started this trip in a stupid temper. I've made stupid scenes. If it's done nothing else it's shown me what a fool I was. Control!" announced Miss Abbott, "and common sense! Complete lack of both leads to murder, it seems."

"And of charity," Father Jourdain added rather wearily.

"That's right. And of charity," Miss Abbott agreed snappishly. "And of proportion and I dare say of a hundred other things we'd be the better for observing."

"How right you are!" Jemima said so sombrely that Tim felt obliged to put his arm round her.

Alleyn moved over to the glass doors and looked out. "We're alongside," he said. "I don't think there's anything more to say. I hope, when you go ashore, you still

manage to find some sort of—what? compensation?—
for all that has happened?"

Mrs. Dillington-Blick approached him. She offered
him her hand and when he took it leant towards him and
murmured : " I've had a blow to my vanity."

" Surely not."

" Were all your pretty ways purely professional ? "

Alleyn suppressed a mad desire to reply : " As surely as
yours were not," and merely said : " Alas, I have no pretty
ways. You're much too kind." He shook her hand crisply
and released it to find that Jemima and Tim were waiting for
him.

Jemima said : " I just wanted to tell you that I've discovered you haven't got it all your own way."

" What does that mean ? "

" You're not the only one to find the real thing on a
sea voyage."

" Really ? "

" Really. *Dead* sure."

" I'm so glad," Alleyn said and shook hands with them.

After that the Cuddys and Mr. McAngus came and made
their odd little valedictions. Mr. Cuddy said that he
supposed it took all sorts to make a world and Mrs. Cuddy
said she'd always known there was something. Mr. McAngus
scarlet and inextricably confused, made several false starts.
He then advanced his long anxious face to within a few
inches of Alleyn's and said in a rapid undertone : " You
were perfectly right, of course. But I didn't look in. No,
no ! I just stood with my back to the wall behind the door.
It was something to be near her. Misleading, of course.
That I *do* see. Good-bye."

Aubyn Dale let Mr. McAngus drift away and then pulled
in his waist and with his frankest air came up to Alleyn and
extended his hand.

" No hard thoughts, I hope, old boy ? "

" Never a one."

" Good man. Jolly good." He shook Alleyn's hand with manly emphasis. " All the same," he said, " dumb though it may be of me I still can *not* see why, at the end, you couldn't warn us men. Before you fetched him in."

" A : because you were all lying like flatfish. As long as you thought he was the innocent observer who could prove you lied I had a chance of forcing the truth from you. And B : because one or more of you would undoubtedly have given the show away if you'd known he was guilty. He's extremely observant."

Dale said : " Well, I never pretended to be a diplomatic type," and made it sound noble. Then, unexpectedly, he reddened. " You're right about the drinks," he said. " I'm a fool. I'm going to lay off. If I can. See you later." He went out. Miss Abbott marched up to Alleyn.

She said : " I suppose what I'd like to say couldn't be of less importance. However, you'll just have to put up with it. Did you guess what was wrong with me, the night of the alibi conversation ? "

" I fancied I did," he said.

" So I supposed. Well, if it's any consolation, I'm cured. It's a mistake for a lonely woman to form an engrossing friendship. One should have the courage of one's loneliness. This ghastly business has at least taught me that."

" Then," Alleyn said gently, " you may give thanks mayn't you ? In a Gregorian chant ? "

" Well, good-bye," she said, and she too went out.

The others having all gone, Father Jourdain and Tim, who had both waited at the far end of the room, came up to Alleyn.

Father Jourdain said : " Alleyn, may I go to him ? Will you let me see him ? "

Alleyn said that of course he would but added, as gently

as he could, that he didn't think Mr. Merryman would respond graciously to the visit.

"No, no. But I must go. He received Mass from me in a state of deadly sin. I must go."

"He was struggling with——" Alleyn hesitated. "With his devil. He thought it might help."

"I must tell him. He must be brought to a realisation," Father Jourdain said. He went out on deck and stared without seeing it, at Table Mountain. Alleyn saw his hand go to his breast.

Tim said : "Am I wanted ? "

"I'm afraid you are. He's talked to me. It's pretty obvious that the defence will call psychiatric opinions and yours may be crucial. I'll tell you what he has said and then ask you to see him. If you can get him to speak it may go some way in his favour."

"You talk," Tim said, "as if you weren't a policeman."

III

"So the priest and the psychiatrist are to do what they can," Alleyn wrote to his wife. "Makepiece, of course, says he would need weeks to arrive at a full report. He's professionally all steamed up over Merryman's readiness to describe an incident that no doubt will be advanced as the key to his obsession and is a sort of text-book shining example of the Oedepus Complex and the whole blasted job. Do you remember there was one curious link in all these wretched crimes ? It was the women's names. All jewels. Marguerite, of course, means Pearl, and the doll's name Esmeralda, Emerald. It was bad luck for Jemima Carmichael that her young man called her Jem. The sound was enough and she wore a pearl necklace, The necklaces were always twisted and broken. And, of course, there were the flowers. This is his story. When he was just seven years old his mother, a stupid woman whom he adored, had a birthday. It was in the early Spring and he spent the contents of his money-box on a handful of hyacinths. He gave them to her but at the same time his father brought her a necklace. He fastened it round her neck with a display of uxoriousness which Merryman describes through his teeth. In raising her hands to his she dropped the hyacinths and in the subsequent embrace, trod on them. Makepiece says the pattern, from his point of view is perfect—jewels, flowers, neck, amorousness and fury. The boy flew into a blind rage and went for her like a demon, twisted and broke the necklace and was dragged away and given a hiding by his father. This incident was followed at ten-day intervals by a series of something he calls fainting fits. Makepiece suspects *petit mal*. Here Merryman's story ends.

" It's as if the fact of his arrest had blown the stopper off a lifelong reticence, and as if, having once spoken he can't stop but, with extraordinary vehemence, is obliged to go through with it again and again. But he won't carry his history an inch further and refuses to speak if any attempt is made to discuss the cases-in-hand. Makepiece thinks his mistaking Dennis for the woman has had a profound effect.

" There's no doubt that for years he has fought a lonely, frantic battle with his obsession, and to some extent may have beaten it off by segregating himself in a boys' school. Perhaps by substituting the lesser crime for the greater. He may have bought and destroyed necklaces and flowers for all one knows. But when his climacteric was reached and he retired from his school, the thing may have suddenly become malignant. I believe he took this voyage in an attempt to escape from it and might have done so if he hadn't encountered on the wharf a girl with flowers and those the most dangerous for him. The fact that her name was Coralie finished it. As for the earlier cases, I imagine that when his ten-day devil arose, he put on his false beard, went out on the hunt, buying flowers for the purpose, and picked up women with whom he got into conversation. He probably discarded many who didn't fit in with the pattern.

" He exhibits, to a marked degree, the murderer's vanity. I doubt if he has made one statement that was untrue throughout the voyage. He was eager to discuss these cases and others of their kind. Makepiece says he's a schizophrenic : I'm never absolutely certain what that means but no doubt it will be advanced at the trial and I hope to God it succeeds.

" Of course, almost from the beginning, I thought he was my man, if my man was aboard. If the others' alibis stood up, he was the only one left. But there were signs. His preferences in literature, for instance. Any Elizabethan play that concerned the murder of a woman was better than any that didn't. The *Duchess of Malfi* and *Othello* were the best because in each of these the heroine is strangled. He resented any suggestion that ' sex monsters ' might be unpleasant to look at. He carried bits of paper and sodamints in his waistcoat pocket. He spilt coffee all over himself when I uncovered the doll, and blamed Miss Abbott for it. He had been to a choir school and could therefore sing. He is an expert in make-up and no doubt bearded himself for the encounters. The beard, of course, went overboard after the event.

" But it was one thing to realise all this and a hell of another to sheet it home. When I saw him, as sound asleep as if he'd expiated a deadly crime instead of committing one, I realised there was only one chance of getting him. He had no doubt decided on the line he would take after the body had been found : I would have to give him the kind of shock that would jerk him off it. I fixed it up with Makepiece. When the right moment presented itself, we would confront Merryman with Mrs. Dillington-Blick. He knew he'd made his kill and of course believed her to be his victim. He was relaxed, eased of his fever and immensely enjoying his act. She loomed up on the other side of the window and—it worked.

" The fact of the D-B being in her own style a *femme fatale* muddled the issues, since she quite deliberately went gunning for any male in sight and thus stirred up Cuddy and McAngus to the dizziest heights of middle-aged fatuity. Dale, of course, had merely settled down to a routine shipboard affair. She's a pretty consistent job-of-work, I must say, and I don't mind betting that when she's got over her vapours she'll take the whole thing as a sort of back-handed tribute.

" For my part, having from the outset been hamstrung by Captain's orders, I hope never to be given such a job again. I can even allow myself one brief bellyache : which is this. Why the hell did the D-B have to dress up a queer steward and put him on the veranda ? And conversely why the hell couldn't she tell me about it ? It could have been turned without harm to advantage. Well, there it is ; by his death he brought about a dénouement grotesquely out-of-drawing to anything in his life.

" Well, my darling, an airmail goes out at noon and will bring you this great wad of a letter. I'm staying in the ship until she sails and will return with the official party. In the meantime——"

He finished his letter and went out on the bridge.

Cape Farewell was discharging cargo. At midnight, having got rid of a bull-dozer, four cars, three tons of unbleached calico and a murderer, she would continue her voyage to Durban.

He supposed he was unlikely ever to travel in her again.

Fontana Books

Fontana is best known as one of the leading paperback publishers of popular fiction and non-fiction. It also includes an outstanding, and expanding, section of books on history, natural history, religion and social sciences.

Most of the fiction authors need no introduction. They include Agatha Christie, Hammond Innes, Alistair MacLean, Catherine Gaskin, Victoria Holt and Lucy Walker. Desmond Bagley and Maureen Peters are among the relative newcomers.

The non-fiction list features a superb collection of animal books by such favourites as Gerald Durrell and Joy Adamson.

All Fontana books are available at your bookshop or newsagent; or can be ordered direct. Just fill in the form below and list the titles you want.

———————————————————————————————

FONTANA BOOKS, Cash Sales Department, G.P.O. Box 29, Douglas, Isle of Man, British Isles. Please send purchase price, plus 8p per book. Customers outside the U.K. send purchase price, plus 10p per book. Cheque, postal or money order. No currency.

NAME (Block letters) ———————————————————————

ADDRESS ————————————————————————————

————————————————————————————————

————————————————————————————————

While every effort is made to keep prices low, it is sometimes necessary to increase prices on short notice. Fontana Books reserve the right to show new retail prices on covers which may differ from those previously advertised in the text or elsewhere.

SINGING IN THE SHROUDS

Dame Ngaio Marsh, one of the world's most popular detective novelists, has written twenty-two of her classical whodunnits since she published *A Man Lay Dead* in 1934.

Now in her seventies, she is New Zealand born and bred. Her first name (pronounced "Nye-oh") is a Maori word which can mean a tree, a bug that lives on it, a light on the water—or simply "clever".

Many of her stories have theatrical settings, for Ngaio Marsh's real passion is Shakespeare. Almost single-handedly she revived the New Zealand public's interest in live theatre, and it was for this work that she received what she calls her "damery" in 1966.

Her most recent detective story is *Black as He's Painted*.